Call Me Yours

ELIZABETH BRIGHT

ABOUT THE CONTENT OF THIS BOOK…

Dear Reader,

There is a man in this book. If you read *A Cowboy in the Streets*, then you already know that Steven McAllister is kind of the worst. I'll be honest: When I wrote ACitS, I had no intention of giving him his own book. But I couldn't stop thinking about him, and men I have known like him.

I believe that you are a reflection of the company you keep. Hang out with assholes long enough, and eventually you become one. But the reverse could be true, too. What would happen if he put in the effort and worked on himself, and changed the company he kept? Could his outlook change, too?

I don't know. Redeeming a man is fucking hard, even in a romance book. I'm never going to try this again, I'll tell you that much. Forgiveness is fine—don't let that anger keep you from your peace—but it doesn't mean letting someone in your life who doesn't deserve to be there.

Other warnings: There is mention of suicide (in the past, off page). Animals sometimes suffer. I hope I dealt with these topics with the sensitivity you all deserve.

Lastly, this is not a warning, but a thank you. Writing is hard and lonely. I am so grateful for everyone who chooses to spend a few hours with my words. Thank you, from the bottom of my heart.

Elizabeth

This is a work of fiction. Names, characters, places, and incidents are products of the writer's imagination or are used fictitiously and are not to be construed as real. Any resemblance to actual events, locales, or persons, living or dead, is entirely coincidental.

Call Me Yours

Copyright © 2025 by Elizabeth Bright

All rights reserved.

Cover Design by Yummy Book Covers

Paperback ISBN: 979-8-9916602-5-9

Ebook ISBN: 979-8-9916602-4-2

*For any woman who ever looked at a hot mess of a man and
thought, I can totally fix that.
Girl, no.
Leave that to the professionals.*

1

STEVEN

Three Months Ago

It had already been a shitty day when the SUV I had tried to flag down slowed its roll just enough to open the passenger door and toss a pig out of it. The pig landed with a splash of mud and a terrified squeal that made every cell in my body cringe.

Now it was a really shitty fucking day.

"Assholes!" I shouted, like that would make them see the error of their ways.

The pig stared at me with its little piggy eyes, and I stared back. It was a still a juvenile, maybe twenty pounds, and obviously in pain, judging from the way it refused to put weight on its left hind leg.

It wasn't my pig. There wasn't a single reason in this goddamn world why I should make someone else's pig my problem. Except...well, it didn't seem like an ordinary pig, the kind that would one day find itself on a breakfast plate. No farmer who raised pigs for food was gonna toss one into a field to become a mountain lion's dinner any more than he'd tear up a hundred-dollar bill. Anyway, it had a pampered look about it. It was weirdly clean for a pig, and someone had painted its hoofs pink. Jesus fucking Christ, it was some asshole's pet.

That still didn't make it my problem. I had enough problems. The dead battery in my truck being one of them. Another was the lack of cell service along this stretch of highway between Aspen Springs, Colorado, and my corner of land four miles from the outskirts of town. Those two problems together made the low rumble of thunder an even bigger problem.

But the pig kept right on staring at me with pathetic piggy eyes.

Goddammit.

I was such a fucking sucker.

"All right," I groused. "All right. Let me see your leg." There was a hand gun in the glove compartment of my truck, so if the leg *was* broken, I could give him a merciful ending. I did not tell him this as I squatted down for a better look.

The pig made sad snuffling noises as I poked and prodded its leg. It didn't feel broken. Dammit. That meant I couldn't just shoot the darn thing and be done with it. I had to actually *do* something.

A fat raindrop splattered on my bare forearm. It was

quickly followed by another, and a roll of thunder directly over our heads.

"We can wait in the truck," I decided. "Someone will be along eventually and give us a jump."

Us. Like we were in this together. Just me and the pig against the world. Fucking hell.

I had zero experience with living pigs—horses were my business—but this one wasn't any bigger than a small dog, so I looped my arms around it and pushed upright.

And it fucking *screamed* like a hellhound had nipped at its tail. My teeth clanked together and my soul damn near departed my body at the sound. I was going to hear that scream in my nightmares. It scrambled my brain long enough for the pig to squirm free and land in the mud with another ear-shattering squeal.

"Goddammit!" I shouted. "Hold still and let me help you!"

I lunged, he dodged awfully quick for an injured animal, and I landed on my knees in the mud. The pig darted through the raindrops to a storm pipe, kicking mud on my gray t-shirt for good measure.

I peered inside. It was dark and cramped. The pig huddled out of reach.

"I'm not going in there after you," I informed the little shit. "You'll have no one to blame but yourself when get eaten by a mountain lion."

I reached for him, just to verify, and he took a step deeper into the pipe. His pink hoof paint glittered in the low light, a reminder that he was someone's pet. Dammit.

"I hate you," I said as I lowered to my belly. It made a gross sucking noise as I flattened against the damp ground.

I wasn't even sure this would work. My shoulders might be too broad for the narrow opening of the pipe. I rolled to my side, stretched my arms overhead, and wiggled my torso inside. It wasn't great. I could fit—barely—but I couldn't move much at all. I was wedged in too tight.

It was a lost cause, saving an animal that wasn't inclined to be saved. But I kept stretching, kept reaching, kept trying like a fucking loser who didn't have enough sense to know he was beat.

Something pushed roughly at my knee, startling me, and I banged my head against the top of the pipe.

"Shit," I muttered. I didn't even have enough space to rub away the ache.

"What are you doing?" a mean woman's voice demanded.

I knew she was mean because I recognized the voice as belonging to Chloe Adams, and Chloe Adams would never say a single nice word to me even accidentally. She said *What are you doing* in the same tone she had said *Get the hell out of here, Steven* not four hours ago at the Aspen Springs Library. She'd followed that with a tirade that had scraped me raw and left me arguing uselessly with her in my brain all these hours later. I'd probably still be searching for a comeback at three a.m.

"There's a pig in here," I grunted. "I'm trying to get it out."

"What a coincidence. There's a pig out here, too."

"Oink, oink, baby," I said sarcastically.

Her laugh ended on an abrupt throat-clearing, like she didn't want to give me the satisfaction of her amusement. "Is there really a pig in there?"

I blew out an exasperated breath and stretched a little harder. Nope. "Why the hell would I lie about that?"

"Who knows why you do anything, Steven? Maybe you listen to too many angry white men podcasts. Maybe your delicate psyche is too fragile for an equal playing field. Or maybe you just weren't raised right." She paused. I gritted my teeth. I still didn't have a comeback, and that one hit a little too close to home. "I guess I can't think of a reason why you would lie about a pig, though."

"Gee, thanks." I wiggled my body back out of the pipe and found myself staring straight into Chloe's pretty, bitchy face under the shelter of a red umbrella. "And don't say shit about my mom. That's out of bounds."

Her head tilted consideringly as she stared down her nose at me. The angle was unflattering. It gave her a triple chin and I could see straight up her flaring nostrils. It pissed me right off that even like this, she was still so fucking pretty.

"What's the problem with the pig?" she asked.

"Some asshole tossed it out of a car. It's hurt and scared. I tried to pick it up, get it into my truck, and now he wants nothing to do with me." Frustration seeped into my tone. "And I'm too big for this fucking hole."

Her lips twitched as the words hung between us.

They'd slipped out of my mouth without a damn thought, but I heard the innuendo now, and I knew she did, too. In that quicksilver moment, I imagined what her laugh would have sounded like and felt some kind of way about never finding out.

"Hmm." When she leaned down to peer into the pipe, her long brown hair brushed my face and I caught the scent of her strawberry shampoo, which only aggravated me more, because of fucking *course* she smelled like a sweet summer day. "Oh! There *is* a pig in there!" she exclaimed.

I snorted. She hadn't really believed me at all. "What are you doing here, Chloe?"

She straightened and met my glare with the barest quirk of her eyebrow. "I saw your truck on the side of the road and figured you might need some help."

There was something in the way she phrased it, something about the way she hadn't been especially gentle when she'd kicked my knee, and the *what are you doing*, not *are you okay* that put me back a step like the earth had tilted under my feet. "You knew it was me and you stopped anyway? Why?"

She looked at me like I was stupid. "I just told you. I thought you needed help. You were lying down in the rain like you'd had a heart attack or something."

"But you hate me."

She twirled her umbrella and regarded me with narrowed green eyes. "Sure do."

"But you stopped anyway." I couldn't wrap my brain around it.

Her eyebrows pushed together like she didn't understand the connection. After a moment of reflection, her expression cleared. "Oh, I get why you're confused. See, I'm a good person. I think people owe each other basic human decency." Her head tilted and her thick hair cascaded down her shoulder. "You still look confused. See, *basic human decency* means—"

"You're such a bitch," I muttered.

Her teeth flashed in a smile. "Only to the deserving. Most people think I'm delightful."

Once upon a time, I'd been one of them. Chloe had worked at Jo's, the only coffee shop in our small town of Aspen Springs, Colorado, since before I'd landed a job training rodeo horses at Lodestar Ranch. I didn't get into town much, but I'd always made a point of grabbing a coffee when I did. I'd looked forward to seeing her. There was something about her wry observations of the most mundane shit that always had me lingering, stretching out my coffee order just a little bit longer than necessary.

All that changed after her best friend, James—who was also the head trainer at Lodestar, so technically my boss— fell off a horse and bruised her ribs, and okay, yes, I'd had something to do with that, but swear to god, I hadn't hurt her on purpose. I would fucking *never*.

But Chloe clearly didn't believe that, because the next time I stepped foot in Jo's, she had kicked me right out again.

I'd tried again sporadically for the next couple months, but Chloe held a grudge like an elephant. If it had been directed at anyone else, I might have considered it a virtue.

Directed straight at me, I didn't like it so much. I liked it even less at the library this morning. Her words were still ringing in my ears like she was screaming them in my face.

I know you. You're the guy who always comes in second and gets mad about it, because no one deserves first place more than you. If someone doesn't laugh at your joke, it's because they don't have a sense of humor. Someone gets promoted over you, they must have cheated. A woman turns you down, she's a bitch. The world never gives you everything you're owed, and your list of grievances is long. It's not fair, right? All of that should be yours. Because you're such a nice guy. *But guess what? No one owes you shit, and you're trash.*

That man she'd described? Yeah, I recognized him. But it wasn't me. It was my fucking father. The man I swore I wouldn't become. Hearing her say I was exactly like him, even though she didn't know she was saying it, felt like a sucker punch to the nuts. I couldn't catch my breath.

And, fuck, I hated her for it.

I held tight to that anger now, despite her smelling so damn edible. "As you can see, I'm not having a heart attack. The battery died." I jerked my chin toward my truck. "And then the pig." I jerked my head in the other direction, toward the pipe. "No cell service."

"You shouldn't be out here without a charged battery jumper," she said, which was true and also, quite frankly, really un-fucking-helpful. "It's stupid."

"I used mine this morning and didn't have time to charge it."

My sister had left the light on in her Subaru. Thank god it was me out here in the rain and not her. I had bought her a rechargeable battery jumper while I was in town today because she would be living with me for the foreseeable future. It was sitting behind the driver's seat.

Also uncharged, of course.

She twirled her umbrella again and stared at me like she was waiting for something. What the hell did she want from me? Rain sluiced down my forehead and dripped into my eyes while she stood there, perfectly dry, twirling her goddamn umbrella like she had all the time in the world, and my truck—

Oh, god*dammit.

I had to ask this woman for a favor? No. Absolutely not. She was a fucking bitch, and I would rather die of pneumonia than give her the satisfaction.

But the dang pig.

And Amy was waiting for me. If I didn't get home soon, she'd decide to come looking for me. I didn't want her out in this storm. She was used to the flat fields of Oklahoma, not the twisting roads of the Rocky Mountains.

"I'd appreciate a jump, if it's not too much trouble," I pushed out through gritted teeth. "I've got cables in my truck."

She stopped twirling that fucking umbrella and her pretty pink lips tilted in a smirk. "No trouble at all."

I grabbed the cables from my truck while she turned

her small SUV around so our engines were facing each other and cut the engine. I popped the hood and waved the cables at her through her windshield so she knew I was ready. Chloe nodded and reached across the passenger seat to the glove compartment, pulled out a notecard, read it over with a little nod of her head, put it away, then pulled it back out and looked over it again before putting it away and shutting the glove compartment.

I cocked my head questioningly as our eyes met through her windshield. She arched an eyebrow and popped the hood.

"Red is positive!" she hollered, her voice muffled behind the glass. "Positive to positive, negative to negative."

"Yeah, I fucking know," I muttered to myself. I clamped the cables from her battery to mine. "Turn on your car!" I shouted back.

I waited a couple minutes with her engine running before starting mine. It roared to life. Thank fuck. I kept the engine running while I darted back into the rain, unclamped the cables, and shut both our hoods.

I rapped on her window, and she rolled it down an inch. "Thanks for your help. I'm good from here. You can go."

With a crisp nod, she rolled the window back up.

The engine needed to run a little bit longer to get the battery charge up, and that fucking pig was still in the goddamn pipe. I squatted down and saw him lying on his side, like he had simply accepted that this was his home now.

"All right, asshole," I muttered as I lowered myself to the mud. "How about you help me help you this time, okay?"

He snorted. It sounded like a swear word.

"You don't fit. Why do you keep trying?"

Chloe's voice came from somewhere down by my feet. I pulled my head out of the pipe to glare at her. "Shouldn't you be halfway home by now? Go on, now. Shoo." I waved my hands at her like she was a mangy stray dog.

She looked at the hole with narrowed eyes, sizing it up, and then back to my face. "I could fit."

"Really." I dragged my gaze up her bare legs, over her tiny denim shorts, up to the white t-shirt that would for sure go see-through in the rain. "You're going to crawl through the mud wearing that?"

She crooked a finger at me and that was all it took because I was some kind of masochist, apparently. I rolled to my feet and prowled toward her.

"Take off your shirt," she said.

Did I ask for an explanation? No.

Did I politely suggest she go fuck herself? Also no.

Did I do exactly what she said like a pussy-whipped sucker even though I would rather put my dick in a hill of fire ants than this woman's pussy?

Look, I wasn't proud of it.

I whipped my t-shirt off over my head and let the rain soak straight into my skin. It was ice cold, which I hadn't expected. Thin though it was, my t-shirt had been better than nothing.

Her eyes didn't linger as she traded me the umbrella for my shirt, and somehow that left me feeling even more exposed. I didn't spend hours lifting weights and working out—actually *working* kept me in good shape—but I took pride in knowing women liked me out of my clothes.

Chloe was not one of them, apparently.

She turned her back to me. "Keep me dry."

And I did that, too, even though it meant my entire backside was left out in the rain. Not that it mattered. I couldn't get more wet than I already was at this point. She pulled her t-shirt off and handed it to me over her shoulder.

It happened so fast. Her shirt in my hand. Her back bare except for the lace band of her beige bra. The umbrella dappling red shapes across her skin like a stained-glass window. The small dark mole on the sharp apex of her shoulder blade.

And then my gray t-shirt tumbled down her spine like a closing curtain and she darted around me into the rain, calling "Don't let my shirt get wet!" while I stood rooted where she left me, light-headed from holding my breath.

"Such a smart pig," Chloe cooed behind me from the pipe. "I wouldn't let him touch me, either."

I huffed an aggrieved sigh, but that made me take a breath and the second oxygen hit my lungs my brain turned back on. I turned around and found her halfway into the pipe, her shapely ass pointed to the sky.

"Darlin', I have as much interest in touching you as I do sticking my hand in a wasp nest," I lied on a thick cowboy drawl. There was a thin line between loathing and lust, and Chloe Adams was unfortunately straddling it with those sweet thighs of hers.

She didn't respond. Maybe she didn't hear me, or maybe she knew I was full of shit. She knew what her ass looked like, after all.

"Got him!" Her triumphant shout was followed by that ass jiggling in those tiny shorts as she wiggled backward out of the pipe. "Open the door."

I jogged to my truck, Chloe speed-walking behind me with the pig tucked protectively against her torso like a football, and opened the passenger door of my truck. She placed the pig on the floor with a lot more care than the asshole who had tossed him out in the first place and then turned to face me under the umbrella.

Because, yeah, I was holding it over her head, even though she was now every bit as wet and dirty as I was, so what was even the point?

She glanced up at the umbrella, then cocked her head like she was wondering the same thing. Her gaze landed on her t-shirt in my other hand.

"Is it still dry?" she asked.

"Yes," I grunted, more than a little bit offended that she even asked me that.

"Great."

She grabbed her shirt and turned around. This time I knew what was coming and stared up at the umbrella as though my soul depended on it because that was how it felt, like I might actually die from it. The next thing I knew she was taking the umbrella handle from me as she shoved my filthy shirt at my chest.

"Good luck with Steve Junior!" she hollered cheerfully over her shoulder as she jogged toward her car.

It took me a second to realize she had not-so-subtly called me a pig again.

God, that fucking woman. I hated her.

But I lifted my shirt to my face and breathed in her sweet strawberry scent like maybe I didn't.

2

STEVEN

Six Weeks Ago

This wasn't where I thought I'd be at thirty years old. For one, I didn't figure I'd be starting my career from scratch for the third time. For another, it never once occurred to me that I'd be a walking encyclopedia about fucking *pigs*, of all things. For example, I now knew that mini pigs were a thing and that *mini*, as it pertained to pigs, did not mean *small*. It meant small*er*.

Like my girl, Stevie. She was an American Mini Pig, which meant she'd never be taller than a medium-sized dog. But pigs, even mini pigs, were a hell of a lot denser than dogs, so at maturity, she'd weigh between 80 and 130 pounds.

She was still a juvenile—I'd been right about that— and she weighed a solid fifty pounds. According to the vet,

Jacob Gunnell, pet mini pigs had recently become a fad on account of some celebrity or other, but once the pig grew out of the cute little baby phase and the owners realized a mini pig was still a whole ass *pig*, it generally got dumped. Apparently pigs made terrible pets if you didn't know what you were doing.

Horseshit. Stevie was a goddamn angel.

Sure, she was every bit as smart as a dog and just as likely to get into trouble if left alone too long. She required intellectual stimulation, entertainment, and friendship.

Which was why I now had three pigs.

In the six weeks since Stevie had been hurled into my life, I had learned a lot of things about pigs. Great and terrible things.

The great: Pigs enjoyed music, and Stevie happened to have good taste. She also liked going for walks, saying hello to people, and belly rubs. She learned how to ring a bell when she wanted to come inside from her pen in the yard, and pigs were easily house trained.

The terrible: Pigs shit right by the water source. That was nasty. They were omnivores and considered anything in reach of their mouth to be food—and they were *always* hunting for food. Roots, bugs, a baby bird that happened to fall from the nest at the exact wrong moment...Yeah. I had to lie down after that one. I still felt nauseous when I thought about it.

But look at that face. How could I be mad at a face like that?

"There's a lock on the fridge."

I looked up from watching Stevie, Lindsey, and Christine devour their morning pellets to find my sister standing in the doorway, still in her pajamas, with her blond hair piled on her head in a messy bun and a steaming mug of coffee cupped between her palms.

"Yeah, you missed a ruckus this weekend while you were fooling around in the mountains," I told her. "Stevie figured out how to open the fridge and made a mess of things. I installed the child lock last night. Code is one-one-one-one."

Amy arched her eyebrows at me over the rim of her mug. "One-one-one-one? Kind of an easy code to crack, isn't it?"

I raised my eyebrows right back at her. "She's a pig, Amy."

"Right. My brain isn't on yet." Laughing, she turned back into the house. "I need more coffee."

I followed her in, knowing she'd gotten up at the crack of dawn for the sole purpose of making me breakfast and packing me a lunch to take with me on the road, and also knowing it wouldn't do any good to tell her she didn't have to, that I was a grown-ass man and could take care of myself, because she'd just remind me she was staying here for free and wanted to earn her keep.

Earn her keep. I hated when she said that. It was an echo of *him*. We had both been raised on the idea that a child should be grateful to have been brought into this world to begin with, and that roof over our heads and food on our plates didn't come for free. Maybe Dad believed kids had to earn the right to exist, but as far as I was concerned, Amy never had to earn the right to be my sister.

"How was camping?" I asked as I poured myself a second cup of coffee.

Amy pulled the egg carton from the fridge, along with a rash of bacon, which neither of us said a damn word about because compartmentalization was part of farm life. "Not camping. Backpacking," she corrected.

"Backpacking? You mean you carried your tent and all your food the whole way?" I shook my head. I couldn't wrap my mind around why anyone would want to do that.

Being born and raised in Oklahoma, I considered myself to be the typical country boy. Outdoorsy to me meant hunting and fishing, both of which I had done my fair share of. Sports meant football or the rodeo, and I had done both of those, too—football in high school, and then rodeo for nearly a decade until I turned my career toward training horses.

Moving to Colorado two years ago gave me a new perspective on outdoorsy and sports. Outdoorsy meant spending long days and even weeks in the mountains, far from roads and hospitals. Sports meant anything from rock climbing to trail running to backpacking.

Honestly, the towering peaks intimidated me a bit. They sure were pretty to look at, but I felt no need to go exploring in them. Those mountains were none of my business.

But Amy, she'd had the opposite reaction. One look at that ridgeline and she'd wanted to know everything there was to know about those mountains. And since I couldn't provide that information, she'd found people who could, joining up with a women-only club for hiking and backpacking.

"It was great." Amy cracked three eggs into the sizzling frying pan. "It ended up being four of us, and all three of them had a lot more experience than me, but they were real nice about it. I took a ton of pictures. I'll show you when you get home from work tonight."

"I'd like that," I said absently, my mind on the more pressing issue of my baby sister out in the Rocky Mountains with nothing for protection but three other women. "No one brought along a boyfriend? Or a brother?"

"It's a women-only group," she reminded me. "That would have been rude."

"Maybe, but being out there all alone doesn't seem safe."

She snorted. "I wasn't alone. Meg, Amber, and Jessica were with me, like I said. Anyway, there's nothing more dangerous to a woman than a man, so it would be kind of reckless to bring one with us, don't you think?" She sent me a smirk over her shoulder before turning her attention back to the eggs.

I glared at her back, but couldn't fault her logic, even though I knew she was joking. Mostly. "What about bears?" I demanded. "Bears are pretty dangerous, aren't they?"

"We were prepared for bears."

"How the hell do you prepare for bears, Amy?"

She slid the eggs, bacon, and two slices of toast on a plate and set it down in front of me. "Do you really want to know? Because I'd be happy to take you out some weekend and show you."

"Nah, I'm good."

Her gaze dipped and the corners of her mouth went right down with it. Was she...disappointed? She didn't actually want me tagging along on her adventures, did she? My eyebrows pinched together, but she turned back to the counter, gathering the ingredients for a sandwich.

"Anyway, bears aren't the scariest thing out there. Moose are worse."

"Moose?"

"Yeah." She nodded vehemently. "Moose are way scarier than bears."

"Well, how do you prepare for a moose, then?"

She grinned. "You don't."

"WHAT DO YOU THINK?" Terry Quinn asked.

Just from the fact that he posed the question at all, I knew I had made a mistake. If I had done the job perfectly, he wouldn't have asked for my opinion. He would have said *nice work*, clapped me on the shoulder with his thick, gnarled hand, and we would have moved on to the next horse.

The problem was, until that very second, I had thought it was good. The old draft mare, Oreo, was a complicated case. Terry had a soft spot for the gentle giants, so he offered his services to Sunshine Rescue at a reduced rate. An interesting choice, because the work was easily four times as hard.

My back ached from the hours I had already spent hunched over these dinner-plate-sized feet, but I crouched so I was eye-level with her knees. "All right. Walk her toward me."

Terry clucked his tongue and tugged the lead rope. The mare ambled forward, her heavy footfall muffled by the wood shavings. She looked fine. Not perfect, but we weren't aiming for perfect, not yet. She had arrived at the farm with cracked, overgrown hooves that hadn't seen a farrier in a decade. This was our second visit with her, and she still had a long road ahead of her before she was fully sound.

But what I was seeing now was a big improvement. No matter how hard I squinted, I couldn't see anything I'd do differently. It was on the tip of my tongue to tell Terry that, but I bit it back.

Six months ago, when I started my apprenticeship after completing the technical program, Terry never asked me what I thought, maybe because my novice experience made my thoughts not worth sharing. He'd go over my mistakes in detail and I was expected to listen and ask questions, not provide insight myself. Somewhere along the way, when my mistakes became few and far between, he started asking for my opinion—even though he already knew the correct answer.

At first it felt like a trick question. Like he was setting me up to look like a fool, so he could yell *gotcha!* and feel good about himself.

It took me a while to understand it wasn't a trap. He was teaching me to slow down and check my work, and he framed it like a question because I already knew the answer, too, if I would simply pull my head out of my ass long enough to see it. With forty-odd years of farrier experience under his belt, he took mentoring seriously.

So I bit back my bad attitude and said, "She looks good from the front. Circle her around and let me see how she moves from a different angle."

Terry nodded and clucked his tongue again. I didn't see anything amiss on the first pass—other than the obvious trauma that would take a few more visits to fully fix—but on the second pass I figured it out.

My knees crackled and popped as I straightened. "All four hooves are fine. Adequate. If I was going to be a nitpicky son of a bitch about it, I'd say the right hind could be better."

Terry smacked the lead rope against his thigh. "You gonna be a nitpicky SOB about it?"

I considered the mare. She had that quiet, wilted look about her of an animal who had given up. I knew that look well, having seen it on my mom's face for most of my life. Like she had spent so many years disappointed that now she couldn't feel anything at all. Most horses would take the opportunity to share their weight with the farrier while they were being worked on, but not Oreo. She hadn't leaned on me even a little. Not on the first visit, and not even now on the second visit.

On the outside, she had improved a hundred times over between the two visits. Her overgrown, split hooves were now healthy enough that she could walk with minimal pain. But on the inside? There was no spark of life in those big, brown eyes. Would she even notice if I went the extra mile on a hoof that was already an adequate job? Probably not.

Probably not.

That didn't much change how I felt about it, though.

I lifted the hem of my t-shirt and dragged it down my sweaty face. "Yeah, I reckon I will."

Terry grinned. "That's what I figured you'd say. Let's get her back on the stand."

"LIGHT DAY TOMORROW." Terry consulted his phone as I steered into his driveway. "Just the Taylor farm."

"That's on purpose," I reminded him. Terry's mind was a steel trap when it came to anything equine related, but dates and scheduling slipped from his brain like water through a sieve. His wife, Angie, controlled his calendar and handled the day-to-day paperwork. "My sister, Amy, is starting at the University of Colorado this fall. I promised her I'd drive her out there and get the lay of it all."

Terry squinted at his phone. "Right, right. Angie made a note right here." He tapped the screen with a blackened thumbnail. "You know, my daughter got her degree there. Did I tell you she has a master's? Smart cookie, that one. Anyway, I'm sure she'd be happy to answer any questions your sister has. I'll give her your phone number to pass on to Amy. I'll tell her to expect her call."

He slid one of his business cards from its holder on the back of his phone, jotted the number down, and handed it to me. I pushed it into my pocket without looking at it. "She won't mind you handing out her number?"

Terry gave me a surprised look. "Nah, she likes being helpful. Did I tell you…"

And he was off and running again, telling me all the wonderful things about his daughter. It never failed to make my chest tight. God, he was so proud of her. Big things, small things, it didn't even matter. He was proud that she was the first in her family to go to college at all, much less graduate. Proud that she came home every Monday, no matter how busy she was, just to help out with whatever needed to be done. Proud that she made the best damn cup of coffee on either side of the Rocky Mountains.

Yeah. That last one would have had my dad hooting about participation trophies. Praise had to be earned in the McAllister house. I agreed with that, in theory. In practice, we had never actually earned it, not once that I could recall. Nothing we did was ever more than adequate, and adequate wasn't rewarded.

I drummed my fingers on the steering wheel and waited for Terry to take a breath and give me an opening to cut him off because I knew from experience that he would segue into stories about her four younger brothers, who he was every bit as proud of, and then we might be here for another hour because goddamn, that man could talk.

There was no denying I felt some kind of way about it.

Gratitude could usually pull me out of a spiral because I wasn't such a shithead that I couldn't look around and recognize that I had it pretty damn good, actually. And when that failed, good, old-fashioned self-loathing did the trick. Because what did it say about me, that I got mad like a fucking toddler when a man showed pride in his sons, just because I knew I would never get that?

You're the guy who always comes in second and gets mad about it, because no one deserves first place more than you. The world never gives you everything you're owed, and your list of grievances is long.

Fucking Chloe Adams. It was hard to say whose voice in my head I hated more, hers or my dad's. At least Chloe made me want to prove her wrong.

My dad? I only ever wanted to prove him right.

"And then—" Terry sucked in air. This was my chance.

"I should get going," I said apologetically and a little desperately.

"Right. Of course. You got time for a snack first? Angie had a good day yesterday. She baked a few loaves of sourdough." His wife had been diagnosed with lupus fifteen years ago, shortly after the birth of her fifth child. She loved baking, but when she had a flare up, her joints ached too much to handle the dough.

"I always have time to eat," I said, unbuckling.

I followed him inside and into the kitchen. We both washed up at the sink. Terry pulled together thick slices of sourdough topped with a generous slab of cream cheese and vine-ripened tomatoes from their garden.

I looked around. It was a typical farmhouse kitchen, with the homey feel of a space well-used. Oak cabinets, green-tiled backsplash, a display of mismatched coffee mugs with hokey sayings like *but first, coffee* and *I'm not arguing, I'm explaining why I'm right*. A collection of moose items. Moose-patterned hand towels. A moose mug. A stained-glass moose hanging in the sunny window over the sink.

"Have you ever seen a moose?" I asked, remembering what Amy said about them being worse than bears.

"Oh, sure. One charged our car when we were visiting Yellowstone National Park. Angie was delighted." He pointed his knife at the refrigerator and chuckled. "That's her photo there."

I paced closer to get a better look. There was a blurred reflection of a hand holding a phone in the window, and then beyond that an angry moose, his lowered nose an inch from the glass.

"Wow, that's—" The words died in my throat as another photo caught my attention.

Four teen boys hoisting a woman in their arms like they were a human throne. All of them were grinning and laughing, dressed in suits, with the beaming woman wearing the cap and gown of a college graduate. Her dark hair hung in long waves and her green eyes sparkled.

My heart dropped into my stomach.

"These are your kids?" I asked. *Please say no.*

"They're mine, all right." The pride in his voice. Goddamn. "Although I'm really a bonus dad to my girl. Her dad died when she was only four. Bad tractor accident. But I've always considered her to be my daughter."

That was why her last name wasn't Quinn, like Terry's, I realized.

I fished Terry's card out of my pocket and flipped it over. There, over the phone number, was her name.

Chloe.

Chloe, who thought I was human garbage, was my boss's beloved daughter.

Oh, fuck *me*.

3

CHLOE

DAD

Your mom had a bad flare up this week. Worried to stay on top of everything, but it got away from me. I'm sorry.

CHLOE

No worries. I'll take care of it.

FUCKING MONDAYS, man. I would cry about it, but who had the time for tears.

I stared morosely down at the mess—*my* mess,

because I had held the door for a harried mom juggling a crying toddler and a stroller and she'd thanked me by accidentally clocking my shoulder with her massive diaper bag, sending my avocado toast and iced mocha careening to the sidewalk. Ice cubes and milky chocolate puddled at my feet, the avocado toast face down. Flecks of green and brown splattered my jeans. Half a cherry tomato landed on the toe of my sneaker.

Dammit. I'd had big plans for that iced mocha. I was going to sit my tired ass in that wicker chair, enjoy fifteen minutes of August sunshine, and let the chocolate and caffeine wash away the remnants of this morning's hangover—courtesy of the Sunday Scaries that had culminated in drinking too much and texting my situationship for one last round of *let's not ruin this with labels* before he left for his *totally epic, bro* motorcycle ride across Argentina—and the stabbing in my uterus that meant my period was inevitable. My period had always been a sporadic motherfucker, so thank heaven for small mercies or whatever.

I put a reminder in my phone to get an STI check in six months, scooped up the empty plastic cup and dumped it into the trashcan, and dropped into the chair with a pathetic whimper. Money being what it was—never enough—I couldn't afford to replace my lunch. I had blown the rest of my weekly fun money on last night's bottle of wine.

Ten minutes. I wasn't going to cry, but I could give myself ten minutes to sulk so I didn't drive mad. And then I needed to pull myself together and get to my parents' house in Evergreen, twenty minutes from Aspen Springs.

From Dad's texts, I guessed there was a small mountain of laundry waiting for me, along with the typical billing and paperwork Mom handled for Dad's farrier business when her joints weren't swollen from lupus. It was how I spent most Mondays after my 6 a.m. to noon shift at Jo's. I didn't mind, but I knew today was going to be a long one, and I still had a pile of my own paperwork to do tonight to prepare for the week's therapy sessions. Two thousand supervised clinical hours down, one thousand to go before I could take the exam and become a Licensed Clinical Social Worker. Just one more year of working two jobs and duct taping my family together in the cracks of my free time. If I could survive it.

Breathe, Chloe, breathe.

I tipped my head back and glared at the world. The Colorado sunshine was annoyingly bright. The morning birdsong was annoyingly loud. The cramps were annoyingly painful. And the cowboy coming my way with a goddamn pig on a leash was annoyingly hot.

I turtled deeper into my gray hoodie with a feeling that the universe was against me. "Get the hell out of here, Steven."

His dark eyes narrowed at me. "Your shift ended ten minutes ago."

"Are you stalking me now? I don't have to be on duty to tell you pigs aren't allowed." My gaze dipped to the animal snuffling my sneakers. "And neither are pets." I leaned my head against the brick wall behind me and closed my eyes with a weary sigh.

"What's wrong with you?" he demanded.

I cracked one eyelid open, decided it wasn't worth the effort, and closed it again. "You're what's wrong with me," I said on reflex, but my heart wasn't in it. Between the pounding in my head and the stabbing in my uterus, I had nothing left for rage, not even for someone as deserving as Steven. Alas.

There was a pause. I knew he hadn't left because Steve Junior was still snuffling my shoes, but I lacked the energy to do anything about it.

"You look like shit," he said. "Are you sick or something?"

The concern in his voice sounded genuine. I must have truly looked like I was knocking on death's door. "I am not sick, Steven. I am hungover. Not only am I hungover, but my uterus has decided that now is the time for a little home renovation and is scraping those walls clean with a rusty knife."

Steven made a disgusted noise. "Too much information. I don't need to hear about all that lady shit."

That was about what I expected from Steven. "Did you know that girls can get their periods as young as nine or ten? If a nine-year-old girl can handle the monthly trauma of bleeding from her vagina for five days straight, then you, a full-grown adult man, can damn well survive hearing about it. Or are you really that fragile?"

There was a beat of silence during which I started to

think maybe he had finally walked away, but no such luck. "So, you're just going to take a nap here?"

"I wasn't planning on it. I was going to gird my loins with an iced mocha and avocado toast before I go to my parents' house, but alas." I indicated the brown sidewalk. "Life had other plans. So now I'm pouting."

Steven blinked. "It's Monday," he said like this had just now dawned on him.

"It really fucking is," I groused. "But I don't know what that means to you."

"Nothing. I just—nothing."

"Great. Can you leave me alone now? I just need ten minutes to get my head on right, okay? Leave me to my wretchedness."

Steven didn't look remotely sympathetic to my plight. His eyes narrowed like my misery was a personal affront. "For fuck's sake, Chloe," he growled. He thrust the pig leash at me. "Don't let Stevie eat anything."

I tipped my head back to look at him as his words trudged through my pickled brain. "Stevie...the pig?"

"No, I talk about myself in third person now," he deadpanned before swinging open the glass door and striding inside.

Leaving me with the leash and a lot of questions.

"What," I asked of the pig, "is going on here?"

Junior did not answer. He—I discreetly peeked—*she* was too busy staring longingly through the glass door like a loyal dog waiting for its master's return.

A moment later Steven reappeared, placed an iced

mocha and hot coffee on the table in front of me without a single word, and went back inside. Junior tugged at the leash like she meant to follow him.

"Listen, honey." I pulled her closer and tied the leash to my chair. Hopefully her love wouldn't drag my seat out from under me. "That man in there? He's no good. Sure, he's nice to look at, but underneath the brown eyes and hard muscles is a steaming pile of hot garbage. He's not a good person."

Junior sat back on her haunches like she intended to be here a while.

I stabbed my straw through the lid, flinching at the horrific squeak of plastic rubbing against plastic, and took a long gulp of my iced mocha. Maybe it was the placebo effect, but my uterus instantly unclenched at the hit of chocolate and caffeine.

The squeak got Junior's attention and she looked at me. I swore her little piggy eyes lingered pointedly on the iced mocha delivering pain relief, courtesy of Steven McAllister.

"Okay, yes, he brought me coffee, and presumably he's getting my lunch, too. And yes, he did save you from being a coyote's dinner—although technically, that was me. His shoulders were too broad."

I frowned, because there it was again, the image branded on the back of my eyelids that had plagued me relentlessly since that rainy night three weeks ago. Steven shirtless, tanned skin slick with rain, nipples peaked and muscles taut from cold, looking like he had stepped out of a cowboy calendar. It was a cosmic injustice that Steven McAllister, asshole extraordinaire, was packaged up like a Wrangler wet dream.

"Sometimes bad people do good things. There's a lot of gray in people."

I frowned again as I fiddled with my straw. There was no reason for Steven to help me. Hell, there'd been no reason for him to save Junior. Actually, there'd been plenty of reasons for him to walk away. The rain. The mud. The pig that definitely didn't want his help. And still, he'd stayed. Even when saving Junior had clearly been impossible, he'd kept trying.

And that was why I hadn't left him there. Well, that and I'd also felt bad for Junior.

"My point is that an iced mocha and a six-pack abdomen do not make up for everything else. Do you know what he did, Junior? He purposefully spooked a horse my best friend was riding. She was bucked off into a fence. Bruised her ribs and a whole lot of other body parts. And do you know why? Because she turned him down. That's the kind of guy he is." I looked up to see Steven shouldering his way through the door and finished on a hurried whisper, "So maybe love him a little less, okay?"

Junior ignored my advice. She trotted right over to Steven and gave him an affectionate head butt on the knee as he set the tray of food in front of me.

"There you go, princess," he said, with an extra dollop of sarcasm on *princess*. He dumped a bowl of salad on the ground and gave Junior a pat on her flank. "There you go, honey." No sarcasm at all.

"Thank you," I grumbled begrudgingly. I had to force the words out. Not because of the nickname—that didn't bother me at all. I hated feeling sick and tended to be insufferable when I had so much as a sniffle. A hangover was even worse because I did it to myself. I deserved the nickname. I was being pathetic, and I knew it.

But why was he being so *nice* about it?

And it was a weird kind of nice, too. Because on the surface, Steven was always nice. He had manners. He knew how to hold a door and all that. But underneath that charming veneer was an absolute jackass who thought the world owed him something, like he had done humanity— and especially women—a huge favor merely by gracing us with his presence.

Now that dichotomy was reversed, and it was making my head spin. He was glaring and grumbling, but he was also bringing me food?

It had to be a trap.

I side-eyed him suspiciously as I popped a piece of bacon in my mouth. "You seriously named Junior after yourself?" I asked.

"You named her Steve Junior, not me." Steven narrowed his eyes at me over his coffee. "And she's not Steve Junior anymore. She's Stevie Nicks. It seemed fitting, since she's a Fleetwood Mac fan."

"Stevie the Pig...is a fan...of Fleetwood Mac." I needed

a moment to digest this information. "How would you even discover such a thing?"

He lifted a shoulder. "The usual way."

"The usual way? As in, you were going for your Sunday drive, windows down, radio on, and she started singing along?"

He laughed. "No. I listen to music while I'm doing chores. She made her preferences known. She likes Fleetwood Mac. She does not like Aerosmith." He leaned down and rubbed her head. "No one's perfect, I guess."

Steven listened to Fleetwood Mac while doing chores? Maybe even sang along to songs of yearning and drama? I could not wrap my brain around it. He had all the emotional depth of a bumblebee. It did not compute. But then, I wouldn't have thought he'd keep Junior or bring me avocado toast, either.

A lot of things about Steven McAllister did not compute.

"JAXSON QUINN, get your butt back here right now," I whisper-hollered to my brother's retreating back. Mom was lying down with a headache, and I didn't want to disturb her. "You're not so big that I can't turn you over my knee and spank you."

At sixteen, Jaxson was the baby of the family, and the

only one of the five of us to still live at home, although we were all fairly close by. Ellis, Garret, Cole, and Jaxson were technically my half-siblings, although we never called each other that. My mom had married Terry three years after my dad's accident, when I was seven. Ellis was born a year later. The rest of them came every eighteen months like clock-work—Garret, then Cole, then Jaxson—and each time I prayed I wouldn't get a sister because I didn't want to share a room. Having all brothers worked out well for me. They were often noisy and smelly, but they were also a lot of fun.

Though right now, this one was being a pain in my ass.

"Yeah, right," Jaxson whispered, pivoting back into the living room. "You've been saying that since I was four, and you've never made good on it."

"I will this time," I threatened. "You literally saw me cleaning this room while you lazed on the couch with your goldfish and now you're leaving me the crumbs and your empty soda can? I don't think so."

"You're mean today," Jaxson muttered as he snagged the can from the coffee table. He tucked it under his armpit and swept the crumbs up into his palm. "I just got home from basketball practice and I still have pre-calculus homework."

"Meanwhile, I slept in until noon and am spending my afternoon here because cleaning is my hobby." Sarcasm dripped on every word.

He dipped his chin so his hair flopped in his face, then looked up at me sheepishly with his big brown eyes. Dammit. Youngest kids always knew how to work their angles. "I'm sorry, Chloe. I just needed a moment to unwind, you know? I didn't mean for you to clean up my mess."

"I know. It's okay. Because I know you're going to do the dishes after dinner even if Terry tries to do it first. Right?"

He blinked but despite the teenager attitude, my brother was a good guy, and he knew our dad would put in ten hours of hard physical labor before finally sitting down to dinner tonight. "Right," he confirmed. "But you're making dinner?" he added hopefully.

My chest squeezed. The kid had probably been living on PB and J sandwiches and hot dogs this week. "Just a frozen lasagna. That's all I have time for today. But I stopped by the grocery store earlier. The freezer is stocked, the pantry has spaghetti and pasta sauce, and I bought your weight in goldfish and apples." Which might last maybe three days, because Jaxson was already six-two and only getting taller.

"You're the best." He dropped a kiss on the crown of my head before heading out with his crumbs and trash.

I took the staircase—dodging the creaks I had long ago memorized—to the gable office, passing my grandmother in the hallway. She had lived with us ever since my grandfather's death eight years ago, and sometimes I marveled at how surreal it must feel to her, living with her daughter-in-law and her new husband and family. My dad had been her only child, so she hadn't had much of a choice in the matter, having no other family who could take her, but she got on well with my stepdad, so maybe it didn't bother her.

"Hi, Grams," I said, on the off chance today would be different, but I wasn't surprised when her cloudy green eyes looked straight past me. There was too much to do to get in my feelings about that today.

The office was, predictably, a mess. Mom usually kept things tidy and followed the organizational system I had set up for them, but Terry, god love the man, was more of the absent-minded professor type. With my mom battling a lupus flare this week, he had been left to his own devices, which meant dumping receipts and handwritten notes in a disorderly pile on the desk.

With a sigh, I rolled the chair to the other side of the desk. Mom liked to face the door, but I liked the view out the gable window. It was the only room in the house where we could still see the mountains beyond the rooftops. This house had been in the family for a hundred years. Five generations of Adams had looked out these windows and saw nothing but green and golden fields of corn and wheat stretching all the way to the Rocky Mountains. Then my grandfather died, and we hadn't been able to hold on. The land had been sold off. Some of it was still farmland, but the acres surrounding the farmhouse had been sold to housing developers. Now the hundred-year-old farmhouse sat on a cul-de-sac with modern colonials on either side.

Six years. That was all it took for suburbia to creep in. Six years for houses to block out the sky. Six years to pave over what we nurtured for a hundred years. Six years for our family graveyard to become someone's backyard nuisance.

Sometimes I couldn't blame Grams for flitting around like a ghost.

AN HOUR LATER, with the last receipt entered into the software, I stretched my fingertips to the ceiling to relieve the tension in my back. My shoulder let out a loud, satisfying pop. Some of those scraps of handwritten notes were *tiny*.

"I thought I'd find you here."

I spun the chair around at the sound of Mom's voice. "You're up?"

"For a little bit, at least. My joints are still achy, but the headache is receding." She stepped further into the room, looking weary and rumpled but still smiling. "I'm glad you're here. You do a much better job with all this than I do."

I made a noncommittal noise that she could interpret any way she wanted to. My parents were so proud of me, but they didn't really understand why I had pivoted to mental health. I knew Mom had hoped I'd put my degree in farm management to use helping Terry with his farrier business or maybe even going to work for another farm. And for a while, after I graduated college and moved back home to sort out the mess left behind by my grandfather's death, I thought I would, too.

But I couldn't shake the anger that all this could have

been prevented. Farmers and ranchers had sky-high suicide rates—two times higher than the average population—but mental health support was almost non-existent in rural communities. It wasn't just a statistic to me. It was a tragedy that had devastated my family. So I started volunteering at a non-profit that connected ranchers and farmers to crisis management resources, including mental health and financial literacy.

When its funding was slashed, I got mad all over again. That anger pushed me through a master's degree in social work while working part-time for Terry and part-time at Jo's. My dream was to bring mental health services back to rural communities through telehealth therapy sessions with social workers who understood the stresses farmers and ranchers faced.

My parents loved me and supported me. But they also had a tendency to question how talking to someone could make any difference at all when the crops were dying from drought for the third year in a row.

Maybe they were right. Maybe the best I could do wouldn't be enough.

But I had to try.

4

CHLOE

By the time I arrived home, it was dark and I was starving. Mom had asked me to stay for lasagna, but that would have meant less leftovers for tomorrow, so instead I made myself a bowl of cereal, peeled open a cup of apple sauce, and called it dinner.

I still had my own work to do, so after a quick shower, I pulled on my pajamas and settled in on the couch. Even though I was exhausted, there was something so nice about the quiet stillness of my own space. I'd started renting this place from Miriam, my landlady, three years ago when I started my master's program. Aspen Springs was halfway between my parents' house and the university, which meant I was always commuting one way or another, but at least neither commute was more than thirty minutes.

The bungalow wasn't very big, but it had loads of charm. More importantly, it did not have four younger brothers, two nosy parents, and one ghost of a grandmother. I loved my family, but my god, I had been taking care of them for so long that I just wanted a place to not take care of anyone. Not even myself, if I didn't want to. I wanted to leave dishes in the sink without worrying that I was adding to my mother's workload. I wanted to eat junk food without worrying that I was setting a bad example for my younger brothers. I wanted to stop worrying about whether my dad was going to buckle under the stress of caring for us.

I finally fell asleep around 10:30 but startled awake at 3 a.m. with the chest-squeezing feeling that I had screwed something up. I lay there for a moment, panting, running through the week's to-do list in my mind. Had I forgotten anything? Maybe. I knew, logically, that nothing I had done or not done was so bad that I couldn't fix it tomorrow but tell that to my extremely illogical 3 a.m. anxiety. Trying to force myself back to sleep was a losing proposition, so instead I reached for my phone. Ten minutes of animal videos usually calmed me down enough.

I never meant for her to get hurt.

The text notification popped up above a video of a rescue emu farm. It was from Steven. I knew it in my gut, even though I didn't recognize the nine digits, and I had never given him my phone number. I typed back, picking up the thread in an argument we'd been having for a solid year now, even if most of it was only in our heads the whole time.

CHLOE

> You didn't mean NOT to. I believe you didn't realize how bad it would be, but you still wanted her to fall. Do you seriously not understand how truly terrible that is?

STEVEN

Why do you think I'm awake at 3 am?

The question gave me pause. Did Steven feel remorse? It had honestly never occurred to me that he might actually feel bad about what he'd done. He sure as hell had never acted like it. Before I could formulate a reply, another text popped up.

STEVEN

> You told Stevie I hurt James because she turned me down. That's not what happened. I mean, yeah, I asked her out and she said no, but that didn't matter. I wanted that promotion, and here was this little girl five years younger than me who got it instead, and when I found out she was sleeping with our boss? I was fucking pissed.

A white-hot bolt of anger streaked through me. James had *earned* her place at Lodestar.

CHLOE

James deserved that job. In case you forgot, no one else got anywhere with Belle, including you. She didn't sleep her way to the top. She did a better job.

STEVEN

I fucking know, okay? But at the time, I was just so angry. About everything. But it wasn't about her turning me down.

CHLOE

Should that matter to me?

I typed the words, but the truth was, it did matter. A very small part of me was relieved that he wasn't *that* kind of guy. But the larger part of me knew he was still an asshole, no matter what his reasoning was.

STEVEN

I don't know if it should matter to you, but it matters to Stevie. She's been side-eying me ever since you told her.

I snorted a laugh in spite of myself. Thank god he wasn't here to see it. He didn't deserve the validation. And then his next text came through and my laughter died in my throat.

STEVEN

Have you ever done something you can't take back, no matter how much you want to? You can't fix it. You just have to live with it like a bad tattoo.

Yes, I knew what that was like. I closed my eyes against the sudden memory. So much blood. Crimson pools of it on the white cotton tarp. The scent of it permeating the air. The acrid taste of it in my mouth.

When I opened my eyes again, the screen had gone dark. A petty part of me wanted to let it stay dark, to let Steven stay in the darkness with it, feeling the heavy weight of his shitty decisions.

But before the thought had even fully materialized, I was already discarding it, typing in my password to wake up my phone. It didn't matter that Steven was my least favorite person. I would never leave anyone alone in the darkness.

CHLOE

You're not the only one awake at 3 am.

Three dots appeared, winking at me in a wave, then disappeared only to reappear a moment later, like he was second-guessing his words. I didn't know what surprised me more: that Steven McAllister was searching for something insightful to say, or that I was waiting with bated breath to see if he could pull it off.

No, not just waiting.

Hoping.

STEVEN

What, the princess isn't so perfect after all? I'm shocked.

The words replaced the dots, landing like a balloon

pop. My head tilted as I stared at the screen for a long moment, my thumb hovering. There were so many ways to respond. I could do the right thing and gently guide him from lashing out to more constructive ways of dealing with his emotions. If I were his therapist, that's what I would do.

But I wasn't his therapist.

And he was such a fucking *jerk*.

It couldn't possibly be my responsibility to fix all the man-babies of the world, could it? Certainly not at 3 a.m. when I had my own shit to deal with.

But I wasn't going to say something mean, either. Because he had texted me first, reached out to me for absolution that wasn't even mine to give, and that told me exactly where to stick the knife.

So I turned off my phone without another word.

5

———

STEVEN

What the fuck was *wrong* with me?

6

STEVEN

IF THE DEFINITION OF INSANITY WAS DOING THE SAME THING over and over again and expecting different results, then I was certifiably insane because for the thirty-seventh time in a year, I walked into Jo's Coffee knowing Chloe was on shift.

Thirty-six times I had walked through that door since James's accident, and thirty-six times Chloe hadn't even taken a breath before kicking me right out again. I had no reason to believe the thirty-seventh time would be any different, but here I was anyway. Looking forward to it, even. The truth was, antagonizing Chloe was the best part of my day.

So maybe I wasn't certifiable. Maybe I was just an asshole.

In my defense, I figured I'd also apologize for being a jerk last night, since I was already here and everything.

Her back was to me as I pushed through the door, but

the bell jangling alerted her to my presence. "I'll be right with you!" she called without turning around.

"Take your time," I muttered, knowing she couldn't hear me.

Halfway to the counter, I squatted down to retrieve a folded piece of notebook paper. *Winter is coming!!!* it announced at the top with an ominous number of exclamation points, followed by a list of chores. Clean the gutters, re-caulk the windows, board up a hole in the attic where a raccoon had chewed its way through.

Two sneakers, white with colorful flowers embroidered down the sides, appeared directly in front of me. I dragged my gaze up the loose-cut denim jeans to the red apron proclaiming *Jo's Coffee! Come for the coffee, stay for the Jo*—a funny slogan considering that Josephine Ramirez, the owner, was not known for her cheerful disposition—and kept going until I found a scowling mouth and meadow-green eyes.

"That's mine." Chloe held out her palm.

My jaw popped. Chloe was going to climb on a ladder to clean the gutters and battle attic raccoons? No fucking way. But I handed her the list anyway.

"Nice shoes," I said, when what I meant to say was *I'm sorry I was such a dick last night*. She had offered me a way in, cracking the door just a little bit, and what had I done? Kicked that door shut in her face because self-sabotage was my specialty.

I didn't expect her to take the compliment at face value, even though it was sincere, so I was surprised when her eyes lit up and she held one foot forward to show off her shoe.

"My friends made them for me for my birthday. Well, they didn't *make* the shoes, obviously. They bought the Converse and then each embroidered a side. Hannah created the design. It's all our favorite flowers together. James is the columbine, Essie is the red rose, Janie is the sunflower, Hannah is the violet, and I'm the pink peony."

I didn't know shit about embroidery, but even I could tell a lot of care and effort went into those shoes. I doubted I had put that much effort into a gift, ever, and sure as shit no one had ever done something like that for me. But that was Chloe. She showed up for people in a way that made them want to show up for her.

"How did they know your favorite flower?" I asked.

Her lips twitched. "They asked. It's not exactly classified information, Steven."

"How did they know your shoe size?"

"They're sneaky." She raised her eyebrows and tilted her head. "So, are you going to apologize or what?"

The look on her face said she didn't believe for one second I would. But she was wrong about that. I wanted to apologize. The problem was I still didn't know what to say that would make any difference.

There was a jagged part of me that believed every nasty thing Chloe had ever said about me, and then some. Maybe that was why I kept coming back for more, why I kept hoping that one day she'd smile at me like she used to. Maybe if I put enough good into the world, the good would eventually outweigh the bad, even if it couldn't erase it. I wanted to believe that there was something worthwhile in the wreckage of my soul, and if she smiled at me again, then I'd know I found it.

"I'm in a coffee shop," I said. "I'm here for coffee."

It killed me a little that she didn't look surprised when she said, "Get the hell out of here, Steven."

That, at least, was something I could do.

THE FEED and supply store called, letting me know that the special pellets I had ordered for Stevie had arrived, so I swung by on my way out of town. Most hog feed was meant for livestock heading to the slaughterhouse, not backyard pets. It was formulated to fatten them up. I wanted my Stevie girl to live a long, healthy life, so I ordered her food from a fancy specialty store and had it sent to Aspen Springs Feed and Supply, since they didn't deliver way out in my area.

"Got it right here for you," Daphne said as walked through the door. She peered over the counter and her face fell. "You didn't bring Stevie with you?"

Daphne loved Stevie, and Stevie loved people in general, so I usually brought her along when I was running errands in town. I never brought her on jobs, though, because cute as she was, she was also a menace, and I wasn't about to let her get stomped by an annoyed horse.

"Not today. I'm going straight to work from here." I hefted the ninety-pound bag over my shoulder and tipped my chin. "Next time."

Daphne grinned. "Tell Stevie I said hi."

"Will do," I said, even though I definitely wouldn't. Stevie might be the smartest pig in the world, but she was still a pig.

I took a step back, pivoted toward the door, and came face-to-face with Blaine Gunnell.

His eyebrows went up in surprise. "Steven."

"Blaine." I shifted the bag. Fuck, this was awkward. Blaine worked summers at Lodestar Ranch. I hadn't seen him since the incident. "How's school?"

"One more year. Then I'm off to vet school."

"Right." I nodded. Blaine's dad, Jacob Gunnell, was the best vet in a hundred miles, and Blaine intended to follow in his footsteps. "Good for you," I said, and meant it. We had gotten along great...until we hadn't.

"It's been a while, hasn't it?" He tilted his head like he was searching his memory, though we both knew damn well he remembered. "I haven't seen you since Adam broke your nose."

I sighed. God, I was so fucking *tired*. "That was it, all right." I stepped around him, pushed the door open with my hip, and went out ass first. "Good luck with school." I still meant it.

But if I never saw a single person from Lodestar Ranch

ever again, I would be okay with that.

I tossed the pellets in the passenger seat and slammed the door shut, hoping like hell the footsteps crunching on the gravel parking lot belonged to literally anyone else.

No such luck.

"I heard you're in the farrier business now," Blaine said behind me. Of course the kid had followed me out. He had never minded his own business a day in his life, so why start now?

I turned slowly. "That's right."

Gossip spread like wildfire in small towns, so I wasn't surprised he knew I had switched careers. The only thing that surprised me was that no one outside the Lodestar Ranch circle seemed to know about the incident with James. The Hale family was one of the oldest and most respected in Aspen Springs. They could have made my life hell, turned every client against me before I had even started, but they didn't.

Maybe that was about to change.

Blaine studied me, his dark eyes serious. "My dad said you were over at Sunshine Rescue a couple weeks ago."

The tension in my shoulders ratcheted up a notch. The Gunnell family had been in Colorado almost as long as the Hales. They had come through here as freed slaves turned cowboys, moving cattle from Texas up to the north after the Civil War, and ended up sticking around, some settling here in Aspen Springs, and others going to Five Points in Denver. As the vet, Jacob's job had a certain synergy with my work. We saw each other frequently, and I respected him. I wanted him to respect me, too.

God*dam*mit.

"I've been a lot of places, Sunshine Rescue included." I leaned against the truck and folded my arms. "What of it?"

Blaine tilted his head. "Just thought it was interesting, that's all. He was impressed with your work. The mare they took on...he said her feet were some of the worst he had ever seen, and wasn't sure a new farrier like yourself would be up to the challenge. He was surprised at how much she's improved."

I grunted. "My mentor, Terry. He's the one overseeing my work until I get certified. He has..." I rolled my lips, searching for the right word. "...*exacting* standards."

"Huh." Blaine's eyebrows quirked. "Well, that's new."

"What's new?" I asked, not following.

"I've never known you to share credit, that's all." He smirked. "Not that there was much credit for you to take, as I recall."

I rolled my eyes and huffed. "I was a good trainer, Blaine."

"James is better," he shot back.

"James is better than all of us," I returned. After a brief hesitation, I allowed, "Myself included."

He laughed. "I'll tell her you said so."

"Don't," I said reflexively. I winced. "I just mean, there's no point. She doesn't want to hear my name." I rubbed the back of my neck. "I didn't hurt her on purpose. It seems stupid to say that, because I made her *fall* on purpose, so what's the difference? I *was* stupid. I didn't fucking think. Just saw her in the ring, doing the thing I couldn't do, saw the bridle, and acted on impulse." I shook my head, still furious and disgusted with my own behavior. How could I have fucking done that? "Seeing her crumpled against the fence like that, unconscious? Worst moment of my fucking life."

Blaine considered that. "I'm not saying an apology will magically make everyone forgive and forget, but it might go further than you think. You should try it sometime."

I barked a laugh. "Oh, hell no. I'm not going anywhere near James."

"Because Adam will beat the shit out of you?" Blaine smirked.

"I think it's fair to say that with all three Hale brothers currently living on the property, my chances of making it out alive are slim. But that's not why." The day at the library six months ago, when Chloe had stripped me raw with her words, James had been there, too. And shit, when she saw me? She fucking *flinched*. It haunted me. "She doesn't need my apology. It would make me feel better, but it wouldn't do shit for her. The best way for me to show her I'm sorry and that I'm not a threat is to stay the hell away from her."

Blaine frowned at the ground, his hands on his hips. "Maybe you're right," he said at last.

"Did you..." I swallowed roughly. I hated asking this, but I couldn't stand the thought of Terry finding out what happened at Lodestar. People wouldn't trust me anymore.

"Did you say anything to your dad about me? I understand if you did. I just…need to know." If he had told his dad, then eventually that information would circle back to Terry. It would be better for him to hear it from me.

"No, I didn't say a word to my dad about your time at Lodestar or what happened with James. I'm not going to wreck another man's livelihood without a damn good reason. In this economy? Fuck no. I figured I wouldn't have to. You'd show your true colors soon enough." He rocked back on his heels, studying me. "Maybe you already are. See you around, Steven."

"Sure," I said, because I liked the kid.

But I really fucking hoped not.

7

CHLOE

DAD

No need to come over Monday. Your mom is feeling much better this week, and you deserve a real day off.

CHLOE

Thanks, but I have a list of things that need to get done around the house before the weather turns.

DAD

The gutters, windows, and attic? Don't worry about it. It's all done.

CHLOE

Seriously? Tell Jax I love him.

THIS WEEK HIT *HARD*. JAXSON MUST HAVE STEPPED UP, AND thank god for that because I would never have survived without the extra help. As it was, by the time Friday rolled around, I was a mere husk of a human, my feet and back aching from my morning shifts at Jo's, my shoulders drooping from the weight of other people's emotions, my brain fuzzy with bone-deep exhaustion. Too tired to eat, I crawled into bed sideways, still fully clothed, my sneakers hanging off the edge of the mattress.

It was pitch-black when I awoke. I stretched my arm out, seeking the nightstand, but found only more bed. For a moment I lay there, utterly discombobulated, before I remembered I was sideways. I shifted, located the night-stand and my phone, and hit the button. 2:57.

Jesus Christ. I had slept for eleven hours.

If I got up now, I might crash at noon, but I had an afternoon shift at Jo's tomorrow and a small mountain of paperwork. I didn't have time for naps. Should I try to go back to sleep for another two? My stomach growled, letting me know that wasn't an option.

Boxed mac and cheese. That was what I wanted. The kind with the day-glow orange powder that clumped together if you didn't add milk. I never added milk. Those damp, tangy clumps of over-processed cheese were the food equivalent of thick, fuzzy socks.

My stomach growled again, an insistent reminder that I hadn't eaten since the handful of pistachios I'd gobbled down between clients yesterday afternoon. I rolled out of bed.

After a cursory shower, I slipped on my fluffy robe and wool socks instead of getting dressed. I wasn't ready to admit the new day had truly begun. Three a.m. was a gray area between yesterday and tomorrow. It was gremlin time. Nothing counted during gremlin time.

I padded into the kitchen, put a pot of water on the stove, and grabbed the blue box of mac and cheese from the pantry. While I waited for the water to boil, I leaned against the counter and scrolled dog accounts on social media. I couldn't have a dog—Miriam, the woman who owned the Craftsman bungalow I had rented for the last three years, was very protective of her hardwood floors—and I wasn't sure I even wanted a dog, but I found their goofy, simple feelings soothing.

I kept right on scrolling with one hand while I used my other to dump the macaroni into the boiling water. Ten minutes later, I drained the pot and stirred in the powdered cheese, leaving it clumpy. I grabbed a fork and the pot and sat cross-legged on the floor. No point in getting extra dishes dirty when I was the one who would have to wash them.

I had just switched from dogs to llamas when Steven's text bounced on the top of my screen.

STEVEN

I'm sorry.

I swallowed the food in my mouth and left the fork there, the tines clamped between my lips, while I typed back.

CHLOE

> For being a jerk a week ago? I might have cared more if it hadn't taken you so long to apologize.

His reply was immediate.

STEVEN

> I might have apologized sooner if I cared less.

My head tilted and my brows pinched as a bloom of sympathy unfurled in my chest. I knew that feeling. It was so easy to let the words roll off my tongue when they meant little, when they followed an accidental shoulder bump or a moment of forgetfulness. But sometimes...

Sometimes when it mattered most, when I *cared* the most, fear clogged my throat until I couldn't push the words past it. Fear that the words would be wrong. Fear that they wouldn't be *enough*. Fear because once they hadn't been enough, and nothing I could say would ever change that.

I knew that feeling so damn well. It knocked me sideways a bit that Steven might, too.

And then he took it one step further.

STEVEN

> I thought about it every day.

My lips parted on a surprised huff and the fork fell in my lap with a harmless thump.

CHLOE

Are you drunk?

STEVEN

I'm not drunk. I'm fucking tired. I haven't slept through 3 am in months.

CHLOE

Your guilty conscience is not my problem.

I hit send before I thought it through, but I meant it. I wasn't the only thing keeping him awake, and as far as I knew, he had never once apologized to James for his role in her accident—although, to be fair, apologizing to James might be physically impossible considering that if Steven came within speaking distance of her, Adam would put him six feet under in a heartbeat.

But I didn't want to be fair.

Steven didn't deserve fair.

I shoveled a forkful of macaroni and cheese into my mouth and chewed with my eyes glued to my phone screen. It took a second before the waving dots appeared. *Go ahead and say something ugly. Prove me right about you.*

STEVEN

So what is your problem? I mean, why are you up?

Concern for my mental health? That wasn't what I expected. My eyes narrowed. I licked cheese goop from the fork tines and then typed back. "I took a nap and now I'm paying for it."

STEVEN

No good nap goes unpunished. My mom says that.

So what do you do when you can't sleep? I'm looking for ideas.

CHLOE

It depends. If I'm anxious, I look at animal videos. Eventually that turns to doom scrolling, which obviously doesn't help with the anxiety. Sometimes I read a chapter or two. Hannah puts a romance book aside for me every week. She's great at choosing things I'll like.

But I'm not anxious now. I'm just hungry because I slept through dinner. So I made myself food.

STEVEN

Sounds like a better use of time than how I usually spend 3 a.m.

CHLOE

What do you do?

STEVEN

Argue with you. ;)

Mostly in my head, but sometimes you're awake and argue back.

CHLOE

Yeah? And how does that work out for you?

STEVEN

Not great, thanks for asking. I never win, even when you're sleeping.

Good night, Chloe.

CHLOE

Good night, Steven.

I put my phone down, finished the last of the mac and cheese and dropped the bowl in the sink so it could be tomorrow's problem, and headed back to my bed, where a book was waiting for me on the nightstand, full of dragons and war and good sex and women who could do anything, even if it hurt.

I rolled into bed, grabbing the book as I went. But I didn't open it right away. I held it to my chest and stared unseeingly at the ceiling, that text he sent me playing over in my mind. *I never win, even when you're asleep.*

I had said terrible things to him that day at the library. True things, but terrible all the same. I wasn't sorry, and I wasn't going to take them back now or try to soften the blow.

But I wondered, lying there, if the cruelest words in his head weren't mine at all.

STEVEN

MONDAY, 3 A.M.

STEVEN
video link

I saw this and thought of you.

CHLOE
A cat hiding in the couch so it can smack a person on the head makes you think of me?

STEVEN
What, you don't see the similarities? It's your goddamn twin.

TUESDAY, 3 a.m.

STEVEN

video link

Talk me out of getting an ostrich.

CHLOE

Did you know that ostriches have 4-inch claws and like to kick? Anyway, you should totally get one. :)

WEDNESDAY, 3 a.m.

STEVEN

video link

What about emus? I don't think I am strong enough to resist an emu in a Sunday hat.

CHLOE

I bet Junior would like a hat.

STEVEN

I already ordered it.

THURSDAY, *3 a.m.*

STEVEN

video link

This cat is your soul mate.

CHLOE

I know you're trying to insult me, but I don't care. She's magnificent. I want to have her babies.

STEVEN

Sleep deprivation has made you loopy.

CHLOE

Maybe I wouldn't be sleep deprived if you didn't text me at 3 a.m.

STEVEN

Did I wake you up?

CHLOE

No

STEVEN

That's what I thought.

It's 3 am. Do you know where your anxiety is?

CHLOE

Sitting right on my chest, motherfucker

FRIDAY, 3 a.m.

STEVEN

photo link

You liked that photo ten seconds after I posted it. Stalker.

CHLOE

Junior is wearing a pink cowboy hat. I believe in world peace again.

9

———

STEVEN

"You're coming home for Thanksgiving, right?" Mom asked.

I scrubbed a hand over my scratchy jaw. "No, Mom. I already told you. Amy only gets a couple days off and she needs them to study for finals."

At the sound of her name, Amy looked up from the map she was studying at the kitchen table. "Don't throw me under the bus!" she hissed.

I rolled my eyes at her. "Plus, I can't take the time off, either. I've got the farrier exam coming up."

"Christmas, then," Mom insisted. "You'll be home for Christmas?"

I couldn't bear the hopeful note in her tone.

"Christmas?" I echoed, raising my eyebrows at Amy. She shook her head frantically. Too damn bad. If she had answered her phone in the first place, I wouldn't be the one having this discussion to begin with. "Yeah, we can probably fly there for a couple days."

I refused to call it home.

It wasn't. Not mine, anyway. He had made that abundantly clear.

Amy glared at me. I turned away but I could still feel the burn of it on my back. "Why don't you come to Colorado for a visit, Mom? I have a spare bedroom. You could go hiking with Amy. You should see the mountains here. They're insane."

"Well, of course we'd love to see your new place, Steven, but you know your dad."

I did know my dad. He'd never put himself out for someone else. He was too busy, too important, to pause his life and visit ours.

"You could come by yourself," I pushed, even though I knew better. "Just you. Stay for a week or two."

Mom gave a startled laugh. "By myself? Oh, I couldn't do that, honey. Who would make your father's dinner?"

I ground my teeth so hard I was in danger of cracking a molar. "He's a grown man, Mom. He can bake a frozen pizza or order takeout."

"Now, you know I won't stand for that ungrateful talk," Mom said sharply. "He provides for me, and I'm happy to do my duty and provide for him."

I thunked my head against the oak cabinet, the first time for punishment and the second to teach me a lesson I seemed slow to learn. In theory, there was nothing wrong with what she said. That kind of partnership could work just fine if both people in it respected each other.

And that was the problem.

Mom loved being a homemaker, and she valued the work. My issue was that Dad *didn't*. There wasn't a damn thing she did that he was grateful for. Every cent she spent, he reminded her where it came from. But somehow when it came to what she gave him in return, he was entitled to all of it. In his twisted mind, she *owed* it to him.

And it still wasn't enough.

"All right," I said quietly. "We miss you."

"I miss you, too, honey. I'll give your love to Dad," she chirped because she liked to pretend that life was a 1950s black-and-white sitcom, when in fact, Dad hadn't spoken a word to me since Amy moved in.

Amy shook her head at me as I hung up.

"What?" I demanded.

"I don't know why you bother. She's perfectly happy being his maid with sex benefits."

"Amy, what the hell?" I nearly spewed my coffee. "Don't *say* shit like that."

She gave me an unimpressed stare. "Dude. Where do you think you came from? Our parents have sex. Mom isn't the Virgin Mary." She pulled a face. "I bet it's terrible. He seems like the selfish type."

I dragged my hands down my cheeks. "I am begging you to stop talking."

"Yeah. I'm grossing myself out, anyway."

I refilled my mug, then held up the pot. "Want me to top you off?"

"Yes, please." She nudged her mug closer to the edge of the table and went back to studying her map.

I filled her cup, took note of the way the fresh coffee lightened slightly from the dregs still in her cup, and grabbed the half-and-half from the fridge. "Just cream, or do you want sugar, too?"

"Just cream." She watched me pour. "That's good, thanks."

I headed back to the refrigerator with the cream. When I turned around again, I found her watching me with her chin propped on her palm. "What?" I asked.

She startled and laughed. "Just thinking, that's all. Dad would never in a million years have done what you just did. He could have been standing right next to the coffee pot, and he still would have expected Mom to refill his cup for him." Her shoulders lifted as she hunched over her mug and took a sip. "It's funny, because I used to worry you'd turn out just like him."

I froze, my fingertips turning white from gripping my mug. There were twelve years between us, so we had never been particularly close growing up. Amy had been eight when I graduated from high school. College had been like a breath of fresh air, and I spent as little time at home as I could, given that Dad still controlled my finances. But I had always made it a point to spend time with her when I was around. Hearing her say she thought I was like him in any way scraped me raw.

"I'm not like him," I said, hating the uncertainty in my voice.

"That's what I'm saying. I mean, sometimes you talked like him, and it always caught me off guard. Remember in college how you were the second-string quarterback, and Dad was so mad because of course his son should have been the starting quarterback, and he said it was the coach playing favorites—"

I winced. "Yeah, thanks, I remember." I remembered breaking the news to my dad, how his anger fed mine, and said something to Julian that was so out of line I couldn't think about it now without feeling like I was on fire.

And I remembered Julian proving me wrong every damn day. When he was one of the first draft picks in the NFL, I wasn't surprised. But did I learn my lesson?

Not a fucking chance.

"You're not Dad, Steven," Amy said quietly. "Dad was mean and angry. You were angry, but you were never mean."

She meant to make me feel better, but I only felt worse. Amy didn't know the truth. She didn't know what happened with James, that she had gotten hurt because of me. And I sure as shit wasn't going to tell her.

I nodded toward the map she had spread out on the table. "Where are you headed?"

"Estes Park with my friend Lila. The aspens are all gold now and the elks are bugling."

"You'll be back in time for dinner? I told Terry we'd be there at six sharp," I reminded her. Terry had invited us for

Sunday dinner, and I only said yes because Chloe wouldn't be there. He still didn't know that I had history with his daughter, and I wanted to keep it that way.

"Don't worry, I'll be home in time to shower and change," Amy said. "We're not doing a big hike, just getting lunch and taking in the scenery. Actually, I've got to get going." She scraped back her chair and pushed to her feet.

I stepped back to let her pass, but she caught me by the elbow, rolled up on her toes, and kissed my cheek. "Thanks, big brother."

My hand flew to my face. We weren't a touchy-feely family. We didn't hug. We sure as hell didn't give cheek kisses. "For what?"

"For the coffee. For...everything."

I stayed rooted to the spot long moments after she had disappeared into her room. The way she had looked at me, with all that love and trust shining from her eyes that looked so much like our mom's...it made my chest hurt.

I wondered how she'd look at me if she knew the truth.

10

CHLOE

MOM

Good news, your brothers will all be home after all. It's been too long since we were all together.

CHLOE

Great, can't wait to see them. Six?

MOM

Could you come at five? We have company coming. Terry invited his new partner. I could use an extra hand.

CHLOE

Sure, no problem. Are you feeling okay?

MOM

Don't worry about me. It's a good day. :)

"She's here!" Ellis, my oldest brother but still younger than me by four years, bellowed over his shoulder before engulfing me in a bear hug. "How's my favorite sister?"

"I'm your only sister, jackass," I said, my voice muffled by his flannel shirt as I returned the hug.

"Good thing. I'm not sure you could earn the title fair and square."

I swatted his shoulder and he laughed, releasing me. Immediately, I was pounced on by the rest of the pack, lifted off the ground, and passed around from one brother to the next while I laughed and hollered.

"Where's Mom?" I asked when they finally set me back on solid ground.

"In the kitchen," Cole said, which is about what I expected, so I was already heading in that direction. "Grams is, too," he added apologetically. "Dad is setting the table."

The second I walked into the kitchen I knew Mom had stretched the truth. It was *not* a good day. She was rubbing her hands, a telltale sign that they ached, and a ruddy butterfly bloomed across her nose and cheeks.

"Mom," I admonished.

She turned, beaming when she saw me. "Hi, honey. Mom, Chloe is here," she added before pulling me into a gentle hug.

"We need more carrots," Grams said, eyeballing the pile of vegetables on the cutting board.

Mom gave me a look somewhere between amusement and annoyance. "We have plenty of carrots."

"What are we making?" I asked, surveying the kitchen. From the smell of it, I was sure there was a chicken in the oven. Grams was chopping vegetables—carrots, onions, and small red potatoes—to throw in with it. Mom, paring knife in hand, was overseeing another pile of potatoes. I took the knife from her and ushered her to the breakfast table. "Go sit down, Mom."

She sat with a relieved sigh that made my chest pull tight. "It *started* as a good day."

"How is it now?" I asked.

"Manageable." When I gave her a suspicious look, she smiled. "Really and truly, Chloe. I'm not playing the martyr here, I promise. I know that the best way to have more good days is to take care of myself on the bad days. My joints ache a bit, that's all."

I studied at her closely, wanting to verify that for myself. Since she had been diagnosed with lupus several years ago, I had learned all the symptoms and what to look for. I didn't see a rash other than the one on her face. On good days, Mom could do almost anything. On bad days, exhaustion and headaches kept her in bed with the lights out.

"Tell her, Grams," Mom said with exasperated fondness. Grams didn't tell me anything, but I never expected her to. Apparently, Mom didn't either, because she barely paused before continuing, "My hands and knees are swollen, which makes cooking hard. That's all."

"All right," I relented. "What are we having?" I asked again.

"Nothing fancy. The chickens are in the oven. I made dinner rolls last night, thankfully. I was starting in on the scalloped potatoes when you got here. Think you can finish up for me?"

Only my mother would describe a full roast chicken dinner for nearly a dozen people as *nothing fancy*. I shook my head, smiling.

"Of course I can do the potatoes," I said. I knew how to cook. I didn't *like* it, but I could get it done.

I got to work slicing the potatoes paper-thin. Scalloped potatoes was one of my favorite dishes, and I suspected Mom had planned them just for me. It was one of those foods that was too labor intensive for me to ever make for myself—although now, of course, that was exactly what I was doing.

"Tell me about work," Mom said. "I want to hear every-thing. How's work going?"

"It's great," I said. "Hard, but rewarding, you know? I'm starting to research options for opening my own telehealth clinic next summer after I'm fully certified. One of the issues with mental health services in rural communities is that we all know each other. There's already a stigma around going to therapy and convincing someone to share their problems and secrets with a person who knows everyone in your life is a hard sell. I—"

Grams turned on the radio. "You don't mind if I listen

to my program, do you, Angie? It's nice to have it on in the background while we're cooking."

Mom blinked. Her gaze darted briefly to me before faltering. "Sure, Mom."

The doorbell rang and Grams set down her knife. "I'll get that."

Mom's gaze followed her out, then she turned to me. "Don't mind her, Chloe. She'll come around."

I snorted. Mom had been saying that for eight years now.

Bracing on the table, Mom rose slowly to her feet. "Let's go greet your father's guests, all right?"

I nodded, rinsed my hands of at the sink, and dried them on my jeans before following her into the hallway.

Where I stopped dead in my tracks.

Because there, standing in my childhood home, a pie box balanced on each hand, was Steven Fucking McAllister, dressed for dinner. His short dark hair was neatly combed, his jaw sharp from a fresh shave, and his crisp white button-down shirt was tucked into dark jeans that hugged his thighs. All of which meant it wasn't the pies that made my mouth water. My stomach swooped like a rollercoaster. It was easy to forget he looked like *that* when he was texting me silly animal videos at 3 a.m.

His pupils flared as he took me in. He didn't look quite as surprised to see me as I was to see him.

"The pies look delicious, Steven," Mom said. "They're from Sweetie Pies, aren't they? I haven't had one of Cat's masterpieces in ages. Let's put them in the kitchen."

Steven nodded, following my mom out of the knot of people. As he passed me, he paused just long enough to murmur, "Please don't."

I didn't know what he meant by that. But I was going to find out.

And then I was going to do it even harder.

Even serial killers had mothers, so I shouldn't have been so surprised that Steven had a sister. But Amy was so sweet and had an air of innocent naïveté about her. She was tall and gangly, with chin-length dark hair and big brown eyes that always looked a little bit surprised, and she was clearly several years younger than Steven. I vaguely remembered his family was all back in the Midwest somewhere, and maybe he had mentioned a sister at one point, but she looked fresh out of high school. Did she live with him?

I had questions. I didn't like having questions about Steven. There was no reason for me to be curious about him.

I excused myself from the crowded room to go finish getting dinner together. Amy volunteered to help and followed me into the kitchen.

"There's not much left to do, really," I said. The chickens had just been pulled from the oven. I opened the door to check on the scalloped potatoes and found them lightly browned but not crisp enough. Five more minutes under the broiler.

I glanced at Amy over my shoulder and found her eyeballing me in the most unnerving way. "So, um, Steven says you're from the Midwest?" I prodded.

"Oklahoma." Her head tilted. "Sorry if you weren't planning to cook for two extra people."

"What do you mean?" I asked, opening a cabinet and pulling glasses down.

"You looked surprised to see us," she said.

"Oh…not exactly. My dad said his new guy—that's all he ever called him, the new guy"—I did air quotes around the phrase—"and his sister were coming. I just didn't know the new guy was Steven." I inclined my head toward the ice maker on the refrigerator door. "If you do the ice and water, I'll put them on the table."

Amy nodded, reached for the first glass, and shoved it under the ice maker. "So, if you don't know Steven through your dad, how did you meet? Because the way you looked at him, it was clearly not the first time you two had clapped eyes on each other."

I paused. Maybe she knew about James, but maybe not. Or if she did, she'd probably heard a different version than the story I'd tell. "We met at Lodestar Ranch. One of my friends is a trainer there. James." I watched her closely for any signs of recognition, but she just nodded. "And Aspen Springs is a small town, so of course we've run into each other now and again. Oh!" I slapped my palm on the counter. "That night his battery died in the thunderstorm?

I gave him a jump and helped rescue Junior. Did he tell you about that?"

"Junior?" She scrunched her nose. "Do you mean Stevie?"

"Right. Stevie Nicks. The pig."

Amy chortled with delight. "That was you? Oh, my god. I kind of thought he made most of it up. Not the part about Stevie because she's obviously real, but all the stuff about a woman coming to his aid and crawling through the mud." She gave me a quizzical look, her head tilting. "It's funny, he didn't mention that he actually *knew* you."

My forehead puckered. I couldn't think of a good reason why he would leave that out. I shrugged. "Maybe he thought it made for a funnier story if I was a stranger?"

"Maybe." But she looked like she had doubts. So did I. Then she shrugged and reached for another glass. "Anyway, I was surprised when Steven first told me he was enrolling in a farrier program, but now I get it. It makes sense. Bronc riding on the rodeo circuit and then training show horses...I don't know. He was good at it, but his heart wasn't really in competition. That's our dad's thing. He didn't care what we did as long as we were the best at it. That was all that mattered. But Steven...he wanted to be outside, and he wanted to be with horses. That was what mattered to him. Honestly, he's too sweet for competition."

I nearly fell over. "Too...*sweet*? *Steven* is too sweet?"

Amy handed me the glass with a laugh. "I mean, yes, he's also grumpy and can be kind of a jerk sometimes. But I wouldn't be here going to college without him. My scholarship doesn't cover room and board or books. He's giving me a place to stay and covering the books I need. He saved me."

That startled me. He sounded like a great big brother, but he *saved* her? From what? Student loans? That seemed a little dramatic. "What do you mean?"

"Oh, I—" Her voice faltered, and she glanced over her shoulder nervously, like she expected to find someone lurking. "I needed a change, that's all, and he made it happen. I was miserable in Oklahoma, and you know Steven. He can't stand to see any living creature suffer, animal or human."

"Hm," I murmured, hoping she might say more, but Amy was clearly regretting that she had said anything.

We gathered in the living room for iced tea while Dad carved the roast chickens, with Steven and Amy sitting next to each other on the sofa across from me. All the wonderful things Amy had said about him kept bumping up against the awful things I knew about him. And muddying the image further were the 3 a.m. text messages.

You know Steven, she'd said. And I thought I had.

But I really didn't know Steven McAlister at all.

11

STEVEN

Organized chaos. That's what this was. I felt like I had been thrust into one of those sappy holiday movies where a down-on-his-luck outsider learned the true meaning of family. It was loud and boisterous, full of teasing and inside jokes. Terry carved the chickens in the kitchen while Cole finished setting the table in the dining room and the rest of us had iced tea in the living room. It didn't seem to matter that everyone was spread out. The Quinns carried on several conversations at once, laughing and shouting over each other from room to room.

Amy watched the Quinns like an anthropologist visiting a foreign land, eyes wide and mouth slightly agape. Our family dinners were nothing like this. No laughter. No teasing. No inside jokes. It was loud, though. Dad had a lot of gripes and dinner was his chance to unload them on my mother. With every beer he drank, he got louder and angrier. Mom focused so much of her attention on pacifying him that she barely got more than a bite to eat herself.

I hated going home, so I used school, football, and rodeo as an excuse to stay away as long as possible. Watching Amy watch the Quinns now, I felt a pang of regret. I should have come home every chance I got. I should have protected her better.

Amy turned to me with an amused, *can you believe families are like this in real life* smile. She had never once given me shit for abandoning her. Hell, she'd been surprised when I told her she could live with me. Surprised, and so damn grateful it made my gut twist with guilt.

I had a lot to make up for with Amy. And if Chloe told her about James? I'd never get that chance. It would be confirmation of her worst fears that I was just like *him*.

I had been worried when they disappeared into the kitchen together, but whatever had been discussed, it wasn't *that*. Amy wouldn't be sitting next to me on the couch right now, sending comically baffled looks in my direction, if she knew about James.

I could feel Chloe's eyes on me, but every time I looked back, her gaze skittered sideways. I'd linger on the curve of her throat rising out of the chunky knit, ivory turtleneck she wore or the small dimple that formed in her left cheek when she smirked at something her brothers said, and then it was my turn to spin away when she felt me looking. My heart pulsed harder during our stupid game of chicken than it ever had in eight seconds on a bronco.

"Birds are on the table," Terry announced, clapping his hands to get everyone's attention. "Let's eat."

I moved slowly, letting the throng file out first, hyper aware of Chloe's simmering presence hovering off to the side. When I fell in line behind Amy, Chloe snagged me by a beltloop just above my ass and jerked me to a stop.

I smirked at her over my shoulder. "Well, hello, there, princess. Something I can do for you?"

"Since you're asking? The lake's not quite frozen over yet. How about you take a walk on it?" Her smile was sweet and sharp at the same time, like how I imagined a sea siren would look before she sank her teeth into a sailor.

My shoulders tightened. It shouldn't have surprised me the way it did. What, did I honestly think that a week of semi-friendly 3 a.m. text conversations meant all was forgiven? Her best friend got hurt because of me. Chloe was never going to let that go.

"What are you doing here, Steven?" she hissed, giving my beltloop another sharp tug.

I rocked back a step to keep my balance and caught a whiff of her strawberry-scented shampoo. "If you wanted me closer, princess, all you had to do was ask," I murmured.

She went so still that the hairs on the back of my neck stood up in alarm.

Fuck, that was a mistake.

There were only two things I cared about in this whole world, and Chloe Adams held them both in the palm of her hand. She could ruin my life if she decided to. I shouldn't be goading her like this, but I couldn't stop myself.

The growl she emitted went straight to my cock. Her hand tightened into a fist around my belt and she shifted onto her toes so she could enunciate every word slowly and carefully into my ear. "I would pull out every single one of my toenails with rusty pliers before I asked you for anything."

It was tempting to prove her wrong. To drag those jeans down her body and lick her until she begged me to make her come. I wanted to make her forget she hated me, make her forget her own name, make her feel even a little of this twisted hunger I felt. Sure, she'd hate me even more for it after, but so what? She already hated me. What was one more thing to add to the list?

Except…I didn't want her to hate me. The only thing I hated about Chloe was how much I *didn't* hate her.

"I didn't think you'd be here," I said. "Your dad said you were too busy with school and work."

"So you knew Terry was my dad," Chloe said flatly.

"Not at first. I—"

"Chloe! Steven! What's taking you two so long?" Angie called from the dining room. "Come eat."

Chloe slowly unfurled her fingers and gave me a little shove to urge me away from her. "This isn't over."

"I know," I said wearily, following her into the dining room.

Chloe claimed a seat next to her mother, and it didn't take long for me to realize she had done that on purpose.

Angie's hands were clearly bothering her. I watched Chloe fill her own plate with slices of chicken breast the she cut into bite-sized pieces, a scoop of roasted veggies that she also cut into smaller chunks, scalloped potatoes, and a dinner roll that she tore in half. Then, without fuss, she swapped plates with Angie, who gave her a tiny nod of appreciation.

Angie caught my gaze and smiled. "You have to try the potatoes, Steven. They're Chloe's favorite."

I smiled back. "I'm not going to pass up cheesy potatoes."

"Hand me your plate," Chloe said, not quite meeting my eyes. "The potatoes are heavy. It's easier not to pass them around."

I gave her my plate across the table and then Amy's. "Thanks."

After also serving Terry and her grandmother, she looked at her brothers. "Who else wants potatoes?"

Of course everyone wanted potatoes, and there was a loud ruckus as her brothers informed her of that, each clamoring to be served first.

"Calm down," Chloe laughed. "There's plenty of food, even for you maniacs."

"Please, miss, may I have some more?" Garret begged like Oliver Twist, his hands clasped. His was the last plate, and Chloe had already plopped a sizable portion next to his chicken.

"No way," Jaxson protested. "It's not humanly possible to eat that much. Not even for you."

Garret smirked. "I ran thirty miles this morning. Watch me."

With a sigh and a laugh, Chloe emptied the rest of the potatoes onto Garret's plate. "Hope no one else wanted seconds, because I'm not cooking more."

"Yes!" Garret pumped his fist. "That's why you're my favorite, Chloe."

"Thirty miles?" Amy asked.

Garret nodded. "I'm training for my first hundred-mile race. Phoenix in November.

"Wow." Amy looked impressed.

I shot her a *don't even think about it* look and then saw Chloe's plate. "You didn't get any potatoes," I said under the thrum of voices.

She shrugged it off. "I have plenty of food."

"But—"

She stared daggers at me. All right, then. I'd mind my own business.

"So, Steven, Terry tells me you will be taking the farrier exam soon?" Margaret—who they all called Grams—asked, pulling my attention away from Chloe.

"That's right, ma'am."

"And what are your plans after that? Will you be going into business for yourself, or partnering with Terry? Terry, pass me the rolls, please."

Terry cast a confused glance at the platter of roast chicken in front of his plate. Chloe picked up the basket of rolls next to her and passed them to Margaret. But Margaret was still watching me, waiting for my response, so after a moment of hesitation, Chloe set the basket down in front of her grandmother with a brief press of her lips.

"Well, I—" I looked at Terry, unsure what to say. A partnership hadn't occurred to me.

"We haven't had a chance to discuss it. I wasn't going to spring it on you over dinner," Terry said, shooting his mother-in-law an exasperated look. "So, thanks for that, Grams." He turned to me sheepishly. "Grams and Angie have been after me to take on a partner, and step back from the more physical parts of the job. I was hoping that might be you."

"Oh, I—augh—" I grimaced as someone's shoe kicked my shin with too much force to be accidental.

"Are you all right?" Margaret asked, her brow puckered with concern.

"Banged my knee, that's all." I rubbed my leg and narrowed my eyes at Chloe.

She glared right back, her hand wrapped threateningly around a knife handle as she slowly and exaggeratingly mouthed the words, "Fuck. No."

"Don't let Margaret bully you into answering now," Terry said. Margaret blinked innocently and sipped her ice water. "We'll talk over the details tomorrow. There's no rush for you to decide."

"I'll definitely think about it," I said. Out of the corner of my eye I saw Chloe shift in her seat, preparing to deliver another blow.

This time I dodged.

IT WAS hilarious watching Chloe boss the hell out of everyone without them seeming to know she was doing it. With dinner over and everyone too full for dessert, she divvied up the chores—clearing the table, putting leftovers away, doing dishes—among her brothers, organized a game of UNO for her parents, Margaret, and Amy, and then reminded me of a promise I sure as shit had never made to put the snow tires on her car.

"Now?" I asked. "You happen to have your snow tires with you?"

She gave a bright, tinkly little laugh. "I keep them here. Usually Terry takes care of it for me, but since you offered..." Her voice trailed off and she arched an eyebrow.

"But it's dark out," I protested. *And cold, being mid-September in the mountains.*

Her head tilted. "Are you scared of the dark, Steven? Don't worry. I'll bring a flashlight."

There was a gleam of challenge in her meadow-green irises. It was hypnotic. I couldn't think of a single reasonable argument with those eyes pinned on me.

"All right," I muttered, shrugging into my coat. "Let's go."

Terry barely glanced up from the cards he was dealing. "Tires are in the shed out back. Tools, too."

Chloe grabbed her coat and a flashlight from the hall

closet. The second the front door closed behind us, she whirled on me, shining the light right in my fucking eyes.

"What the hell is going on here, Steven?" she demanded.

"Chloe—shit—" I squeezed my eyes shut and batted her arm down, but I could still see the afterimage of her face on my eyelids. "This isn't some nefarious plot to weasel my way into your life. It's a coincidence, like you finding me when my battery died. I started working with your dad six months ago. He's well respected in the community and has taken on interns before. It's not my fault he didn't tell you about it."

"Well," Chloe hedged. "He *did* tell me about it. He just never mentioned your name."

"You have different last names," I went on. "I don't really know anything about you. Why would it even occur to me that you were related? But about two months ago, I saw a photo of you on his fridge." I rubbed my eyes and cleared away the floating Chloe. Unfortunately, the real one was still right here, and she was not happy.

She rolled her lips together. "Two months ago? Is that why you've been so nice to me?"

"Nice?" That caught me off guard. What did she know? "When was I nice?" I asked cautiously.

"That day at Jo's when you bought me coffee. That was nice. Or how about all those funny animal videos you send me at three a.m.?" She jabbed the flashlight at me like a pointer, the light down this time. "You were trying to butter me up!"

I wasn't really into social media, but I followed a handful of farriers I respected to bounce ideas off of. It wasn't a huge stretch for the algorithm to guide me from diseased hoofs to cute animals, but until Chloe told me it helped with her anxiety, I had scrolled right past without watching. Now my whole feed was full of those fucking videos.

"No, Chloe, I was not trying to butter you up. It never occurred to me that you *could* be...buttered." Goddammit, my mind was in the gutter again. I rubbed the back of my neck. "I saw those videos and thought of you, that's all."

She reeled back half a step, her bottom lip falling open. "You saw those videos and thought of me?" Her eyes searched my face. "And you don't think that's nice?"

"I was up. You were up. That's not nice, Chloe. That's... what did you call it? *Basic human decency.*" I leaned in, and my voice deepened when I murmured, "When I'm being nice, you'll know it."

Her eyes dilated until they looked almost black in the dim light as she stared back at me. Her cheeks were flushed pink, which might have been from the cold, but I knew it wasn't. When her gaze dipped to my lips, it took all my self-control not to do something very un-nice, like kiss her. If it were anyone else looking at me like that, I would have done it. But this was Chloe. She hated me. Her body might want me, but her brain sure as fuck didn't.

"It's fucking cold out here," I muttered. "Let's get your tires done."

"Right." She swallowed hard. "Right."

We didn't say a word as we rolled the tires from the shed to the driveway. Fortunately, Terry had an electric car jack kit, so doing all four tires would probably only take thirty minutes, tops.

"Thanks for doing this," Chloe said. She leaned against the car, aiming the flashlight at the first tire. "I'd do it myself, but I promised my mom."

I grunted as I shoved the jack in place. "You promised your mom you'd trick her dinner guest into freezing his ass off doing manual labor in the dark?"

She laughed and it was all worth it. I would have changed a thousand tires in sub-thirty temperatures to hear that sound. "No. I promised her I would never change my own tires. She's weird about it, but I understand. That's how my dad died," she added quietly. "He was helping a friend repair his tractor wheel, and his friend didn't secure that tractor properly. It rolled over on him and crushed him. He died instantly."

I froze. What the hell was I supposed to say to that? Terry had told me her dad died in an accident, but he hadn't shared the details. "Christ, Chloe. I'm sorry."

"Thank you." She nodded. "And, just so you know, my mom doesn't want you to get crushed by a tractor, or Terry or my brothers, either. She knows it's dumb, but she's worried I'll die like that because my dad did. She knows tractor accidents aren't hereditary, but anxiety isn't rational. We both struggle with it."

I turned back to the lug nuts. "That's what wakes you up at three a.m.? Worrying you're going to die by tractor?"

For a moment I worried that I sounded like an asshole, being flippant about something that was entirely serious, but she laughed under her breath.

"No. Evil tractors are my mom's thing, not mine. I'm more concerned that I'm going to forget something vital or screw up something small that has huge consequences." Her face shadowed for a moment, but then she laughed again. "Like, I hardly ever use my oven, but I'm always paranoid that I forgot to turn it off. So I'd check the knob every morning before I left the house and say out loud *I am checking the knob. The oven is off*. Because that makes it real to my brain. And then one day I was in the middle of an English exam and it occurred to me that maybe I was gaslighting myself, and I hadn't really *looked* at the oven knob, I had just sort of faked it. So now I take pictures of the knob."

I blinked up at her. "Jesus, Chloe. Maybe you should see someone about that."

She nudged my knee with her boot, not hard enough to knock me off balance. "I *do* see someone about that. It was one of the requirements for my master's degree in social work. We can't be good therapists without knowing what therapy feels like from a patient's point of view."

"That makes sense." One tire down, three to go. I maneuvered the tools to the rear tire and Chloe pivoted to follow me with the light.

"My dad likes you, you know," she said. "But he likes everyone, even the people he shouldn't. Quite frankly, he's a shitty judge of character."

Something in her voice made my gut tighten. I peeked at her over my shoulder. Pinched brows, squinty eyes, flat lips. That was not the face of a trusting woman. Goddamn it. She was going to ruin my life.

"What is it you want, Chloe? To protect your dad because you think I'm going to hurt him? Or do you just want to keep punishing me for James?"

She considered that. "Both," she decided.

I snorted. "Of course you do," I muttered. I rolled the old tire out of the way and lifted the new one into place. "If you really think I'm going to somehow hurt your dad, then go ahead and do what you have to do. Hell, I'll do it for you. But here's the thing, princess." I pushed to my feet. "If you just want to punish me, this isn't the way. Because it punishes your dad, too. He needs a partner, and I'm good at this and getting better. We work well together. Do you really want to take that from him?"

Her eyes spit green fire at me. "How do I know you've really changed?"

"Changed? I haven't changed, Chloe. I'm still the same guy I was two years ago." I cocked my head, considering. "Maybe I'm less angry. I wasted a lot of time feeling like the world had done me wrong in one way or another. It took me a while to realize I was paying attention to the wrong things. The world is unfair to everyone in some way or another, and fuck, I got sick of hearing myself whine about it. It sounded like—" *Him.*

Chloe looked at me. "Like what?"

"It sounded like someone I don't want to be. Now, I just

want to do my job. I want to keep horses sound and pain-free. I want to put some good in the world instead of worrying about what I can take out of it. But spooking James's horse? It wasn't some other guy who doesn't exist anymore. That was me making a huge, thoughtless mistake that I can't take back."

For a long moment, she stared down at the flashlight, rolling it between her palms, frowning. Then she heaved a sigh. "Goddammit. Why do you have to make it so hard for me to hate you? *Fine*. I won't say anything to my dad."

"And Amy?" I asked gruffly.

Something flashed across her face, there and gone again before I could decipher it. "No. But I think you should."

I grunted noncommittedly. "I'll think about it."

But I already knew I never would. I could live with Chloe hating me. But Amy? Not a fucking chance.

12

CHLOE

This week was kicking my ass and it was only Tuesday. All I wanted to do was change into my comfiest sweats and eat my weight in olives while bingeing a TV show I had already watched a hundred times. I didn't care what it was, I just wanted something familiar. Something that wouldn't require brain cells—because mine were currently barely operational—but would still make me laugh.

But no, I couldn't do that because I had to be an adult and go to the grocery store and buy real food like chicken strips and sweet potatoes, which I had planned to do over the weekend but instead I had napped, lazed around, and napped some more. That had been delightful and exactly what I needed, but now I didn't have so much as a box of cereal in my house, and Aspen Springs was not the kind of town that had an abundance of takeout options.

I hadn't felt this tired since I had first started taking on clients. Back then, it was hard not to carry the weight of their emotions home with me. Eventually my brain learned to set emotional boundaries and got into a rhythm. I loved my work. I woke up every morning with a sense of purpose. This was what I was meant to do. What I wanted to do. What I *needed* to do.

And yeah, maybe I needed it a little too much, cared a little too much, and that was why I came home bone-tired every day, and the past eighteen months of working 5 a.m. to noon at Jo's, and 2 to 7 p.m. at the clinic had finally caught up with m.. But I also suspected I was coming down with something. I didn't feel feverish, but every now and then my stomach flipped around a bit.

I drove straight to the grocery store from work because if I went home first and changed out of my "therapist on duty" uniform, as I liked to call my blazer, embroidered Chucks, and nice jeans, then I wouldn't leave the house again until tomorrow, even if it meant dining on ice cubes for dinner.

Damn, being an adult sucked.

I rattled the shopping carts, trying to pull one free of the line, but it wouldn't budge. With a pathetic whimper, I folded over the handlebar, resting my cheek on the handlebar of the attached cart.

"For fuck's sake, Chloe," a familiar voice growled behind me.

Well, wasn't that just perfect. Steven and I hadn't talked since declaring a fragile truce at dinner last week. He hadn't even sent me a single animal video. And now here he was, once again right on time to see me at my worst.

I stayed where I was. "Everything sucks and I'm dying."

There was a pause, followed by the kind of gusty sigh most often heard from parents of rambunctious toddlers. "Move, princess."

Steven nudged me with his body, hip to thigh to knee, and I sort of oozed aside and braced my back braced against the brick wall of the grocery store while he figured out the shopping cart situation with annoying competence.

"Here you—" Maybe it was the way I was glaring at the shopping cart like it had ruined my life, but his sentence died with another sigh. "All right. One cart. Text me your list."

"What list?" I asked.

"Your shopping list."

"I don't have a shopping list. I don't do that."

He looked truly aghast, like I had told him I enjoyed swimming in the creek with open wounds. "Then how do you know what to buy?"

I shrugged. "Vibes. I buy what looks good, things that don't involve cooking, and throw in some fruits and vegetables. Boom, done." I looked up at him. "Do you have a list?"

The offended look on his face gave me great joy. "Of course I have a list," he said. "I'm not here to fuck around, princess." The glass doors slid apart as he pushed the cart forward. "Just keep your vibes to the back half of the cart, all right?"

I opened my mouth to say something hilarious, but instead found myself struggling to hold back a vomitous hiccup as we passed a pungent garbage can and a wave of nausea rolled through my body. I clawed at Steven's forearm.

"What—" He glanced down at me and his eyes widened. "Shit—" With one arm looped around my waist, he hustled us out of the doorway and over to the citrus display. "Are you okay?"

The glass doors slid closed. I inhaled the sharp, sweet scent of oranges and grapefruit and my stomach settled. "I think...yes?" I said hesitantly.

His brows pinched as he studied me. "Are you hungover again?"

"No, of course not. It's just been a long week."

"It's Tuesday," he pointed out.

"Well, it's possible I'm coming down with something. I've been tired and feeling off."

He put the back of his hand to my forehead. "Do you have a fever?"

His hand was warm, dry, and a little rough. I was pretty sure the surface temperature of my skin had increased by another degree or two from his touch and the liquid feeling I wouldn't let solidify that I might like that feeling against the bare skin of my hips.

My eyebrows arched, pushing against his knuckles. "You're the one touching my face. You tell me."

"I don't know." He lifted his other hand to his own forehead to compare. "We're both warm."

"Like...feverish warm? Or mammal warm?"

"Huh," he said, looking perplexed.

I laughed.

He grinned and dropped his hands. "My mom always knew. She's like a human thermometer."

"Mine, too. Maybe it comes from practice."

"That makes sense. I don't think I've touched a lot of sick people. Not on purpose, anyway."

I shuddered at the thought. "Ew."

He shrugged. "It's no worse than a diseased hoof. I've seen some nasty shit. I just go into robot mode and do what needs to be done."

"Having four younger brothers, I, too, have seen some nasty shit. I was never good at robot mode. I did it anyway, but with a lot of internal screaming, and a lot of external screaming, too." I grabbed a five-pound bag of clementines and dropped them in the cart.

"The vibes want oranges?" he asked. His dark eyes sparked with amusement.

"The vibes don't *want*," I corrected him. "The vibes *are*."

One corner of his mouth hitched up and he chuckled. "I'm not sure any of that was English." But he grabbed another bag of clementines and placed it in the opposite end of the cart.

I arched a brow. "Is that on your list?" I teased.

He smirked. "The vibes are too strong to resist."

Maybe he was referring to just the oranges, but the words felt like they were about us, too. Or about me, anyway. Because suddenly I wasn't tired anymore. His touch on my forehead had jolted me awake like a shot of espresso and I was buzzing head to toe from it.

And that was bad. That was very, very bad.

Because these vibes? These were first-date-I-want-to-get-to-know-you vibes.

I felt *giggly*. I had no business feeling giggly for Steven. I had no business laughing and joking around with him, grocery shopping together like a couple. This was *Steven*. Yes, I knew he wasn't the same guy he was a year ago, but so what? The enemy of my friend was my enemy. That was how friendship worked, right?

Between 3 a.m. texts and grocery store vibes, I had forgotten that.

Steven liked to shop the perimeter, focusing on fresh fruits, vegetables, and meats. The smell of seafood made me gag again, so he tossed bulk packages of chicken thighs and cuts of steak, and we hustled through to the breakfast aisle, which was where I sourced most of my meals anyway. I grabbed three different kinds of cereal and a package of apples and cinnamon instant oatmeal.

He didn't say anything, but I saw him look from his side of the cart to mine and shake his head, so I threw in a box of strawberry frosted toaster pastries as well. He blanched and I grinned.

"I should have known you were a health nut," I said, laughing.

He gave me a quizzical look as he reached for the round canister of plain, non-instant oats. The tasteless kind. "Why would you have known that?"

"You don't get abs like that eating strawberry frosted toaster pastries," I said without thinking, doing an air circle around his abdomen with my index finger. "You get abs like that by working out in the gym for two hours every day and eating nothing but chicken and carrot sticks."

He looked genuinely flummoxed as he looked down at his midsection. "How do you—You were checking me out." His head jerked up. "That night in the rain. You were ogling me while I was wet and shirtless."

"I was not!" I protested. My face felt hot and tingly. Maybe because I was imagining it all over again. Steven, shirtless. The rain literally streaming down the indents between his muscles. "I *saw* you. I did *not* ogle."

His full lips tilted in a sexy smirk that made my belly flutter with something that definitely was not nausea. He reached for the powdered donuts behind me, leaning in so close that his warm breath brushed my cheek.

"You've got me all wrong, princess. I have a sweet tooth, and I don't spend hours at the gym," he murmured into my ear. Goosebumps broke out on my neck. "I don't work out. I *work*."

Oh, fuck.

I was so wet between my legs that all my feminism slid right out of my pussy.

"That's, um..." I cleared my throat. "Nice."

He tossed the donuts on his side of the cart. His lips quirked. "I'm glad you think so."

God, he was so...*smug*. Self-satisfied.

"Haven't you ever heard it's what's on the inside that counts?" I scoffed.

All the laughter drained from his face. Shit, I felt like I had kicked a puppy. He turned away, the muscle in his jaw popping. "Yeah, I might have heard that a time or two."

"Steven—" I tried but stopped. What could I really say? That I forgave him for what happened with James? I didn't. I wouldn't hit him with my car, but we were still a long way from forgiveness. And what did it matter, anyway? Even if I forgave him, James never could, and I didn't blame her.

He steered the cart past me, refusing to look me in the eyes. "Let's go, princess. It's getting late."

I shuffled behind him. How had I gone from nauseous and pissy to happy and horny to...fucking *wretched*...in twenty minutes? I felt so off kilter. I needed a nap, a snack, and a good cry. And then another nap.

"How do you keep those clean? The world is disgusting," he said.

"What?" I glanced at him and saw he was looking down at my feet. "My shoes? Do you mean the embroidery? With very gentle liquid soap and a toothbrush."

He grunted and turned down the personal care aisle and pulled out his phone to consult his precious list. "Shaving cream," he muttered. "Shampoo, deodorant, pads." He stopped in front of the sanitary supplies and scanned the shelves with wide eyes. "Jesus Christ." He looked down at his phone again. "Large. Okay. Is that a size or amount?"

My jaw flapped open.

"What?" he asked.

I shook my head and peered over his shoulder at his phone. "Maybe she meant long? Get the long size in a large pack. With wings. It protects your underwear better."

He grabbed a pack, studied it, and tossed it in the cart. Then he grabbed a multipack and threw it in, too. "Just in case," he said. "She couldn't find a store that delivered to our house, and I only come out here every couple of weeks."

I stared at him.

"What?" he asked again.

"You've changed," I said.

He snorted. "Trust me, princess, I haven't. I told you that already."

"Remember that day outside Jo's? You told me you didn't want to hear about all my *lady problems*," I mocked in a sing-song voice. "And now here you are, buying maxi pads for your sister. No flinching. No pretending to gag. You've changed."

He looked at me for a moment, then shook his head with a disbelieving huff. "I didn't change, Chloe. I'm still the same guy I always was. I considered a new perspective, that's all."

"Mine?" I asked, somewhat stupefied by the notion that *anything* I had said that day had been worth paying attention to. He had not found me at my best, to put it mildly. I had been fucking *sloppy*.

"Yours, yeah. And Amy…" His chin dipped and he rubbed the back of his neck. "I lived with two women most of my life, you know. My mother and my sister. And I still didn't have a fucking clue about periods, other than I knew they existed. They never talked about it. I never saw feminine hygiene products anywhere because they had their own bathrooms. My dad…" His voice trailed off on a disgusted laugh. "Amy told me he never let them throw their pads and tampons away in the house. They had to use the outdoor trash can."

"What the fuck," I whispered.

"Yeah. He said he didn't want to see it or smell it. And, you know, I had girlfriends. I knew they had periods. They just…never talked about it. Or maybe…maybe they did, and I said something like I said to you, and…I don't know. I hate wondering if I made them feel like shit. I don't remember. It didn't mean anything to me at the time. It should have."

"Yeah, it should have," I said flatly. I chewed my lip for a second, thinking. "But you know, what you said? I've heard shit like that before. All women have. And even if you said that to your girlfriends, you probably weren't the only one."

He gave a noncommittal grunt. "Doesn't make it any less stupid."

"No," I agreed. "It doesn't."

"Anyway. Sorry I was a dick to you when you were

having period cramps." He tilted his head so he was somehow looking up at me even though he was taller than me.

"You bought me an iced mocha. It's already forgiven. I don't know why my cramps were so bad. Usually I get a really heavy flow, but all I got from that was light spotting."

I said it to see if I could gross him out, just to test him. But he looked at me like he was doing a complicated math equation in his head.

"What?" I asked.

"You've gotten your period since then, though, right?" he asked. "It was six weeks ago."

"No, but that's normal for me," I explained. "I don't get regular cycles."

He cocked his head. "Is it normal for you to get nausea spells when you're not really sick?"

"I..." *Six weeks ago I had unprotected sex.* "Shit," I whispered.

Steven looked at me for a long moment, then scrubbed a hand over his face. He grabbed a pregnancy test from the shelf and dropped it in the cart.

"I don't need that," I said. A whole team of doctors had assured me of that.

But the universe decided that was the perfect time to prove me wrong because a rancher smelling like he had rolled in cow patties cut brushed past us. It was too much, and I had been fighting it for too long. I didn't have a snowball's chance in hell of stopping it.

The vomit was instantaneous.

"Your shoes!" Steven hollered, lunging forward, palms outstretched.

I puked directly into his bare hands.

OF COURSE I was wide awake at 3 a.m., alternating doomscrolling analysis of the vicious drought hitting the western states with soothing videos of dogs guarding ducks, trying *not* to picture Steven's hands full of my vomit and how I had made my humiliated escape while he was washing up in the grocery store bathroom because that made me feel ill all over again, when his text came through.

STEVEN

Well?

CHLOE

Well, what?

STEVEN

Did you take the test?

CHLOE

No

STEVEN

Why not?

CHLOE

I don't want to.

STEVEN

For fuck's sake, princess.

Text me your address.

CHLOE

36 Second Street

STEVEN

I'll be there in 20.

13

———

STEVEN

WHAT THE HELL WAS I THINKING?

I wasn't thinking. That was the problem. But Chloe texted me her address, so clearly I wasn't alone in the One Braincell Club. We weren't friends. She was never going to forgive me for what I did to James. No, she was going to hate me until her dying breath, and even then, I'd hazard a guess that she'd carry that grudge to heaven with her and give the angels an earful. I knew this.

But I also knew this: Chloe Adams wouldn't leave her worst enemy wounded and stranded by the side of the road, so I wouldn't either.

Not that she was my enemy, even though I was hers. And she wasn't wounded. Or stranded, for that matter.

Whatever. It was a fucking metaphor.

My headlights illuminated her yard as I turned into her driveway. I cut the engine. I had half expected her to change her mind during my twenty-minute drive here, but there was a faint light coming from one of the windows. Still, I texted her, just in case.

STEVEN

I'm here.

CHLOE

Door is unlocked.

I exited my truck, shutting the door as quietly as I could. Unlike me, Chloe lived in town, and she had neighbors. I didn't want to give them something to talk about.

"Chloe?" I called softly as I stepped into her dark living room.

"In here," she called back.

I fumbled around her furniture toward the sound of her voice, bumped my knee against a table and swore quietly, until I found the hallway. Light spilled out from an open door. I headed toward it.

I paused in the doorway to her bedroom, feeling like I needed an invitation to cross the threshold, and folded my arms across my chest and leaned one shoulder into the frame. "Hey."

She didn't so much as lift her head from the pillow, just looked down her nose at me before returning her gaze to the ceiling. "Hey."

I had never seen her look like this. So still and quiet. Like all the life had been sucked out of her. I didn't like it. "Did you take the test?" I asked.

"No," she said.

"Why not?" I asked.

"I can't pee," she said. "I'm not hydrated enough."

There wasn't a glass or water bottle on the nightstand, and from the way she lay completely still on her queen-sized bed, her hands clasped over her abdomen, I figured she didn't intend to rectify that herself.

"I'll get you a glass of water," I said, pushing away from the door frame.

"You don't have to," she said, not moving a muscle.

I paused. "Are you going to do it yourself?"

She didn't answer, but she didn't need to. We both knew she wouldn't. It was funny. At dinner, I had watched her take care of her mom, her dad, her brothers. Six months ago, she'd rescued me and Stevie in the middle of a thunderstorm. But when it came to helping herself, it was like she couldn't be bothered.

And then I thought of all the Monday afternoons she spent doing chores and paperwork for her parents after a six-hour shift pouring coffee at Jo's. I thought of the way she had heaped the last of the potatoes on her brother's plate, taking none for herself even though it was her favorite.

So maybe it wasn't that she couldn't be bothered. Maybe she gave so much to everyone she loved that when it came to herself, she had nothing left to give.

I located the kitchen off the hallway. It was small—everything about the bungalow was small—and it took only a moment to find the cabinet with the glasses. I grabbed one and filled it to an inch from the brim with tap water. There were dirty dishes in the sink. A blue porcelain bowl with a shallow moat of milk rimming the bottom, a spoon, and a coffee mug that looked like it had been there since at least this morning.

I shook my head, annoyed that she had either eaten cereal for dinner even though she had just gone grocery shopping, or she hadn't eaten anything at all. I took a minute to wash them by hand since she didn't have a dishwasher before heading back to her room.

Chloe was right where I left her. She probably had every centimeter of the ceiling memorized by now. "Sit up," I ordered.

Her eyes narrowed to annoyed green slits, but she huffed an aggrieved sigh, pushed up on her elbows, and wiggled backward until her back was pressed to the tufted headboard. I handed her the glass, and she took five long swallows before setting it down on the nightstand.

"I can't drink it all at once. I'll puke," she said.

I felt a tiny twinge of guilt. Maybe I should be gentler with her, but I hated seeing her like this. "Do you want something to eat? Would that help?" I asked, trying to be nice, but the words still came out gruff.

She was already shaking her head before I finished speaking, in an automatic kind of way, like saying no was a reflex, but then she suddenly stopped. Her eyes lit up. "A cheese sandwich. That's what I want."

She bounced off the bed, brushing past me so close that I caught the strawberry scent of her shampoo. I snagged the glass of water and followed her into the kitchen. She didn't bother with a plate, just slapped two slices of generic white bread—the squishy, underbaked kind that you could squeeze into a quarter-sized ball—on the hopefully sanitized countertop before spinning to the refrigerator. I winced when she pulled out the package of individually wrapped slices of American cheese. Two floppy slices went between the pasty bread. No condiments. No tomatoes or lettuce. Just...cheese, if it could be called that.

She held it up triumphantly with a huge smile on her face, like she had just caught a fish. "Want a sandwich? It's delicious."

"That's not a sandwich, princess. I'm not sure it even qualifies as food. It's just a pile of preservatives."

Undeterred by the truth, she took a big bite and chewed. Silently, I handed her the water glass. She took a few sips and handed it back.

"I didn't have you pegged as a food snob. Although now that I think about it, I don't think you put a single pre-packaged food in the cart." Her head tilted. "I take it you don't have a favorite struggle meal?"

"What's a struggle meal?" I asked.

"You know, the thing you make when you're struggling financially or just struggling in general to hold things together. Something cheap and simple."

I shook my head slowly. Money had never been an issue for us. My dad's job overseeing a factory made us solidly middle class in a low cost of living area, and if Mom had ever had a problem holding her household together, she never showed it. We didn't struggle—not the way Chloe meant, anyway.

Chloe shrugged. "I used to make cheese sandwiches for my brothers all the time. Served it up with a heap of eggs—scrambled to make them go farther—and hotdogs if they were particularly hungry, which they always were because they were growing boys. It was back when we were still trying to save the farm, so money was short. And on Mom's bad days, it felt like *everything* was short. I hated to cook, and my brothers learned quickly that you get what you get and you don't get upset. And if you did get upset, you were the new cook." She grinned, like she thought maybe struggling was fun.

Maybe it *was* fun, in a weird way. Maybe struggling wasn't really so bad when you loved the people struggling with you. My chest pinched.

I handed her the water again, because I hadn't forgotten what we were doing here, even if I couldn't quite wrap my mind around the fact of it all. That Chloe might be pregnant, and the man responsible for that wasn't here. That I was here instead, and somehow that felt both wrong and right at the same time.

"Are you struggling now?" I asked, because why else would she be eating that god awful "sandwich."

Her warm laugh curled around me like heat from a fire on a cold night. "I'm okay. I'll never be rich as a social worker, but my rent is ridiculously cheap and I can cover it with two jobs. Anyway, I actually enjoy struggle meals. That helps." I made a face that told her exactly what I thought about that and she laughed again. "No, really. It's good."

She took another sip of water, and her gaze fell on the sink. Her brows pushed together. "Did you do my dishes?"

"It only took a minute."

"You didn't have to."

For some reason, that annoyed me. Was that what she expected of me? I only helped someone if I *had* to? "You're welcome." There was a bite to my words.

Her lips pursed, but then she nodded. "Thank you." After another sip of water, she said, "This might be the first time all week I haven't felt nauseous. It's nice."

There was no delicate way to phrase it, so I didn't try. "You about ready to pee on a stick?" I asked.

She snorted. "Yeah, I think I'm hydrated enough now." She popped the last bite into her mouth. "I'm not pregnant, you know."

"I don't know that," I said. "And unless something has changed in the last hour, neither do you. So how about you take the test and find out?"

"If I take the test, it will be like I'm admitting that it's possible. Which it's not." Her gaze narrowed on the glass in her hand, and she chewed her lip. "It's *not*."

"Hey," I said. I took the glass from her and set it on the counter. "Hey, it's going to be okay. Even if you are pregnant, you don't have to stay that way if you don't want to. There's a clinic a couple hours from here. I'll drive you."

Chloe blinked up with me with startled green eyes. "You would do that for me?" She shook her head as though to clear it. "No, I mean, that's not what I'm worried about. I haven't even gotten that far in my thought process. It's just that…I've never been in this situation. I've never had to take a pregnancy test. It's never been a concern at all for me. It just wasn't possible. And I was fine with that! But I don't know how I'll feel if I take that test and it's negative. Because it *will* be negative. I know that. But maybe I won't feel fine anymore."

I studied her. She was babbling in circles, and none of it made any sense to me. "Do you *want* to be pregnant?"

She huffed. "Well, that would be ridiculous. It's the worst possible timing. I'll be done with my supervised clinical hours in May, and then I'll be launching my career. I'm not in a committed relationship, and I don't want to be. Of course I wouldn't choose now, with this guy, to be pregnant." And then, so softly that I almost missed it, she said, "I never thought I'd get to choose at all."

Shit. I didn't know what to say to that. Didn't know what to do with my hands, either. Should I hug her? Christ, no. She'd probably bite me if I tried that. I patted her shoulder, testing.

She reeled back, eying me suspiciously. "What are you doing?"

I barked a laugh. "I don't have a fucking clue what I'm doing here. I've never had a pregnancy scare, either. What am I supposed to say? What would *you* say to a friend who was stalling on taking a pregnancy test?"

She cocked her head, thinking. "I'd gently but firmly insist she take it."

"Take the fucking test, Chloe," I said.

She gave me an unimpressed eyeroll. "Your delivery needs work."

"Where's the test?" I asked.

"In the bathroom. I really was going to take it, but I couldn't squeeze out more than a drop."

"For fuck's sake, princess," I grunted. I took her by the elbow and escorted her down the hallway to the bathroom and practically tossed her inside. I took note of the disposable plastic cup sitting on the sink counter. The test was next to it. "You want me to hold the cup for you while you pee? I'll do it," I threatened.

She glared and gave my shoulder a not-too-gentle shove. "Get the hell out of here, Steven."

I smirked. "There she is," I murmured, stepping into the hallway and closing the bathroom door behind me.

And then I paused, listening for the sound of her going like a damn pervert. When I heard pee hit plastic, I headed back to the kitchen. Might as well clean something while I waited.

A minute later she found me wiping down the inside of her butter-splattered microwave. I had the feeling she made a lot of popcorn. "Well?" I asked tersely.

"Thirty more seconds," she replied.

We stared at each other for every single one of those seconds. Longest thirty seconds of my fucking *life*. Why the hell was I so invested? It wasn't my baby. *She* wasn't mine. And yet I couldn't imagine how changing either of those facts would make a damn bit of difference. I couldn't imagine caring more than I did right now. It was already too fucking much.

The alarm went off on her phone. She silenced it, then looked at the test. Surprise, then joy, a quick lightning strike of emotion before her features went blank again. She held up the test so I could see the single word on the digital screen.

Pregnant.

14

STEVEN

TWO UNANSWERED TEXTS, SENT TWENTY-FOUR HOURS APART, was where I draw the line. A third would be an invitation for her to block me. Maybe she already had, and I was too dense to get the hint.

"She's fine," I muttered to my phone. Stevie plopped her head in my lap and I absently rubbed the silky spot between her ears.

"No pigs at the table," Amy said, pushing Stevie aside

as she placed a stack of pancakes in front of me. Stevie whined in protest, which worked on me, but Amy had a heart of stone. "Who's fine?"

"Just a…" Friend? No. "Just a person I know. I offered to help her with something, but she didn't text back. That means she's fine, right? She doesn't need help."

"That means she doesn't want to talk to you," Amy said bluntly. "Someone else is probably helping her."

She had a point. Chloe had friends. The kind of friends who knew her favorite flower was a pink peony and gave her hand-embroidered shoes. The kind of friends she held a grudge for. She didn't need me. I was just the guy who happened to be awake at 3 a.m.

I should have been relieved. Chloe was fucking *pregnant*. I didn't need to be a part of that mess. I should be glad she didn't text back. Instead, I was fucking pissed.

Anger is a mask.

I heard Chloe's voice clear as day, like she was sitting right next to me, and if I closed my eyes, it was a sure bet I'd see her withering green stare branded on the back of my eyelids. I solved that problem by not closing my eyes.

Alright, fine. I wasn't actually pissed. My feelings were hurt, and I'd break every damn plate in this house before I'd admit that out loud.

"Yeah," I mumbled. "She's got plenty of people to help her."

I pushed my plate away, then pulled it closer again. Big breakfasts weren't my thing. I preferred to start the day with a banana and a large coffee and then have a solid lunch after I'd worked up an appetite. But if this was what Amy needed to do to feel okay about living here and taking my money, then fine. I'd eat the fucking pancakes and anything else she made me.

"Who's the girl?" Amy asked.

I cut a deep triangle through all four pancakes and shoved the whole thing in my mouth, then shrugged and gestured to my face like, *oh, well.*

She smiled sweetly, but her eyes glinted. "I can wait."

I chewed extra slowly. She raised her eyebrows, unimpressed with my effort to stall her out.

I swallowed the mush in my mouth with a gulp of orange juice. "It doesn't matter. You've only been here a couple months. You don't know anyone."

Her eyes narrowed speculatively. "I know people. And I'm beginning to think I know *her*, or else you would tell me her name."

I smirked. "Maybe I'm not telling you her name just to annoy you."

"Or maybe you're not telling me her name because you have a big ol' crush on her," Amy sing-songed. "Oh, that's it, isn't it? You have an unrequited crush."

I scoffed and swallowed another bite of pancakes. One more and I could get out of here without hurting her feelings. "I'm too old for crushes. But I'll never be too old to annoy my baby sister."

I folded one last pancake into my mouth and pushed to my feet. "Gotta go. Be good at school." I ruffled her hair to prove my point and smirked when she swatted my hand and jerked away.

"Bye, honey," I cooed, cupping Stevie by her fat cheeks. So fucking cute. She snorted affectionately. So did Amy, with considerably less affection.

"This isn't over," she warned as I scooped my lunch from the counter and pivoted toward the door. "I'm going to figure it out."

OREO SNUFFLED the sugar cube in my palm with flaring nostrils, but she didn't take it straight away. I waited patiently for her to recognize it as something tasty. The fact that she showed any curiosity at all was leaps and bounds ahead of when I'd last seen her. That was thanks to Bernadette, the woman who ran Sunshine Rescue. Still, when the mare finally lipped it up, it felt like I had accomplished something.

"That might be her first sugar cube," Bernadette noted, tucking a frizzy gray curl behind her ear. She reminded me of a bristlecone pine. Weathered and gnarled, but strong. Like she had seen some shit and wasn't too impressed by it. "I usually stick to carrots and apples. Too much sugar makes a horse founder. Except for kisses." She planted a loud, smacking kiss on Oreo's cheek. "Isn't that right, baby?"

Oreo nickered and bobbed her head like she was

agreeing, but since horses didn't speak English, I suspected she was really asking for another treat. I held up my empty hands, fingers spread wide. "No more."

"Let's get her moving," Terry said. "I expect we won't do more than a trim and new shoes today, but I want to see how she's coming along and make sure there isn't anything we need to be concerned about. Walk her around the ring and then straight down the middle."

Bernadette nodded and clucked her tongue. "Let's go, sweet girl."

Oreo ambled forward. The pep in her step was new. Her flank had filled out nicely, too. No more jutting hip bones.

"Hard to believe it's the same animal," I remarked. "You're a miracle worker, Bernadette."

She waved off the praise. "Team effort. I couldn't have done it without you boys. It's hard to summon a will to live when every step hurts like hell. Once the pain stopped, she woke up a bit."

At the top of the ring, Bernadette turned Oreo down the center like Terry had requested, steering her straight for us so we could get a head-on view of her gait. "But you know what really lifted her spirits? The chicken."

For one horrifying moment, I remembered Stevie's baby bird incident, and thought she meant Oreo had been eating baby chicks for protein. "The chicken?" I repeated cautiously, squatting down so I was level with the mare's knees.

Bernadette nodded. "Henrietta. She gets bullied by the

other hens and one day she hopped up on Oreo's back to escape them. They've been thick as thieves ever since. Oreo doesn't like wide-open spaces—they make her nervous, I think—so we keep her in the small pasture by the garden, which also happens to be next to the chicken coop. When Henrietta gets chased away from the garden bugs by the other hens, she hitches a ride with Oreo out in the pasture and gets her fill of bugs there. Sometimes Oreo will find a sunny spot to rest in and they'll take a nap together. As I said, team effort."

Terry scratched his jaw. "Seems like there's a lesson in there somewhere," he mused.

"You would think that because you're a sentimental old fool." Her tone was full of fondness despite the insult. "I don't anthropomorphize animals, so don't go spouting nonsense about world peace. Even chickens and horses need a friend, that's all."

"Everybody needs a friend," Terry echoed. He grinned. "Well, no lesson there, eh? Everyone needs a friend...or partner." He raised his eyebrows at me.

Subtle, Terry. Real subtle. I had told him I needed some time to think aver his partnership offer. Honestly, I already knew what I wanted to do. It was Chloe who needed some time to adjust to the idea.

Bernadette snorted. "If you are just now learning that everyone needs a friend, after sixty turns around the sun, well, Terry, I honestly don't know what to tell you. Look both ways before crossing the street, I guess."

Terry chuckled. "I'll do that." He pulled out his phone

and tapped something into it. "I gotta remember to tell my daughter about Oreo and Henrietta. She'll get a kick out of it."

The reminder was a sudden smack upside my head.

Chloe.

His daughter.

His *pregnant* daughter.

And since he hadn't said a single word about that, I would hazard a guess he didn't know that part yet. Fuck. *Fuck.*

15

CHLOE

Honestly, I forgot it even happened. Well, not forgot, exactly. But 3 a.m. and the pregnancy test took on a hazy, surreal quality, vanishing in the bright light of day like fog burned off by the sun. When I found myself pulling over to the side of the highway to puke, my first thought was, *dammit, I'm getting the flu.*

Then I remembered I was pregnant.

And then I promptly forgot again.

When I threw up the chicken nuggets I'd eaten for lunch, I picked up my phone to let my advisor know I needed to cancel my afternoon clients before remembering I wasn't sick, I was pregnant, and pregnancy wasn't contagious. I called my ob-gyn instead and made an appointment for Monday, the earliest day she could squeeze me in.

Every problem had a solution. But it was a lot harder to find a solution when I couldn't seem to fully grasp the fact that I had a problem. Steven texted a couple times over the next few days to see how I was doing, and each time I was stunned anew with the realization that I was pregnant.

I wasn't in denial.

I just couldn't believe it was *true*.

Until the server set a mimosa in front of me at our post-sewing club brunch.

"I'm pregnant," I said through that same hazy fog. I blinked and looked up, startled awake by my own words. "I'm *pregnant*," I said again, awed, like this was brand-new information to me.

James, Essie, Hannah, and Janie stared back at me with slack jaws.

"Well, shit," Janie said.

"You don't have to drink that," James said next to me. She pulled my mimosa closer to her plate. "Should we get the server back? Ask her for plain orange juice? Unless you want a mimosa." She pushed my mimosa back to me and blinked rapidly. "I mean...what are you going to do?"

"About the mimosa?" I asked stupidly.

"About the *baby*," Essie said.

"Oh." I stared at the mimosa.

"Chloe?" Hannah nudged gently.

"Yeah." I huffed and pushed the mimosa back to James. "I don't know what I'm going to do. I have an appointment with my ob-gyn on Monday to confirm it's viable. Until then...it just seems fake, you know? I mean..." I looked around helplessly. "This wasn't supposed to be possible. I've never had a normal cycle. Sometimes it's long and bloody, sometimes it's a trickle, and mostly it's not there at all. I could go a couple months without anything and then have two periods in three weeks. Doctors have run tests and ruled some things out, but they never could give me a reason. All they could tell me was that I would be very unlikely to get pregnant without intervention. Even with intervention, it would be a long shot. That's what they *said*."

I felt like I had been lied to.

"Chloe," James said quietly. She reached for my hand and squeezed it.

I shook my head. "It's fine. I've known this since I was fourteen. And at fourteen I was so busy helping with my brothers that being a mom sounded terrible, anyway. And then...I just never let myself think about it. Why hope for something you can't have?"

Chewing my lip, I looked up and found nothing but love staring back at me. "It would be selfish of me to have this baby, wouldn't it? The dad...We're not together. He's off riding his motorcycle across Argentina, so I can't even talk to him about this. I'll try to call him after my appointment on Monday. But I know I screwed up. I had drunk, unprotected sex."

Janie's eyes narrowed. "So did he," she pointed out.

"Yeah, yeah." I waved dismissively. "In theory, it takes two to tangle and all that. In practice, women suffer the consequences, financially and physically, so in the end it's our responsibility."

Essie snorted. "Oh, honey. My husband is a lawyer and

I'm unhinged. We can make him suffer consequences both financially and physically if that's what you want."

I laughed even though I knew she was completely serious. Fuck around with Essie Price or someone she loved, and you would find out. "He's not a bad guy. I appreciate the offer, but I don't want him to suffer. I just wish I knew what he wanted."

James shook her head. "He doesn't decide what you do with your body. Let him worry about what he wants. What do *you* want?"

A baby. This *baby.* The answer unfurled in my chest with feather-light softness. It felt like hope. Fragile, furtive hope.

I rolled my lips together, afraid to say it out loud, like if I admitted I wanted it, it would be taken away from me in some cruel cosmic reckoning.

"I never let myself hope for this." I looked down at my stomach. My hand pressed against my lower belly like I could make it stay. "And now that it's happening, it still doesn't seem real, that I could actually have this. Part of me feels like I shouldn't even consider it because it's not really mine to keep. But I want—" My voice cracked, and I pushed the words out in a rush. "I want it."

No one at our booth said a damn word. I could hear the low hum of indecipherable words from the tables around us, and somewhere in the distance a fork clattered against a china plate. And then—

"We're going to be aunts!" Essie crowed. She leaped to her feet and lunged across the table at me. She couldn't quite reach for a hug, so instead she grabbed me by the shoulders and shook me.

"Don't shake me!" I wheezed. "I can barely keep anything down as it is." That made everyone lean away from me real quick. "And holy shit, keep your voice down. I haven't told my parents or my brothers."

Janie's mouth hooked upward. "Don't worry. I can keep a secret."

I believed her. She wasn't the one I was worried about.

"I won't even tell Zack," Hannah promised. "I love him, but if he knows, then everyone in Aspen Springs knows."

Essie bobbed her head in agreement while sipping down her mimosa. "Brax, too. I swear the Hale brothers are thirteen-year-old girls in hot cowboy bodies."

"Not Adam," James said. "He's like a vault. Me, on the other hand…I'm a terrible liar. How am I supposed to pretend I don't know you're pregnant?"

I did a quick mental calculation. "It's only another five weeks until I'm in the second trimester." *If it's real. If it stays.*

James's big brown eyes got even bigger. "Five weeks?" she squeaked. "You're cooked, Chloe. Why is that a rule, anyway? It seems arbitrary."

"Most miscarriages happen in the first trimester," Hannah said, fiddling with the string of her teabag. "It's not that you *can't* tell anyone. It's just a guideline to share your joy with the same people you would tell if you miscarried."

"Oh," James said softly. She looked at me. "So…us?"

"You," I agreed, and damn those pregnancy hormones because my eyes got misty.

She nodded firmly, like she was making an oath. "I'll keep my mouth shut even if I have to use duct tape."

Janie cocked her head, studying me. "You're not going to tell your family yet?"

Hell no! my brain shouted.

"I wouldn't want to trouble them if it doesn't work out." I said it as lightly as I could, but the thought of telling my mom I had miscarried the only grandbaby my body might be able to conceive sat like a lead brick on my chest.

Back when we were making the rounds from doctor to doctor, trying to get an answer as to why my periods were so wretched, Mom had taken the news about my fertility—or lack thereof—much harder than I had. I had locked the information away in a dark corner of my mind where it couldn't hurt me. My mom couldn't do that.

Mom had always wanted a daughter, and she was so damn glad to have had me first. So of course she'd also dreamed of being a grandmother to her daughter's daughter. Sure, her sons might one day have children of their own, but it wouldn't be the same, in her mind. She had cried when the doctor told us I probably couldn't have kids. Not just for my sake, but for her own. For the loss of *her* dream.

If I told her that dream might actually come true after all, only to snatch it back later, she would be devastated.

And then there was this, too: My mother would tell my grandmother, and my grandmother would say nothing.

That would be bad enough, but it would be even worse if I then lost the baby. My mother would weep, I would comfort her, and my grandmother would still say nothing.

Our family would never recover from that, and we had already been through so much. *Too* much.

I must have been making a face because Hannah's mouth twisted in a sympathetic grimace. "Families are complicated. I wouldn't tell my parents, either," she said in the understatement of the year.

"Well, no shit, you wouldn't," Essie said. "They illegally married you off to your uncle when you were still a kid. Assholes," she muttered under her breath. "I'd tell my mom right away. My dad…I guess I'd text him eventually. If I knew where he was."

I blinked down at my soft, but still relatively flat belly. There was an innocent bundle of cells in there. "So many ways to fuck up a kid. Maybe I should worry less about who I tell and focus more on being the kind of parent who gets told."

James nudged my shoulder with hers. "That's why you're going to be a great mom, Chloe."

"Maybe." I blew out a shuddery breath. *If it's real. If it stays.* "I hope so."

We fell quiet as the server reappeared with our food. Waffles for me because it seemed like the brunch equivalent of a Saltine cracker, avocado toast for James, French toast for Janie and Essie, and an omelet for Hannah. The sudden array of smells hit my stomach immediately after my nose, and not in a good way.

"Can I get a ginger ale?" I asked the server as she set down the last plate.

"Sure, hon. Coming right up." She spun away again, heading back to the kitchen.

"Morning sickness?" Janie asked sympathetically.

I nodded queasily. "More like all-fucking-day sickness. I'll be fine. Just keep talking. The distraction helps." I took a tiny sip of water and an even tinier bite of waffle. I was starting to learn that an empty stomach only made the nausea worse.

"Tell us everything," Essie said, digging into her stuffed French toast. I tried not to gag as cream cheese filling oozed out. "Who's the dad? How long have you known?"

"The dad is…" My voice trailed off as I thought better of it. "Actually, I'm going to keep that to myself for now. I'll tell you after I tell him, okay? I don't think he should be the last to know he's going to be a dad."

"Fair," James said. "So how did you find out you were pregnant? How long have you known?"

"A couple days. I…um…" Shit. Steven. She hated Steven, as much as James was capable of hating anyone. I couldn't just say, *oh, hey, remember that guy who purposefully startled your horse so you would fall off and then threatened to sue the ranch? Funny story, he came over in the middle of the night so I wouldn't have to take the test alone.*

Which might beg the question: why?

A reasonable question, because I hadn't told them about any of it. I hadn't told them about Stevie the Pig and our roadside rescue, or that he had bought me coffee, or that he was working for my dad, or the 3 a.m. text conversations. I definitely hadn't told any of them that he'd caught *literal vomit* in his bare hands to protect the shoes they had embroidered for me.

I hadn't told them that of all the people who could have been there, I wasn't mad that it was him. Maybe I was even *glad* it was him.

Another wave of nausea hit, but I was pretty sure this one at least had more to do with my guilty conscience than growing a baby inside me.

"Here's that ginger ale." The server placed it in front of me and then backed up a step. "Anything else I can get you, ladies?"

"No," we chorused.

I stuck my nose into the glass and breathed in the spicy-sweet smell. The bubbles tickled my nose, and I coughed, but my nausea dissipated somewhat.

I looked up at my friends, who were still waiting for an answer. "The nausea sort of gave it away." That was true. "It had been about two months since my last period, which was still within the normal range for me, but I took a test anyway, fully expecting it to be negative. It wasn't." Also true. "And here we are."

They didn't need to know the Steven parts. We weren't dating. We weren't even really friends. We had just...accidentally stumbled into each other's lives for a moment, that was all. Now we would stumble right out again. Heck, I hadn't even responded to either of his last two texts—the first one being "You need anything?" and the second being "Hey"—and that was three days ago.

I should text him. Just so he knew I was okay, and I wasn't his problem. I wasn't *anyone's* problem, but really and fucking truly, I wasn't his. I should tell him that.

And then we'd never speak to each other again.

That was the truth.

So why did it feel like another lie?

16

———

STEVEN

Aspen Springs went all out for Halloween. With two weeks to go, there wasn't a single undecorated shop or home on Main Street. I rolled through town at a crawl, taking it in. Witches with green-striped stockings careened into lampposts. Fat orange pumpkins, dusted with last night's snow flurries, lined the porch steps. Skeletons were big this year. Two were taller than the gold-rush-era buildings, but most of them were human-sized and placed in ridiculous positions: rocking on a porch swing, checking the mail, getting chased by a skeleton dog.

And there, striding down the crumbling brick sidewalk, bundled up in a thick puffer coat and green knit hat, was the most terrifying thing I'd ever seen, given how my heart damn near jumped up my throat at the sight of her.

I slowed even further, rolled my window down, and hooked one elbow over the door. "Chloe Adams, as I live and breathe," I drawled.

Her eyes darted sideways to take me in. "Pity," she murmured.

I smirked. "Sorry my existence disappoints you."

She kept walking, so with a quick glance at my mirrors to ascertain no one was behind me, I did a u-turn in the middle of Main Street and pulled up next to her. "Where are you headed?"

She pulled her coat collar higher, like it could save her from me. "Doctor," she grumbled.

I frowned. There wasn't a doctor in this part of town. The hospital was forty-five minutes from here, and the closest medical office was a fifteen-minute drive. "You're walking?" I asked sharply.

She stopped and turned to face me, annoyance stamped all over her pretty face. I hit the brake. "Well, driving makes me nauseous, and I can't drive and puke at the same time, so yes, I'm walking."

"I'll take you," I said.

She started walking again. "No, thank you."

"Come on," I argued. "You can lie down in the back seat, or hang your head out the window, or go ahead and puke if you need to. I've got a trash bag for you." Fuck me, now I was begging her to let me do her a favor? This woman had me by the balls and didn't even know it.

She stopped again. "You're going in the wrong direction."

Goddamn, this woman.

"I'm going wherever you are," I growled. "Get in the

fucking truck, princess. It's freezing out here. You're not walking."

The belligerent purse of her full lips told me she was not done arguing. "Don't test me, Chloe," I warned. "I'm used to dealing with nine-hundred-pound ornery animals. I can deal with you the same way." I stretched across the cabin and pushed open the passenger door for her.

With a petulant sigh, she got in, slamming the door closed with more force than necessary. "It's five miles, Steven. I can walk five miles."

"It's ten miles, there and back, and it would be dark by the time you were walking home. I don't want you walking next to a road in the dark." I waited while she struggled out of her coat and buckled her seatbelt and then hit the gas.

She squirmed lower in her seat, smashing her knees against the dashboard, then grabbed the lever next to the seat and pulled it. The backrest jolted flat with a bounce.

"Are you gonna be sick?" I asked, alarmed. With one hand on the steering wheel, I flicked open the center console and pulled out one of the plastic bags I kept balled up inside. "Here."

She took it but dropped it in her lap. "Not yet. We're about to pass the library and Hannah gets off work soon. I don't want her to see me."

With you. She didn't have to say it. I knew that was how the sentence ended. It stung. Another reminder that we weren't friends and never would be. We sure as hell would never be more. And that didn't just sting. It burned. Because sometimes…

Sometimes she looked at me with those green eyes glinting like she saw right into my soul, and I saw the ghost of a future we would never have. A future we maybe *should* have had, if I hadn't fucked everything up before we even got a chance to know each other.

I didn't know what the hell I was doing with Chloe Adams. I just knew I couldn't stop myself.

I unlocked my phone and handed it to her. "Put in the address." I had a pretty good idea of the direction we were headed, since all the medical buildings were clustered by the highway, but I didn't know the exact location.

"Ohhh, you're giving me access to your phone?" she asked, opening the maps app. She tsked. "Not very smart, Steven. Who knows what I'll find?"

"You already know the worst thing I've done. No point in keeping secrets now," I said. When she didn't respond, I glanced over and found her scrolling through my photos. "Wow, you're nosy," I muttered.

"It's all pictures of Junior," she complained. "Where are all the vanity selfies?"

"Vanity selfies?" I repeated, merging onto the highway.

"You know. Fresh out of the shower, a towel wrapped around your waist, flexing your abs but pretending you're not. Maybe a little steam for atmosphere. You seem like the type."

"Oh, I do, do I?" I smirked at her over my shoulder. "Why are you so obsessed with my abs, Chloe?"

She pulled the seat lever and popped upright. Apparently her reputation was safe now that we had left downtown Aspen Springs. "Why are you so obsessed with your pig, Steven?"

"She's cute," I defended.

"It's weird," she replied. "You know that, right?"

I hummed noncommittally. When I looked at her, she was still thumbing through my photos, hearting her favorites and smiling to herself. My chest pinched with the knowledge that I was going to spend some time tonight looking through those photos myself, trying to see her favorites through her eyes. Something was definitely wrong with me.

"So," I said cautiously.

"So." She circled one wrist in a gesture for me to continue.

"You didn't text me back."

"Right. Sorry about that." She worried her bottom lip. "I didn't know what to say because I didn't know what to do. So I ignored you because I wasn't ready to think about it. I needed some time to work through it."

We were treading through something delicate now. I still didn't know what this doctor appointment was for. I didn't know what she had decided to do about the pregnancy. No matter what she had decided, no matter what was going to happen at the doctor's office, I was in it with her. If this was a regular checkup, I was driving her there. If this was an abortion, I was driving her there. No regrets either way.

My gaze flicked to her face and immediately sought the open road again. "And did you? Figure it out, I mean?"

She blew out a breath. "I'm keeping it. If I can." She scowled at a perfectly adorable photo of Stevie wearing a pink sweater. "It still feels fake, you know? Like fate, the universe, whatever"—she did jazz hands—"is playing a joke on me. They're not *really* going to let me have a baby." She sighed again. "Anyway. We'll see what the doctor says today."

I frowned. She had said something similar the night she took the test, that pregnancy hadn't ever been a concern for her. No wonder she didn't want me to drive her. This was a high-stakes doctor appointment, not just another box to tick.

I pulled into the parking lot in front of a gray, square building and cut the engine, then twisted in my seat to face her. She had a white-knuckled grip on herself, her hands folded tightly in her lap, her eyes staring straight ahead, her mouth a grim slash of pink.

"I can wait here for you," I offered.

She paused. I swore I could hear my heartbeat in the silence. "You might as well come in with me," she said finally.

That was as close as Chloe would ever come to admitting she needed something from me. I wasn't going to make her say it twice. I unbuckled without another word.

THE WAITING room was packed full of women, about a quarter of whom had protruding bellies and a man by their side. I settled next to Chloe in the world's most uncomfortable chair and watched her fill out the intake form, glancing from the other women to her stomach. Very soon that would be her.

"Are you imagining me with a baby bump?" she hissed, smacking my thigh with the clipboard. "Stop that!"

Busted. "Why? It's going to happen."

She sneaked a peek at the woman cattycorner to us, who looked like she had swallowed a basketball. "God, I hope so. I would be so cute, right?"

I could picture it. "Cute. Yeah." Why did my chest suddenly ache like a motherfucker? It wasn't even my bun baking in her oven. The only reason I was here was because *he* wasn't. She'd probably trade me for him in a heartbeat if she could.

The nurse appeared in the doorway. "Adams?" she called.

I turned toward Chloe and opened my mouth to ask if I should wait here, but her sudden death grip on my thigh made me snap it shut again. I managed to pry her fingers off my leg and interlocked her hand with mine. "Right here," I called back, tugging Chloe to her feet.

The nurse held the door open wider so we could join

her in the hallway. "I'm Renee. I'll be assisting Dr. Davidson today in examining you. Is that all right?" Chloe nodded and Renee beamed. "Great! We will be in room three."

She ushered us inside and handed Chloe a folded blue paper hospital gown. "Put this on so it opens to the front, then hop up on the table and lay the cloth over your lap. Daddy, your job is to stand there and look handsome. No pressure." She gave me a wink. "Dr. Davidson will be right with you."

The door closed behind her with a quiet snick, leaving us staring after her with slack jaws.

Chloe pivoted to me with a scowl. "I can't believe she was flirting with you right in front of me. That's so rude."

I blinked. Apparently we had very different viewpoints of what just happened. "She wasn't flirting with me." Although I did kind of like the idea of Chloe being mad about it. I wasn't so delusional as to believe she was jealous, but a man could dream, couldn't he?

Chloe rolled her eyes like she thought I was trying to pull a fast one. "She called you daddy."

Laughter roared out of me. "Fuck, Chloe," I wheezed. I couldn't breathe, I was laughing so hard. "You're pregnant. She meant *baby daddy*, not *spank me daddy*."

Her cheeks flushed. "Oh." She blinked rapidly. "*Oh.* She thinks we're together. That's crazy."

"It's not crazy. I'm here at the appointment with you. Of course she thinks I'm your baby daddy."

The flush on her cheeks darkened and she narrowed

her eyes. "Say that phrase again and I'll cut out your tongue. Now turn around so I can get undressed."

I obliged, spinning toward the wall. A row of posters hung at eye-level. I focused every brain cell I had on those posters—and not Chloe getting naked—like there would be a test on it. The middle poster was a fetal growth chart that compared the baby to a type of fruit. Chloe's fetus was probably the size of a radish. Next to the chart were hazy photos of sleeping babies dressed as flowers and, disturbingly, salads. Jesus fucking Christ. What kind of parent allowed this shit to happen?

There was a telltale rustle of paper and squeak of vinyl as Chloe got situated. "Okay, you can turn around," she said.

I shifted to face her. Chloe sat at the edge of the examination table, her legs dangling between the stirrups and crossed at the ankles, the paper gown drawn tight across her chest. She looked nervous. And then her gaze fell on the posters behind me and her expression changed to downright appalled.

"Are they promoting cannibalism?" she wondered.

"Maybe that's why they compare fetus size to fruit."

"It's creepy," she said.

I was going to have nightmares about it. "Promise me you will never put your baby on a bed of lettuce. I don't want you to get confused."

She choked out a horrified laugh. "I'm not going to eat my baby, Steven."

"Not on purpose," I agreed.

"I don't even like salad. The risk is very low." She paused, her gaze going to middle distance. "Although now I kind of want one. With lots of Caesar dressing."

I bent down and whispered to her lap, "You hear that, Radish? Your mom wants a salad. Better stay inside where it's safe. Hold on tight, okay?"

Chloe made an odd sort of honking sound, somewhere between a laugh and a sob. "You are so weird, Steven."

But she looked at me like that wasn't a bad thing.

And there it was again, that feeling of nostalgia for something that hadn't ever happened, that would never happen. How could I ache for something that had never been real to begin with?

The knock on the door startled us both. I back up three quick steps, putting space between us.

"Come in," Chloe said, her voice hoarse.

"Hi, there." Dr. Davidson entered with Renee right behind her. She was a petite woman with a bouncy red ponytail and a warm smile that instantly put me at ease. "It's good to see you again, Chloe, although I have to admit, never in a million years would I have expected to see you under these circumstances. Congratulations."

Chloe's cheeks reddened. "Thank you. It was definitely a surprise."

Dr. Davidson tilted her head. "A happy one, I hope?" When Chloe nodded, she smiled. "Good. So, here's what we're going to do. Your vitals look good, so I'm going to do a quick pelvic exam. Then, because of your history, I want

to do a transvaginal ultrasound to rule out ectopic pregnancy. Is that all right with you?"

Chloe nodded.

"Great." Dr. Davidson patted Chloe's knee and took a
seat on the rolling stool. "You know the drill. Lie down and
slide your butt all the way to the edge. Feet in the stirrups."

I shoved my hands in my pockets. Chloe's clothes were
in a folded pile on the only other chair in the room, so I
just stood there, feeling like I was in the way.

"*Steven*." Chloe stared daggers at me. "You are not
going to watch Dr. Davidson put her hand up my vagina.
Get over here by my head."

Dr. Davidson chuckled as I leaped forward. "Must be
your first time, too."

"Yeah," I said sheepishly.

"Don't worry. First-time dads are always a little
awkward about everything. Women's bodies are such a
mystery to men that sometimes I wonder how the human
species still exists."

"He's not the dad," Chloe corrected. "He's just..." *Friend*
would have been the obvious choice, but she didn't say it.
"Steven."

I clenched my jaw and pretended it was fine.

"Hm." Dr. Davidson's eyebrows went up and my
hackles went right up with them. That judgmental look on
her face made me want to throw something. "Will the dad
be in the picture?"

Chloe swallowed audibly. "I don't know. If he wants to
be. I haven't told him yet. I figured it would be better to

find out if there's even a picture to begin with before I asked him if he wanted to be in it."

Dr. Davidson nodded. "Well, your cervix feels high, firm, and closed. I'd know you were pregnant even if I hadn't seen the results of your urine test." She slowly withdrew and Chloe's knees collapsed inwards. "Let's see how the ultrasound looks." She reached for the machine next to her and unhooked a slender probe the length of my forearm. "I'm going to slide this inside—"

"I beg your finest pardon?" Chloe squawked, lifting her head off the table. She clawed my arm like a lifeline.

I had to work to cover my laugh. It was long, but not *that* much longer than something else I could put inside her, and I was thicker. "If that thing scares you, don't come running to me for protection. I'm the wrong man for the job."

She craned her neck to stare at me, and when I smirked back at her, her gaze dropped to my crotch—conveniently right at eye level for her. And then I wished I hadn't teased her because the way she looked at me made my jeans tighten.

Dr. Davidson cleared her throat. "It's only the first four or five inches that goes inside you. It's not comfortable, but it's not painful, either. Just breathe, okay? Squeeze Steven's hand if the pressure is too much."

Chloe nodded and closed her eyes. Her hand found mine. I rubbed my thumb across her knuckles in what I hoped was a soothing gesture. Dr. Davidson kept her eyes on the machine's rectangular screen as she worked. She was quiet for so long that I started to worry. Chloe wanted this baby so badly. I didn't believe in a god or higher power, but I sent a prayer to the universe anyway. *Please.*

"All right," Dr. Davidson said brightly after what felt like an eternity. "Everything looks exactly as it should. The embryonic sac is definitely in your uterus where we want it, so it's not ectopic. You're about eight weeks along. And I think if I...yes...there it is. Do you hear that?"

Lub-dub. Lub-dub. Lub-dub.

"It's the heartbeat," Dr. Davidson explained.

Chloe's hand spasmed in mine. "The heartbeat?" she whispered.

Dr. Davidson nodded. "Listen."

Lub-dub. Lub-dub. Lub-dub.

I looked down at Chloe. She stared back at me with eyes as shiny and green as a spring meadow. "That's my baby," she said, awed.

Lub-dub. Lub-dub. Lub-dub.

The beat was quick but strong and steady.

And so was mine.

17

CHLOE

CHLOE

Hey! Hope you're having an epic adventure. When you have cell service, give me a call.

CHLOE

I really need to talk to you about something. Call mo when you can.

CHLOE

Dude, are you alive??

Since Gabe and I only texted when we were home, I wasn't too surprised I hadn't heard from him. Still, I hated that he was out there, taking all kinds of risks because that's what he loved to do, and had no idea he was going to be a dad in seven months. I didn't know any of his friends or family, so there was no one I could get in touch with to make sure he was okay.

Other than that niggling worry, I was surprisingly calm. Better than calm, I was in solution mode. Solution mode was where I thrived. Not that Radish was a problem. Babies were always a blessing, blah blah blah, but they sure did *cause* problems. Such as: space, and the lack thereof. Child care, and the lack thereof. Money, and the lack thereof.

But every problem had a solution. Luckily, I had seven months to find it.

In the meantime, I whiplashed between bliss and nausea.

Radish will be born in May. She'll be a summer baby. We'll rock together on the porch while the peonies I planted are in bloom. Bliss.

Ugh, someone microwaved fish in the office. Nausea.

Steven nicknamed my fetus Radish and now I can't call it anything else. I landed somewhere in between bliss and nausea with that one. How had Steven gone from being the person I wanted to drop kick off the earth to the person I wanted holding my hand during my baby's first sonogram?

It had to be the baby hormones, making me latch on to the first big, strong man in my vicinity like I was some cavewoman in need of masculine protection. Evolution had programmed me for this. Feminism was no match for his sharp jawline, broad shoulders, and all that fucking *competence*.

Fuck evolution. I could do this on my own.

I walked the entire floorplan of the bungalow, measuring tape in hand, for the ninth time. Nine hundred square feet wasn't a lot to work with, but babies were, what, twelve inches? Of course I wanted my little Radish to have everything in this world, but we could make do with the bare necessities. A crib (twenty-eight by fifty-two inches), a high chair (which I wouldn't even need until Radish was a year old), and a dresser (with a changing table on top). Three items. I could find space for three items.

Somewhere.

The closet, maybe? The walk-in closet in my bedroom was crammed full of who knew what, but I was pretty sure it would fit a crib if I cleaned it out.

I pivoted to my bedroom just as my cell phone rang. I pulled it out of my pocket, saw my landlord's name, and put it on speaker. "Hi, Miriam. How are you?" My lease was up next month, so I wasn't surprised that she was calling to check in. I was hoping she would be willing to sign a two-year agreement this time around. "Perfect timing."

"Good, honey, good." Miriam heaved a long sigh—which, quite frankly, did not *sound* good. "As for the timing...that's not so good, I'm afraid."

I frowned at my phone, my hand flexing around the measuring tape.

"Listen, honey, I know how much you love the place, so I wanted to tell you right away. My daughter needs the bungalow. She's getting a divorce, and she doesn't have a lot of options."

I stared dumbstruck at my overflowing closet. "But... but *I* need the bungalow," I stammered.

"I know the timing is terrible. But you have family in the area who can help you out. And you have two months until you need to be out. That's plenty of time to find other arrangements."

Right. Because Aspen Springs had an abundance of affordable housing. I was so screwed.

After we hung up, I wandered the house in a daze. For the last two years, this had been my sanctuary. Close enough to the clinic that I didn't have to find a more expensive apartment in the city. Close enough to my family that I could help them anytime they needed it, but far enough away that I finally had some breathing room. I loved this place.

I stepped out onto the porch, wrapping my arms around my midsection to protect myself from the sharp autumn breeze. My gaze landed on the peony bushes I had planted when I moved in. The branches were bare now. Radish would never see them bloom.

I sank into a pathetic ball there on my welcome mat and burst into tears.

"Chloe! Chloe, what the fuck!"

The pure panic in Steven's voice had me scrambling to my feet, but I was crying too hard to get out more than a hiccupping sob. Through the blurry teardrops in my eyes, I saw him toss a package on the porch swing before gathering me into his arms.

"What happened, princess? Are you hurt?" He pushed my hair off my damp cheeks. "Is it...is it the baby?" he asked hoarsely.

"We're homeless!" I wailed.

His eyes darted frantically over my face. "The baby is... still in there?"

I nodded, hiccupping.

His forehead dropped to mine and I felt his chest expand on a deep breath. "Okay. Okay. Let's get you inside and you can tell me all about it."

"Okay." I pulled my flannel over my palms and wiped my eyes on cuff. "What are you doing here, Steven?"

"Delivery. It's from your mom." He snagged the package from the swing and followed me inside. "She baked it this morning."

I peered inside the brown paper bag and then back at him. "A loaf of bread? She asked you to bring me a loaf of bread?" I asked dubiously. "You don't even live in my neighborhood. Why would she ask you to bring me this? It doesn't make any sense."

He rolled his eyes. "Okay, you caught me. The bread is a ruse. I figured, why not drive an extra hour today just so I can see how you're doing? It's not like I have anything better to do on a Saturday." He shook his head. "For fuck's sake, princess."

Sometimes Mom did things that didn't make sense. She always felt a little guilty after a bad flare, even though we'd all told her she had no reason to. "Fine. Whatever. I'll call her later to say thank you." I headed straight for the kitchen because if there was one thing that was good at sopping up tears, it was my mom's sourdough bread.

Steven was right on my heels. "So, what do you mean, you're homeless?"

"I mean, I am without a home. I am devoid of shelter. I am—"

"Dramatic," Steven muttered. "You're fucking dramatic, that's what you are." He took the knife from me, slid the loaf down the counter, and cut off a thick slice. "Do you like the end piece?"

I shook my head. "And don't tell me it has more nutrients because it has more crust. I know that's a lie."

He smirked but set the piece aside and sliced a second one. He handed it over and then said, "Now, tell me what happened."

I took a large bite and chewed. "My landlord just called. Her daughter is getting a divorce and needs a place to stay. I have two months to find a new home."

"Two months? But you're pregnant. Did you tell her you're pregnant?"

"No, of course not." I ripped off another bite of bread with my teeth. "What difference would that make? It wouldn't change the fact that her daughter is in a rough spot and needs a place to stay. All it would do is make her feel bad."

"She *should* feel bad. This is unacceptable. Call Brax."

I squinted at him. "Brax Hale? Essie's husband?"

"Do you know another lawyer?" he snapped.

"For heaven's sake, Steven. I'm not going to sue Miriam. One of the nice things about living here is that I actually *like* my landlord. She let me paint the bedroom any color I wanted. I have the feeling our relationship would change if I sued her."

He growled.

I laughed, then my head tipped forward on a groan as a new, terrible thought occurred to me. "I'm going to have move back home with my parents. Oh, hell."

"Would that be so bad?" he asked cautiously.

I shook my head. "My parents are great. But I want a life of my own. Would *you* want to move back home?"

His mouth twisted and I suddenly wished I had kept my own shut. Amy had told me enough about their child-hood that I already knew the answer.

"My parents are too far from school, anyway. I'd spend three hours a day driving. I guess I could try to find something in the city, but everything is so expensive. I'm not sure I can afford anything more than an effi-ciency there." I scrubbed my hands over my face. "God, I'm so fucked."

Steven leaned against the counter and wrapped one hand around the back of his neck, his eyes focused on the linoleum tile. "I have a spare bedroom."

I gave him a narrow-eyed look. "This is not the time to brag, Steven."

"I'm not bragging. I'm offering it to you."

My jaw flapped open on a shocked laugh. "What?"

"You heard me. You need a room. I have a room." He said this like it was perfectly logical instead of fucking insane.

"Move in with me, Chloe."

18

———

STEVEN

It wasn't like I expected Chloe to be *overjoyed* by the prospect of living under the same roof as—how had she phrased it to Stevie? *Hot garbage*—but shit. A little gratitude would have been nice.

"Steven," Chloe said, slowly and patiently like I was an idiot, "I cannot live with you."

"No," I said, matching her tone, "you cannot be homeless. You *can* live with me. You *can* cut your commute to work by fifteen minutes. You *can* still be close to your family without having them all up in your business. You can save money on rent so that when the right opportunity comes along, you can take it."

That gave her pause. Her head tilted and her gaze slid sideways as she considered. "How much would rent be?"

"No rent."

She straightened, her gaze snapping to mine. "I'm paying rent."

I shook my head. "It's in both of our best interests that you don't. The more you can save, the faster you can find a permanent place to live."

She folded her arms and frowned at the floor while she thought it through. I didn't rush her. Chloe wasn't unreasonable. She'd do the right thing for her and her baby. I cut another slice of bread and pushed it to her. She stared at it for a moment before taking it. Then she looked up at me.

"At least let me help with food and utilities," she said.

I shrugged. "Sure."

Her shoulders tensed. "What if I can't find a place before Radish is born? You really want a newborn baby living with you?"

Radish. She'd kept my silly little nickname. Warmth spread through my chest. "I happen to like kids, Chloe." Probably. I didn't actually know any, but I'd seen several from a distance and they seemed fine. "I wasn't a huge fan of Amy when she was born but in my defense, she cried a lot. I think she's great now."

Chloe stared at me. "Amy is eighteen. She's not a kid. And babies *do* cry a lot. That's what they're known for. They cry when they're hungry, they cry when they need a diaper change, they cry when they're sleepy, they cry when they wake up. Oh, god." She squeezed her eyes shut. "This isn't going to work."

"It will be fine," I insisted. "I won't even notice. My room is at the opposite end of the house. The room you're taking has its own bathroom, too, and it's big enough for a bed and a crib, so you don't have to worry about waking me up in the middle of the night. And if I hear the baby cry, so what? You cannot be homeless, Chloe. Your baby cannot be homeless."

Her forehead creased as she searched my face. "Why are you doing this?"

Because when I think of anything bad happening to you, I want to tear the world apart. But that didn't seem like the kind of thing I should say out loud. "I don't know," I said. "It must be that basic human decency I've heard so much about."

"No." She shook her head slowly. "No, that's not it. You're—"

I cut her off. "Yeah, I know what you think I am, princess. I don't need to hear it again." I jerked away, bracing my palms on the countertop.

There was a beat of silence. Fuck me, why did I go and say that? I felt so fucking exposed.

And then her hand ghosted over my shoulder, skimming against my thick flannel shirt, no weight to her touch. I would have thought she was flicking away a fly or schmutz if she hadn't hesitated, the barest flex of her fingers grazing my collar.

I couldn't breathe for hoping.

"I was going to say," she said quietly, pulling her hand away, "that you're doing so much more than that. This isn't basic human decency. This is—" She sucked in a deep breath. "Anyway. Thank you."

"It's fine," I said, when what I wanted to say was *please put your hand back on my shoulder immediately.*

We stood there for a moment, neither of us speaking.

Then she cleared her throat. "Would Amy be okay with me moving in?"

I turned so I was facing her again. "I don't see why not. She likes you. I'll talk to her, though."

Chloe chewed her lip, twisting her fingers together. "Seven months is a long time. I'm sure I can find something else before the baby comes, but what if I can't? I don't want Amy to feel like she was tricked."

"Do you want me to tell her you're pregnant?" I asked.

"Yeah." She sighed. "She's going to figure it out pretty quickly, anyway. I'm so nauseous all the time that I can't hide it, so she'll know I'm either pregnant or dying. We might as well tell her the truth straight off."

I studied her for a moment. "You don't seem very happy about that."

"Steven." She huffed my name. "I'm a therapist. I'm supposed to have my shit together. Of course I don't want to tell people I'm pregnant from a one-night stand. I can't even claim the condom broke. It's embarrassing. I should know better."

"Well, yeah, Chloe. You *do* know better. So does everyone else. It still happens. What would you say to one of your clients, if they were pregnant from a one-night stand because they didn't use a condom? Would you tell them they should be embarrassed?"

Her eyes rolled to the ceiling. "No, of course not. A lecture wouldn't do anyone any good."

"So stop lecturing yourself. It's no one's business how this baby came into the world. You can't take back the past, and you want this baby. Let yourself be happy about it. Anything else, all the regrets and what ifs, it's all noise. Don't listen to it."

She blinked rapidly. "That's…Wow. What a…beautiful…thing to say." A tear trembled on her lower lash line before splashing onto her cheek.

I stared at her in horror. "Why are you crying again?" I demanded. "Everything is fine now. You have a place to live."

She sniffled. "Baby hormones. I can't help it. You're being so nice to me."

"Would it help if I were mean to you?" I asked, stepping closer. "Because I'd be happy to oblige, princess."

Her eyes narrowed as she shifted toward me. "Really, Steven? You're going to be mean to a pregnant woman?"

"If you want me to." My voice came out low and rough. Somehow the space between us had dissolved. We were at kissing distance now. Her face tipped up to look at me.

"I want…" Her gaze dipped to my mouth and she licked her lower lip. Every cell in my body took note. "I want…"

All I could feel was want.

All I could hear was her breath.

All I could smell was her strawberry hair.

All I could see was that mouth.

I fucking *whimpered*.

The fragile moment splintered. Chloe blinked the lust from her eyes and stepped back. She looked around as though searching for an explanation of how we had gotten here.

"Bread," she said. "I want more bread."

Without a word, I reached for the knife. What the hell else was I supposed to do? This woman hated me, and I still wanted to give her every damn thing she wanted.

And now she was going to live with me.

I was fucked.

"Tell me again why we're moving all your shit into the basement?" Amy panted as we carried the solid pine dresser that had occupied one wall of my bedroom for the last two years down the hall.

"I already told you." I glanced over my shoulder to make sure I wasn't about to bump into a wall. Amy was supposed to be steering us, but she seemed more interested in talking than keeping me upright.

"You garbled a bunch of words at me that made no sense. So try again," Amy said.

I sighed. "Chloe needs a place to stay for a couple months. She's moving in until she finds something more permanent."

"Yes, I understand all that. Landlady's daughter, divorce, blah, blah, blah. Got it. What I don't get is why

Chloe can't just stay in the guest room since it's not permanent. Why are you giving up your bedroom?" Her brown eyes lit up and she dropped her end with an unceremonious thunk against the braided rug, making me swear loudly. "Oh, my god. Chloe's the girl, isn't she?"

I grunted as my fingers started to lip against the wood and I carefully set the dresser down. "What girl?"

"*The* girl. The one who didn't want your help. The one ignoring your texts. Although I'm guessing that part changed, judging by that dopey smile you get every time you look at your phone."

Sisters, goddamn. So gossipy. Never letting shit go. Did I sometimes look back over my text messages with Chloe? Yes, but only because I wanted to watch the animal videos again. That would make anyone smile. "What makes you think it's about a girl?" I asked.

Her eyes narrowed suspiciously. "Well, it's definitely not our parents making you smile. And it's not a guy, either. I'd know if you were gay." She pursed her lips, thinking, and then clapped her hands to her cheeks. "Oh, god. You're not getting another pig, are you?"

I couldn't categorically deny that. "Pigs are social creatures," I defended. "Stevie needs friends."

Amy groaned long and loud, the sound bouncing off the cement walls. "Steven, *no.*"

"Pretty sure it's a tax write off if we call it a rescue," I mused.

"You're crazy." She shook her head. "But that doesn't explain why Chloe is moving to the master bedroom and you're taking the crappy guestroom at the back of the house."

"It's not crappy," I protested. "It's small, but it's comfortable. I figured Mom might come to visit eventually."

Amy's pitying look made my jaw clench. She cleared her throat. "Okay. Well. You're going from a queen-sized bed to a twin. Do you even fit in a twin?"

To be honest, I hadn't tried but it was too late now. "All right, break time is over and I'm not going to talk about this while carrying a hundred-pound dresser backwards down the stairs." I hefted my end. "Let's go."

She smirked at my blatant attempt to dodge the question but hooked her hands under the beveled edge and lifted. "Okay, I've got it."

Our height difference made the descent slow and awkward, but Amy was strong and disinclined to let me be crushed by a falling dresser, so we made it safely. I wiggled the dresser against the back wall where it would be out of the way. I still needed to wrangle my bed down here, along with the nightstand and any clothes I couldn't cram into the tiny guestroom dresser because the room didn't have a closet.

I turned around and yelped at finding my sister an inch from my nose. "Amy, what the hell?" I moved to pass her, but she poked me between the ribs.

"What's the deal with Chloe?" she demanded.

Why was I so reluctant to talk about this? "It's not a big deal. Chloe is pregnant. I figured she would want the extra privacy of having her own bathroom."

"Holy shit, Steven. Holy shit," Amy whispered, which was a bit overly dramatic for the situation, in my opinion. "You knocked up your boss's daughter?"

"What? No. *No.* Jesus, Amy." I scrubbed a hand over my face. "I'm not the dad. But that reminds me. Chloe hasn't told her parents yet, so keep it zipped, all right?"

I side-stepped her while she stood there slack jawed. I was halfway up the stairs when she pivoted.

"I have more questions," she said.

I grunted. "Of course you do."

Amy fired them off one after the other. "When is she due? Where's the dad? Why is any of this your problem?"

"May. On a bike in South America somewhere. I didn't think it *was* a problem." At the top of the stairs, I turned around and leaned against the doorway with my arms crossed. Amy stomped up the stairs behind me. I quirked an eyebrow at her. "Is it a problem for *you*?"

"It would have been nice to be asked," she said. "I live here, too, don't I?"

That got my attention. The last thing I wanted was for her to feel like this wasn't her home. She'd had enough of family making her feel like an unwanted obligation. "Chloe told me to ask you. I didn't because I thought I knew the answer. Don't you like Chloe? Are you telling me you would let her be pregnant and homeless?"

"Of course not," Amy grumbled. "It still would have been nice if we'd had an actual conversation about it before you started moving furniture around."

"I'm the one giving up my room," I pointed out.

"And I'm the one who now has to share a bathroom with a yucky boy," she tossed back.

"I'm not yucky," I protested.

She wrinkled her nose.

I sighed. "I promise I won't piss on the toilet seat, and I'll wipe down the sink after every shave. Satisfied?"

"Maybe." She tilted her head, clearly waiting for more.

This time my sigh came from the depths of my sister-wearied soul. "Amy, Chloe is in a tight spot. What do you think about letting her stay here for a while? If you're not okay with it, we'll find another solution."

"Really?" she asked.

"Of course, really. You're my sister. This is your home for as long as you want it to be."

"In that case..." She dragged the words out slowly just to fuck with me but couldn't stop her shit-eating grin. "I think I would like that a lot."

CHLOE

CHLOE

Anyone want to blow off sewing circle tomorrow and help a friend pack up all her worldly goods? (It's me. I'm the friend.)

HANNAH

You're moving?? We're not going to be neighbors anymore?

JAMES

What happened? I thought you loved the bungalow and you were going to ask for a two-year lease this time.

ESSIE

Chloe Adams, I know you're not telling us over text that you're leaving Aspen Springs!

JANIE

Where are you going?

CHLOE

> I'll tell you everything tomorrow, I promise.
> This is an in-person kind of conversation.

"Oh, my god." James stepped over the threshold and looked around my disheveled home with wide eyes. "You're actually moving. I kind of thought you were teasing us, but no. You're really doing it."

I blew a lock of hair out of my eyes, dumped the armload of sheets and towels into the open box, and straightened. "I'm really doing it," I confirmed.

"Tell me everything."

Oh, shit.

I had asked James to come over twenty minutes before everyone else so that I could tell her alone. Essie, Hannah, Janie—they all had strong opinions about Steven, but James was the one I was really worried about. Radish was literally eating my brain cells. That was the only reasonable explanation for how I could have said yes to sharing a roof with the man who had gotten my best friend bucked into a fence before talking it over with her.

I had to tell her. A tiny, cowardly part of me briefly considered not telling anyone. The move was temporary, after all. Maybe I'd only have to live with Steven for a month, and then a perfectly priced, two-bedroom house would miraculously fall into my lap. But I knew that wasn't going to happen. More than likely, I wouldn't find anything until the summer.

Anyway, I believed that if you had to keep a secret from a friend, that meant either they weren't *really* a good friend, or you were doing shit you knew was wrong. James was a good friend. Moving in with her worst enemy? That made me a bad friend, I couldn't deny that, no matter how good my reasons were. I just hoped it didn't make me an *ex*-friend.

I had to tell her. I knew that. It was just so dang hard.

"Bedroom," I said. "I'll tell you all about it while I clean out my closet."

She followed me into the bedroom where I pulled my suitcase from the closet and tossed it onto the bed. "So, first of all, I'm moving because I have to." I told her about Miriam's daughter while I unzipped the suitcase and flipped it open.

James made a sympathetic sound. "That sucks. I feel bad for everyone involved, but especially you." Her forehead pinched with obvious worry. "It's not like Aspen Springs has an abundance of housing options. This is a ranching town. What are you going to do? Are you going to have to move to the city?"

"No, I...I found a place. Not in town, but close by." I stared unseeingly at the contents of my underwear drawer. I needed to reserve a week's worth of clothes to hold me until I was fully moved into Steven's house— everything else was going in boxes—but for the life of me I couldn't figure out how much underwear that meant.

"Chloe," James said softly, like she knew I was on the cusp of a minor meltdown. "How can I help? Put me to work."

But I couldn't let her lift a finger with the weight of my lies sitting on my chest. I shook my head. "Let me tell you first. Then...we'll see what you want to do."

James toed off her sneakers and sat on the bed cross-legged. "Okay. Let's hear it."

"I don't know where to start." I scooped up the entire drawer's worth of socks and underwear and dropped everything into the suitcase. Better to be prepared.

"Start with now. Where are you moving?"

Here we go.

"I'm moving in with Steven McAllister." I pushed the words out and backed up a step like I had tossed a grenade.

James snorted. "Haha, Chloe. Very funny. Now tell me what's *really* going on." She looked at me. I looked back. Her eyes widened. "Oh, shit...you're serious? But you...you hate him, Chloe." That was so like James, to think about my feelings before her own. "Are you—holy shit, are you *dating*?"

"No!" I said, the word coming out louder than I intended. "*No*. He's...I don't know what he is, to be honest. We're not friends, exactly. He's just always around." Getting me food. Making me take a pregnancy test.

Holding my hand during a sonogram. I shook my head. "I can't explain it."

"Okay. Okay. Okay," James chanted, like she believed that if she said it enough, she could magically make it true. "Start from the beginning."

I tilted my head back to contemplate the ceiling. What was the beginning? Was it before James's accident, when I thought maybe he might be worth talking to? Or was it the first time he walked into Jo's after James's accident and I told him to leave? "So there was this pig..."

James was quiet while I told her all of it. Rescuing Junior, the 3 a.m. conversations, finding out he was working with my dad, the pregnancy test and doctor's appointment, and then how he offered to let me stay with him.

Her silence held for a long moment after I stopped talking. I waited, my heart in my throat.

"So...you don't hate him?" she asked finally.

"I..." I blew out a long breath. "I hate what he did to you. That's the same thing, isn't it?"

"Honestly, I don't know. People make mistakes. What he did was terrible, and he can't take it back, so now what is he supposed to do? Yeet himself off a cliff?"

"I'm not opposed to that idea," I said reflexively. My chest tightened and I frowned. Apparently I *was* opposed to Steven yeeting himself off a cliff. When had that changed?

James squeezed my hand. "You don't have to hate him on my behalf, Chloe," she said gently. "He's giving you a place to stay. Do what you need to do to take care of yourself and your baby."

I worried my lip. "But Adam…"

"Yeah." James sighed. "That's a problem. Adam isn't going to forgive or forget. I can't…He would be furious if he found out I was anywhere near Steven, and quite frankly, I don't *want* to be near him. I'm not going to waste my time hating him, but I'm not hanging out at his house, either."

A big, fat tear rolled down my cheek. "It's just until I can find something permanent. I can go to you at Lodestar. We can still do the sewing circle together, too, right?"

"Of course." James pulled me into a fierce hug. "I'm going to be your baby's favorite godmother. We're friends. Steven won't change that."

"It's temporary," I whispered again, snuffling into my sleeve. "I'll find a place of my own."

"It's going to be okay, Chloe. I promise."

I wanted to believe her, but right now, nothing felt okay at all.

I OFFICIALLY MOVED to Steven's the following Sunday. It took all morning and a good chunk of the afternoon, but I got it done with the help of my friends. Janie, Essie, and Hannah—not James, for obvious reasons—had each loaded up their cars with boxes.

Things had been…tense…between my friends and

Steven. Essie, being Essie, had deliberately shoulder checked him more than once. To his credit, Steven had simply apologized for being in her way, even though we all knew she had gone *out* of her way to bump him, but I saw the muscle flicker in his jaw each time.

This is temporary, I reminded myself. Steven wasn't my boyfriend. They didn't have to get along or like each other. They just needed to be minimally civil for a couple months. Surely everyone could do that, right?

Ellis, Garret, and Cole claimed the bigger furniture I couldn't take with me, like the couch and dining room table, on the agreement that they would return them when I found a place of my own. It had been a little awkward keeping my pregnancy a secret, and once I almost let it slip when Steven wouldn't let me carry a box of books to my car.

"Trust me," Garret had said as he and Cole went by with the couch. "She's stronger than she looks."

"Don't even think about it, princess," Steven growled in my ear. "If you carry that box, then I'm carrying you."

It had to be the pregnancy hormones that made me feel light-headed and flustered at the mental image of Steven carrying me out of there with a box of books in my arms.

When the last box had been unloaded and my friends and family were gone, I collapsed onto the couch with a groan. "I'm going to be so sore at Jo's tomorrow. It will be a miracle if I can steam the milk."

"You work at Jo's?" Amy asked. She was star-fished on

the floor, as worn out as I was. Steven's little sister had truly busted her ass for me today and I was grateful.

I nodded. "For about the last four years or so."

"Interesting. Steven has a huge crush on a girl there. They have this whole enemies-to-lovers thing going on, except they haven't become lovers yet. He goes in there just so she can kick him out again." Amy laughed. "You probably know her. Give me all the dirty details."

A crush? Steven didn't like me any more than I liked him. My gaze darted to the kitchen, where I could hear him opening cabinets. "Maybe they're really just enemies," I dodged. "It sounds like he's trying to piss her off. That's not a crush."

Amy shook her head. "You don't know my brother like I do. He's a quitter."

I thought of that day in the rain eight months ago, the way he refused to leave Junior to the mountain lions. "Steven is a lot of things, but a quitter isn't one of them."

"He is," Amy insisted. "When things get hard, he quits. Football, rodeo, horse training. He'll self-sabotage or just stop trying. There's no way he would ever care enough about pissing someone off to show up every week. He's got better things to do. Trust me on this. My brother does not put in effort when he doesn't care." She lifted her head off the floor and looked past my shoulder. "Isn't that right, Steven?"

"Isn't what right?" he asked, rounding the couch with a glass of ice water in each hand. He set one down on the coffee table. "That's for you, Amy." He handed me the other one. "Pregnancy adds fifty percent more blood to your body. You need to stay hydrated."

My eyebrows went up. "Look at you with the random pregnancy facts."

"I might have flipped through a book or two." He shrugged. "I was curious." He nudged Amy's hip with his boot. "What were you saying?"

Her eyes darted between us as though she were watching a fascinating tennis match. "I was saying that you half ass everything."

"Not everything. But most things." He smirked. "Very few things out there are worth my whole ass. It's too good to waste on petty shit."

Amy rolled her eyes at me. "See, I told you. He has to really care about something to give it his all, and then..." Her voice trailed off and she split another look between us. "And then he's relentless."

20

CHLOE

Olives were amazing. Take out a tooth-chipping pit, replace it with a perfectly uniform red pepper, and boom. Fucking genius.

"What are you doing up?" came a sleep-roughened voice behind me.

I yelped in surprise and banged my elbow on the open refrigerator door as I whirled around. The jar of olives slid from my fingers, bounced once against the linoleum tile but thank god did not shatter, olives and briny juice erupting from its open mouth like a volcano before it spiraled across the floor, rolling to a stop at Steven's slippered toes.

He looked at it for a long moment, so I looked at it, too. It was kind of pretty, actually, the way the pale green liquid glistened in the refrigerator light. I did not like the cold, sticky feeling of the juice on my bare feet, however.

"Did you eat half a block of cheese last night?" he

asked, still staring at the jar, as though one thing had everything to do with the other.

"Which cheese?" I hedged.

"The cheddar."

"Yes." I had also eaten the feta, but he hadn't asked specifically about the feta, so it seemed unnecessary to share that information. "It turns out that the only time of day I do not have morning sickness is three a.m. My body has traded anxiety for hunger, apparently."

He looked up. "You're hungry?"

"Starving."

The olives mocked me from the floor, plump and green and shiny, their adorable red pimentos winking at me like a dare. I had only eaten two. I bit my lower lip. Steven kept a pretty tidy house. Sure, Junior had free rein of the place, but how dirty could the floor really be? It looked fine from here.

"Chloe." Steven's voice sliced through my thoughts. "You're not actually thinking about eating olives off the floor, are you?"

I huffed. "Until you find yourself famished and nauseous at the same time, twenty-three hours a day for six weeks, don't you dare judge me."

"For fuck's sake, princess," he growled.

My hand was inches from an olive, but I paused. It was the damnedest thing, the way my heart bounded hopefully at those words, like Pavlov's dog salivating at the ring of a bell. Because I *knew*. Whatever stupid, inconsequential problem I had, if Steven grunted those words at me, it meant he was going to fix it. And hell yeah, I was going to let him.

Maybe he thought he needed to run to my rescue because I was incompetent, but I knew I wasn't. My whole life, I had taken care of other people. My brothers, my mom, even my stepdad. Between mom's lupus diagnosis and the financial strain of medical bills on top of farm bills, and the emotional upheaval from losing my dad and then my grandfather, all of us had to give one hundred percent. And we did, every last one of us.

But I had learned early on that my hundred percent went a little further. I was older than my brothers, healthier than my mother, and had more time than my stepfather. I could give more.

And so I did.

I wasn't incompetent. Not even now, when exhaustion had settled so deeply into my bones that I couldn't remember what it felt like *not* to be tired. I took my prenatal vitamin every single day. I hadn't had a sip of caffeine or alcohol since the positive pregnancy test. I might not have six months of savings socked away like those finance dudes were always yapping about, but I paid my bills on time. I gave every client my full attention and only puked between sessions.

I could take care of myself, and—mostly—I did. But sometimes, I really didn't want to. Sometimes I just wanted to be coddled. My parents took care of me, truly they did, but they never babied me. If there was something I could do for myself, I was expected to get on with it and not waste time fussing. They would never have gotten me an iced mocha when I was hungover or pushed the cart around the grocery store when I was tired.

And if they saw me standing in a puddle of olive juice, contemplating eating food straight off the floor, they'd hand me a rag and expect me to use it. That's what my parents would do.

But not Steven.

Because Steven growled "For fuck's sake, Chloe," and the next thing I knew he wrapped his arms around my bare thighs, the curve of my butt resting on his forearm, and hoisted me out of the mess and onto the clean countertop.

It felt symbolic somehow, like it meant something bigger than the act itself, and maybe I should pay attention to that. But pregnancy hormones had a way of making everything seem more vital than it really was. Steven wanted me out of the way and didn't trust me to get there myself, that was all.

I shifted my weight from one butt cheek to the other, tugging my minuscule sleeping shorts back into place. "You want some help?" I offered half-heartedly. I didn't really want to help. I wanted to sit there on the pristine countertop and watch shirtless Steven clean up my mess.

He shook his head as he tossed the empty olive jar into the trash can. "You're barefoot."

"That doesn't matter. I'm already sticky."

He frowned at my feet and shook his head again, his annoyance clear in the tick of his jaw. "I've got it."

But he didn't start in on the floor right away. Instead, he unlocked the fridge and pulled things out of it. Steak, butter, green beans. My stomach clenched and rumbled. After setting a pot of water on the stove to boil and placing a cast-iron pan on the burner next to it with a fat slab of yellow butter in the center, he finally grabbed a handful of paper towels and went to work sopping up the olive juice.

Hot damn. Steven multitasking cooking and cleaning might be the sexiest thing I had ever seen.

After dumping the mess in the garbage, he ripped off one more paper towel, dampened it under the faucet and wrung out the excess, and pivoted toward me.

"Foot," he grunted.

I kicked out my right foot. He caught it, encircling my whole ankle with his large hand, and held it up to his abdomen while he wiped the stickiness from my foot. My whole body flushed. I could feel heat rising off me like steam.

He let go of my ankle and tapped my left knee. "Other foot."

I gave him my left foot and he wiped it clean, his forehead furrowed like the task required his full concentration. The damp towel was a cold shock against my heated skin. I wondered if I felt hot to his touch, if he knew I couldn't catch my breath.

I wondered what it would feel like to touch him, too.

So I put my hands on his shoulders to find out. He sucked in an audible breath and froze, not moving a muscle as I slowly, lightly, skated my hands over the boulder-like bulge of his shoulders, across the ridgeline of his traps, and settled them in the crook of his neck.

Wonderful.

That was how it felt to touch him. Soft and hard and wonderful.

His eyes dipped to my mouth and dilated slightly when I licked my lower lip before rising to meet my gaze.

"Chloe," he said quietly, my name half-plea, half-warning. He exhaled a long, shuddering breath and then captured my wrists with his hands, gently but firmly prying them from his body. "I don't want to be something you regret."

I wanted to reach for him when he stepped away, pull him back to me, whisper lies in his ear. *I won't regret this. I forgive you. It's all right.* But we both knew the truth.

"You have to stop being so nice to me," I teased lightly, a pathetic attempt to regain the equilibrium between us. "It confuses my brain. Sometimes I forget I hate you."

"I don't," he said in a voice like barbed wire.

His back was to me as he seasoned the steak and placed it in the sizzling pan. I was glad for that, glad I couldn't see his face when those words spiked out of him, and glad he couldn't see mine when they cut me.

He cooked the steak to a perfect medium rare. The green beans were crisp and tender. He sat with me at the table while I ate every bite. We talked about Stevie and the other pigs, and the weather, and whatever else crossed our minds.

And the next night he made me chicken and sweet potatoes.

The night after that it was pizza.

I wondered what it said about him that he got up at 3 a.m. to make me dinner, with that jagged barbed wire between us, ready to cut the person who dared to cross it.

I wondered what it said about me that I let him.

21

STEVEN

The hardest part about working with animals was that you couldn't save them all. Most of the horses I shoed were healthy and had healthy hooves that only needed basic care. Some were healthy but had feet issues that we could mitigate or even solve with specialized shoeing. But occasionally, we saw a horse with feet so bad that nothing we did could save him.

It fucking sucked.

"Jacob made the right call." Terry laid a hand on my shoulder. "We did everything we could."

"It wasn't enough," I grunted.

"That's life. Sometimes your best isn't good enough. Don't let it eat at you or this career will burn you out."

Jacob Gunnell, the vet, inserted the needle into the gelding while its owner stroked its neck. I grimaced.

Pedal osteitis wasn't usually a death sentence, but this had been a particularly severe case. When Dr. Gunnell brought us on six months ago, he had explained that this was a last-ditch effort with a low likelihood of success. The coffin bone in both front legs already looked moth-eaten on the x-rays. But I had taken it on anyway under Terry's supervision, and for a while I had even been hopeful. I built the gelding customized shoes to keep the pressure balanced and protect his weak points, but now even that wasn't working. The horse was in too much pain. It was the end.

Dr. Gunnell approached, looking weary. "Thank you."

"For what?" I asked. "I couldn't save him."

"I never expected you could." His dark eyes were kind as they looked at me. "He needed an expensive operation years ago, and we don't have those kind of facilities around here. You gave him six months of life with minimal pain. You gave his owner time to come to terms with it. You did good work, McAllister. I couldn't have asked for more."

I nodded, but I felt like shit.

I still felt like shit an hour later, standing on my front porch with my keys in my hand.

Amy was inside—I could hear her music blasting—and I knew the moment I stepped through the door she'd be on me, chatting a mile a minute about school, her new friends, and whatever hike she was planning next. Chloe tended to get home later, so it was just me and my sister for an hour or so. I'd make dinner while she bounced around like the extrovert she was, pretending to help cook but mostly just talking.

I loved our evening routine, but right now I couldn't face it.

Fuck, I didn't want to be my dad. I didn't want to be the angry man who dumped all his problems on the people who loved him. Dad would walk in that door after work and drop straight into his chair. He'd stay there until dinner, shouting all about the terrible things that had happened to him that day—some real, some imagined—a beer glued to his hand. He'd go right back to that chair after dinner. The drunker he got, the louder he got, and the quieter my mom and sister became. Mostly I disappeared to my room. Once I looked more like a man than a child, Dad tended to leave me alone. Mom and Amy weren't so lucky. If Amy tried to escape, he called her back. Mom never even tried to leave.

Damn. A bottomless beer and shouting at the world would feel fucking great right now.

I didn't want to be him, but I didn't know if I had it in me to be anything else.

My chin dropped to my chest. The cold November air bit at my neck.

The door flew open and I jerked in surprise. Chloe stood in the doorway, backlit by the light, looking every bit as startled as I felt.

"What are you doing here?" I asked gruffly.

"I live here, sorry to remind you. Also, my last client of the day cancelled so I came home early." She stepped back to let me in.

I shoved my hands in my pockets and stared at my boots.

"Bad day?" she asked.

I grunted.

"Come inside," she pressed.

I shook my head. "I'm in a bad mood. I don't want to take that out on…" I gestured to Chloe, the house, and my sister singing offkey somewhere in there.

Her head tilted as she studied me. Then she took another step back and shut the door in my face.

That didn't make me feel any less shitty. In fact, now I felt shitty and annoyed. Maybe that was irrational. It wasn't her job to fix my shitty mood. But, damn. She could have been a *little* nicer about it.

I glared at the door, and suddenly it opened and I was glaring at Chloe, a blanket in her arms and a bag of gummy bears clamped in her teeth. I blinked.

"Sit," she said.

The word was garbled around the bag of candy, but I got the message, partly because she was pushing me toward the swing with her body. I sat. She sat next to me and tucked the blanket around us.

"Some of the best advice I've ever gotten boils down to this: If you feel like everyone hates you, take a nap. If you feel like you hate everyone, eat something." She popped open the bag and offered it to me. "You look like you feel a little bit of both."

"What if you're just sad?" I asked. I took a gummy bear. Green. My favorite flavor.

"Cry about it." She shrugged.

I snorted. "You don't want to see a grown man cry. It's pathetic."

"It's human." She bit off the head of a red bear, then put the whole thing in her mouth.

"That's not what my dad would say."

"Oh, yeah? What would he say, then?"

I didn't have to guess. I knew. "*Suck it up. Don't be such a girl. It's just a dog.* That's what he said when he was drunk and backed his truck over my dog in the driveway." I could still hear Milo's scream of pain, and then his soft whimpers as he died in my arms.

Chloe stilled next to me. "That's fucked up, Steven."

"Fucked up? Is that your official diagnosis?" I smirked before tossing the green gummy bear into my mouth.

She studied me. "That's not really what I do. I *can* diagnose mental illness—or I can after I am fully licensed as a clinical social worker—but mostly I focus on temporary life upheavals and how to navigate the emotions around them, and community solutions. Like, farmers and ranchers have a high suicide rate because their livelihoods depend on many factors outside their control, and you couple that with a toxic masculine culture of not talking out problems and deep feelings of shame for not being able to provide for your family, and...boom. I focus on getting them talking and moving their life past whatever event it is they feel they can't live past. I help them find a solution that isn't suicide."

She ate another gummy bear head first, still watching

me. "I'm not your therapist, just to be clear. But if I were, I might point out that you have a tendency to hide deep feelings behind sarcasm, smirks, and general grumpiness."

My eyebrows went up slowly. "You mean, if you were my therapist you might point it out like you just did?"

"Did I? Huh. How about that." She smirked and shook the bag at me. I grabbed another bear. Orange this time. "What was the name of your dog?"

"Milo." My chest squeezed. I hadn't said his name out loud in years.

She nodded. "That's a good name. Tell me about him."

I shifted, putting an extra inch of space between us. "You said you weren't my shrink."

"I said I wasn't your *therapist*," she corrected. "And I'm not. I'm being your friend, weirdo."

"I don't talk to my friends about this shit. Work gripes, women, weekend plans. That's what we talk about. Not childhood trauma and feelings." I didn't talk about that with anyone, ever, actually.

"Is friendship another one of those girly things your father wouldn't approve of?" she asked drily.

I blinked.

Well, shit.

Seeing my face, Chloe laughed. "Surprise! The patriarchy doesn't do men any favors, either." She paused, reconsidering. "Well, it does, obviously, but at what cost, Steven? *At what cost.*" She raised her fists to the sky and shook them.

"Fucking dramatic," I muttered, but I was smiling.

She arched an eyebrow at me. "In my experience, there's nothing more dramatic than a man who truly believes he's successfully repressing his emotions when in reality they're leading him around by the balls."

It was hard to argue with that when I was sitting out here in the cold November air instead of inside where it was warm, spending time with someone I loved.

I blew out a breath, sending a white cloud of steam into the air. "A horse died today," I said quietly. "I really thought I could save him, even though everyone told me it wasn't likely. I thought if I just didn't give up, that would be enough. It wasn't. But I still wonder if maybe I should have tried more. Maybe I could have done something to convince Dr. Gunnell that I could do it. I shouldn't have quit on him."

She shook her head. "Dr. Gunnell is the best, and he isn't going to put a horse down if it's not necessary. If he said it's time, then it was time."

"Maybe." My leg vibrated restlessly. "But maybe I could have..." My mind drew a blank. I couldn't think of single thing I could have done that I hadn't tried. Dammit, there had to be something. I just didn't know what it was.

"Relentless," Chloe said softly. She placed her hand on my leg under the blanket and I stilled. "That's what Amy called you. She said when you care about something, you're relentless. She was right. Even now, you're still running it through your mind, trying to solve the problem, aren't you? The horse is dead, and you still haven't quit."

"Yeah." I scrubbed my hands over my unshaven jaw. "That's what makes me stupid."

"No, Steven. That's what makes you great." She scootched lower into the blanket and rested her head on my shoulder. "I'm sorry the horse died today. I'm sorry you're hurting."

I stared down at her dark hair spilling over my chest, genuinely shocked to my core. Chloe Adams...was *sorry*...I was hurting? I hesitated, waiting for a *gotcha!* that never came.

"Thank you," I roughed out.

We sat there a moment longer. I kept hurting.

But it felt a little lighter, somehow, with Chloe there beside me. A little more bearable.

"All right," I said. "Let's go inside."

Pregnancy Week 12: Radish is the size of a plum.

Nice Chloe was a goddamn problem. I had thought living with a woman who hated me would be miserable, but living with a woman who *didn't* hate me was so much worse. Because nice Chloe still teased me, still made biting, sarcastic remarks, still walked around looking like *that*, but now it felt like foreplay. How the fuck was I supposed to keep my hands to myself?

Three weeks of living with her and I was a wreck of a man, a live wire of energy buzzing through my veins with no outlet to provide relief.

I needed to get laid. Something—*someone*—to take the edge off. Allow my blood to return to my brain where it was desperately needed. Because my brain *knew* that Chloe would cut off my balls if I tried something with her.

She was pregnant with another man's baby, for fuck's sake. But with all that blood flowing south, my brain had gone fucking stupid.

There was only one bar in Aspen Springs, so that Friday night, I sat my ass down on an ancient barstool that had witnessed many a bad decision, so why the hell not add mine to the list. I hadn't stepped foot in here since the mess with James two years ago. The original Hale had built the Painted Cat as a brothel during the Colorado gold rush. It had changed hands a generation ago, but it was still considered their stomping ground. I half expected one of them to be here tonight. Hell, maybe I even hoped for it. Fighting could be as cathartic as fucking.

"You shouldn't be here." The bartender braced her palms on the scarred pine bar top and glowered at me.

Shit. She was one of Chloe's friends. I didn't know she worked here. "Janie. The one who likes sunflowers," I muttered. Fuck my life.

Her head tilted, a cascade of red hair falling over her shoulder. "How did you know I like sunflowers?"

"Chloe's shoes. James likes columbine, Essie likes red roses, Hannah likes violets, you like sunflowers. Chloe likes peonies," I said. *Chloe.* I had come here to get her out of my head, but she was proving to be surprisingly stubborn about it. She was probably home from work by now. The thought made me antsy, like I wanted to jump out of my skin and go find her.

Damn, I needed a drink.

Janie narrowed her eyes. "That's right." She studied me

for a moment, then shook her head. "No. You still shouldn't be here."

I glanced around. I couldn't blame her for not wanting trouble. "Any of the Hale brothers here tonight?"

"You got a problem with the Hale brothers?" a man two barstools down asked.

Something about his tone made the hair on the back of my neck stand straight up. He wasn't anyone I recognized, and I knew most everyone in Aspen Springs by now. "No. The Hale brothers have a problem with me."

"Why is that?" he asked. He turned on his barstool to look me squarely in the face, as casual as a lion surveying a herd of zebras and debating whether he could go for a little snack.

No, I did not know this man, but I was sure as fuck I didn't want to fight him.

"A misunderstanding," I muttered. Janie guffawed loudly. "On my part," I clarified.

"The Hale brothers are pretty good at judging charac-ter," the man noted.

Like she sensed a sudden change in the wind, Janie's head whipped toward him. "Just drink your beer, Jack. I'll handle this." At his surprised look, she rolled her eyes. "I knew who you were the moment you sat down. Essie has a photo of you on her fireplace mantle."

"Did you tell her I'm here?" Jack asked, not sounding particularly pleased about it.

Janie's brow furrowed. "She doesn't know?"

"I wanted to surprise her."

"Then it's a good thing I didn't tell her, I guess." Janie turned back to me. "I haven't decided what to do about you yet, so don't get too comfortable on that barstool." She sank a hand on her hip. "Maybe I should follow Chloe's lead and tell you to get the hell out. That's what she always did."

"And now she lives with me, so..." I spread my arms wide. "Seems like a risk on your part. You might actually end up liking me."

"Doubtful." Janie pursed her lips. "Still not sure she wasn't under duress."

I huffed and rubbed my palms over a crack in the wood. "Chloe could tell me to get the hell out of my own home, and I'd go," I grumbled. She could have the damn place if she wanted it. It smelled too much like her, anyway. "I'm not forcing her to share space with me."

I glanced up and found Janie staring at me with wide brown eyes and more than a little pity.

"One beer," she said. "That's it." She didn't ask me what I wanted, just grabbed a bottle of IPA from the fridge, popped the top, and handed it to me.

Not my favorite, but I wasn't in a place to complain. "Thanks."

I sipped the beer and glanced over at Jack. He'd been awfully quick to jump to the Hales' defense, and Essie had a photo of him. What did that make him? He was too young to be her dad, despite the gray at his temples. Was he her brother? Which would also make him Brax Hale's brother-in-law. Probably not a person I wanted to strike up a conversation with.

"You got a favorite flower, Jack?" I asked.

He paused, the brown beer bottle dangling from his hand. "Why do you want to know?"

"The flowers they embroidered on Chloe's shoes. Apparently that's the kind of thing friends know about each other." I jerked my head in Janie's direction. "I don't think that's normal. Hell, I'm not sure I even have a favorite flower." *Sissy shit*, my dad's voice whispered in my ear. But then I remembered the way Chloe's eyes lit up when she looked at her shoes. Why did he always make me feel like I should be embarrassed by happiness? Maybe *that* was the thing that wasn't normal.

"We're not friends," Jack said.

"No, we're fucking not," I agreed. Everyone in Aspen Springs had chosen a side even if they didn't know it, and it wasn't mine. Janie shot me a warning look as she swiped by with a towel. I swigged my beer. "What are those colorful flowers that look like balls?"

Janie scrunched her face like she was thinking. "Dahlias?" She tugged her phone out of her back pocket and tapped the screen a couple times, then turned it to face me so I could see the picture. "Is this what you mean?"

"Yeah." I studied the image for a moment. "I like those."

Jack moved to the barstool next to me and leaned toward Janie's phone. "Those are nice. My mom grows dahlias."

A woman down the bar lifted her hand to get Janie's attention. Janie stuck her phone in her pocket and pushed away from the bar. "Holler if you need something."

Jack watched her leave, then turned to me. "Why are you at a bar, talking to strangers about fucking flowers, when you want to be home with her?"

I rolled the bottle between my hands. "It's complicated."

"Nah, that's lazy." Jack shook his head. "It's pretty simple. If you want to be with her, hooking up with a random woman at a bar is self-sabotage."

My specialty.

I glanced around the room. A couple girls were here tonight, single by the looks of it. Pretty. One of them met my gaze with a smile and flick of her eyebrow. I waited for a feeling of *something*, but it never came. Nope, not interested. "You got a better option?"

"My advice?" He tipped his beer to his lips, appraising me over the rim, and took a swallow. "Go home. Take a cold shower."

CHLOE AND AMY were in their pajamas by the time I got home. They faced each other from opposite ends of the couch, their backs against the armrests and their fuzzy-socked feet meeting in the middle. Chloe had a stack of notecards in her hands and read out loud from the top card.

"Okay, true or false? A decrease in the unemployment rate will shift an economy's production possibilities curve outward." Chloe looked up at Amy expectantly.

I blinked. That sounded like a lot of gobbledygook to me.

Amy's forehead puckered. "Hm. False? Not directly, anyway."

"Why?" Chloe prodded.

"Economic growth or technology improvements can shift the curve. Decreased unemployment *might* lead to the kind of economic growth that can shift the curve, but it might not."

Chloe nodded. "Excellent." She slid the card to the bottom of the stack. "Okay, next—oh, hey, Steven," she interrupted herself, catching sight of me. "You're home." A faint flush bloomed on her cheeks, and she cleared her throat. "I wasn't sure when you'd be back. We had pizza for dinner. Leftovers are in the fridge."

"Thanks," I said.

Her eyes darted around, not quite meeting mine. I wondered if she suspected where I'd gone and why, and that I hadn't planned on coming home tonight, and figured she probably did. Why did that make me feel like shit? We weren't together. There was no reason for me to live like a monk just because I couldn't stop thinking about her.

I shoved my hands in the front pockets of my jeans. "What are you two doing?"

"Studying," Amy piped up. "It turns out that Chloe also had Econ 101 with Professor Garcia when she was a freshman. We made some flashcards from my notes and now she's quizzing me."

I glanced at Chloe, who was smiling at my sister like doing Econ flashcards was her idea of a fun Friday night. And that…Hell. I didn't know what that was.

Maybe Chloe didn't know what it meant to Amy to have someone pay attention to her like this, but I knew. Our mom loved us, I was sure of that, but our father was a jealous man, even when it came to his own kids. Time spent with us was time stolen from him. Every spare moment she had was spent on pacifying him and ensuring that the house was exactly how he wanted it so that nothing would set him off once the beers hit.

Chloe didn't know any of that. She took care of people. That was simply who she was. It didn't surprise me that she had found a way to take care of Amy. But somehow, it felt like she was taking care of me, too. And damn, it felt good.

Feeling my eyes on her, Chloe's gaze bounced to me and then away again with a little shrug. "Professor Garcia loves to give really tricky true-or-false questions, the kind that seem like the answer is a little bit of both. The only way to get through his exams is to know the material front, back, and sideways." Her fingers fidgeted with the cards.

"I could make popcorn," I offered. "If you're going to keep going for a while."

"Yes!" Amy pumped a fist, and I laughed. Popcorn was one of her favorite snacks.

I headed for the kitchen. Behind me, I heard Chloe say, "Okay, true or false..." I glanced back over my shoulder at them and my chest tightened. Maybe this was what family should feel like.

Well, fuck.

Cold showers it was.

23

CHLOE

No one warns you that in the second trimester, all that first-trimester nausea? It gets replaced by straight-up horniness.

What a terrible time to be in forced proximity with walking, talking cowboy porn that I was only allowed to look at and not touch. Every room in this damn house, there he was. Leaning in doorways. Rolling up his sleeves to his elbows to expose his forearms. Making me snacks at all hours of the night. I couldn't escape him. My vibrator hated to see me coming at this point. If it survived this pregnancy, it would be a miracle.

And what the heck was going on with my breasts? I knew they would get bigger, but it was like they had taken on a life of their own. I was so *aware* of them. They felt so full, and my nipples were constantly tingling. It took my thoughts from merely horny to downright depraved.

Which was why I was staring out the kitchen window, ogling Steven while he made repairs to the pig pen. He had tossed his coat aside in the bright Colorado sunshine and worked in a dark gray henley and plaid puffer vest, shirt sleeves pushed back to his elbows, baseball cap backwards, two nails clamped between his lips. He hammered a third nail into a fence rail and my god. My *god*. All I could think was *please come inside and pound me*.

Amy reached around me to shut off the faucet that I had turned on to wash the dishes that now lay forgotten in the sink. Her nose wrinkled as she looked out the window. "Gross."

"What?" I asked innocently. Steven disappeared from view and I couldn't check my sigh.

"I can't watch this. I'll have nightmares," Amy muttered and bolted from the kitchen right as Steven walked in.

"Hey," he said. He unlocked the fridge, pulled out a Coke, and popped the top. "You hungry?"

You hungry? had become his standard greeting the past week. Clearly my cheese sandwich had scarred the man for life. Steven did not believe I possessed the skills necessary to feed myself and my growing fetus, and I was disinclined to correct him on that.

My brain glazed over as I watched him lift the can of soda to his lips and tilt his head back, the strong lines of his throat moving in deep swallows.

"I could eat," I said huskily. *You. I could lick up every last drop of* you. My tongue swiped my bottom lip like I could taste him there.

He slowly dragged the heel of his palm across his mouth, his eyes darkening as he stared at me. "Chloe..."

"Hmm?" Somehow I had swayed closer. Somehow my fingers were toying with the zipper of his vest.

"Fuck," he muttered.

He captured my wrists and pushed my arms down to my sides, then gave me a wide berth as he stalked past me. The bathroom door slammed.

A second later, I heard the shower turn on.

I came home from sewing circle on Sunday to find Steven out front, a horse hoof propped between his leather chaps. A gorgeous blonde woman held the lead rope clipped to the horse's bridle.

"What's going on?" I asked. My tone was undeniably testy. Seeing this very pretty, very unpregnant woman looking at Steven in a very interested way set my teeth on edge.

"Annabelle here threw a shoe while Lydia was riding the property line." Steven rasped the hoof gently. "Lydia figured she might as well swing by for a new set since Annabelle was due anyway. I'm on the last hoof now."

"Steven is such a lifesaver," Lydia cooed. She smiled at

me. "You must be Amy. I'm happy to finally meet you, neighbor."

Damn, she was friendly. I eyeballed her. She was also a wee bit overdressed for ranch chores. Unless she always fixed fences with perfectly curled hair and the kind of girl-next-door makeup that looked natural but took a good half hour. I bet Annabelle hadn't thrown a shoe at all. Lydia had probably pried it off with her bare hands. Honestly, I wouldn't blame her if she had.

"I'm Chloe, actually," I corrected sweetly. "I moved in a couple weeks ago."

Lydia's forehead creased as she looked me up and down. I kind of wished I had a more obvious belly bump, just to make her wonder who the father was, but I was squarely in the *maybe she's pregnant, maybe she ate a burrito* stage. "You live here?"

"With Steven," I confirmed.

Her lips turned down, which had a direct and opposite effect on my own.

"He didn't mention that," she said.

Like puppets on a string, our heads swiveled in unison to look at him.

He released Annabelle's hoof and gave her a brisk pat on the neck. "It didn't come up," he said.

Well, what *had* come up while he played hot farrier with the hot neighbor? I could think of at least one thing I really, really hoped had stayed down. And that was stupid. I had no business feeling all surly and proprietary about Steven.

He headed to the forge he had set up on a metal table next to his truck, pausing as he passed me. "You hungry?"

My gaze ate him up. The leather farrier's apron with medieval-looking tools tucked into the pockets. The black smudges on his hands. The lines of sweat running down his neck. Slowly I lifted my eyes to his. "Starving," I whispered.

A muscle popped in his cheek and his eyes darkened. "You're going to be the death of me, Chloe. You know that?"

I didn't know what he meant by that. I pivoted to watch him use forceps to grab the hot steel shoe from the forge, then pivoted again as he brought the shoe to Annabelle and settled her leg between his knees again. I knew my ogling was obvious and I didn't care. Someone could have been throwing hundred-dollar bills behind me, and I still wouldn't have been able to tear my gaze away from him.

Steam hissed and billowed as he placed the hot shoe on Annabelle's hoof. A bead of sweat trickled down his temple and followed the sharp curve of his jaw. I wanted to lick it up.

Lydia and I sighed in unison and pretended we hadn't.

Steven only let the shoe stay against the hoof for a few brief seconds before taking it away again and dropping it in a pail of cool water. After a final pass of tidying the hoof, he nailed the shoe in place. Annabelle nibbled on his hair as he bent over her hoof, making him laugh, but he never lost focus on perfectly aiming the nails and hammer.

"There you go, honey," he murmured, setting her hoof

down, and I melted a little further. The way this man loved animals made my knees weak.

"Thank you so much," Lydia said, as though he had brought Annabelle back from the dead. "How much do I owe you?"

"Same as always. I'll send you the bill," Steven said.

"Oh, but it's your day off," she said. "At least let me pay for the overtime with dinner."

I was too afraid I would dunk her head in the dirty water to wait for his answer. I strode past them and into the house.

It didn't take even thirty seconds for Steven to storm in after me.

"What's gotten into you?" he demanded.

"Nothing," I said in a voice that definitely meant *something*. "You can go out with whoever you want."

The way he looked at me made my chest ache. "I said no, Chloe."

That was even worse, and I couldn't explain why. "Well, that was dumb, Steven," I spit out. "She's pretty. She seems nice enough. She definitely wants to fuck you."

His jaw worked as he turned his head so all I could see was his profile. "What if I don't want her? What if I want... someone else?"

Anger and hopelessness swirled in my chest. God, I hated wanting something I couldn't have. And I couldn't have Steven. Not now, and not ever. "Don't waste your time waiting for someone else. I doubt anyone else wants you."

I regretted the words before they had even fully left

my lips. These fucking pregnancy hormones had me lashing out like a toddler. I started to apologize but it was too late.

He jerked back like I had slapped him. Shocked hurt flashed across his face before disappearing behind a smirk. "Fine. I guess I'll give her a call right now and tell her I changed my mind."

It felt like a punch to my already aching chest. My eyes watered. "I don't care," I scoffed, as though he couldn't plainly see the tears rolling down my cheeks. Goddammit, everything made me cry these days. It was humiliating enough to want him. But crying about it? There was no coming back from this.

We stared at each other for a long moment.

"Fuck!" he roared. He disappeared into the bathroom and slammed the door shut.

A second later, the shower turned on.

AFTER THAT, we managed to go a full seventy-two hours without seeing each other. I half convinced myself I wouldn't see him again until I moved out.

And then it was 3 a.m. and I was up for a little snack and bumped into him, nose to sternum, as he was coming out of the bathroom, fresh from a shower with a towel wrapped around his lean waist.

Oh, my god. His *abs*.

I rubbed my nose and winced. "You know, this is how all the good pornos start," I said hopefully.

He didn't even pretend to look anywhere but my chest. In his defense, my breasts had never looked better, and I was braless. My nipples could not be more prominent if they waved little flags. "You hate me, Chloe. Remember?" The barbed wire was back in his voice.

I scowled, mostly because it wasn't true and I wished it were. "I can hate you and want to fuck you at the same time, Steven. It's called multitasking."

He speared one hand—not the hand holding his towel, unfortunately—through his hair and tugged.

"Fuck," he growled, and stepped backwards into the bathroom, swinging the door shut in my face.

A moment later the shower turned back on.

FUCK THIS. I needed sex.

In less than six months, my life was going to revolve around a hungry, screaming, pooping baby that was helpless without me. I was okay with that—more than okay, I was so happy it frightened me—but I also recognized that once this baby was born, I wasn't going to be dating or having sex for months, if not years. For now, my body was still mine. My *life* was still mine.

Dammit, I was going to enjoy it while I still could.

I saw Steven's reflection zip past my open bedroom

door while I was giving myself a last look. I fluffed my knee-length skirt—jeans would have been better on such a cold night, but none of mine buttoned anymore—and tugged at my denim vest, then turned to the side. I didn't *look* pregnant. The denim fabric was thick, the neckline a low V that drew attention to my chest, and the silver buttons down the front disguised my soft belly swell.

Steven's reflection returned, filling my doorway, arms crossed over his chest, scowling. I shot him a fake, sweet smile over my shoulder. "Can I help you?"

His scowl deepened. "You can tell me why you're all dressed up. It's eight o'clock and you have to be up at five a.m." He sounded exactly like a dad reprimanding his teenage daughter for sneaking out to meet her boyfriend on a school night. Or so I imagined. I had been too busy helping raise my younger brothers to earn that lecture.

"I'm going to the Painted Cat." I slicked on an extra coat of pink lipgloss and pouted at the mirror.

"Why are you going to a bar? You can't drink."

"No, but I can fuck, and the Painted Cat happens to be the place people go to *find* someone to fuck."

Steven fell out of the doorframe in shock. "What the hell, Chloe? You're pregnant. You can't let some stranger put his dick in you. There's a goddamn baby up in there."

I stared at his reflection in the mirror, then slowly turned to look at the real thing. "Steven, you know the baby is in my uterus, right? The uterus has only one opening. It's called the cervix. Right now, my cervix is shut tight. Nothing is going in or out. Not that dicks can reach that far anyway." I suddenly remembered what he said about the sonogram wand and my gaze dropped to his crotch. My cheeks felt hot.

"Eyes up here, Chloe," he barked. "I can't think straight when you're salivating for my dick."

I jerked my gaze to his face. "I am *not* salivating," I huffed. "I am *considering*."

"Well, don't. Don't consider something tonight that you're going to regret tomorrow. I can't..." He raked a hand through his hair and made a noise of pure frustration. "Dammit, Chloe. I want to be a good man, but I'm still just a man and I've used up all my good jacking off in a cold shower every goddamn day this week."

God, I would have paid good money to see that. Heat unfurled in my center, winging out in all directions until I was flushed from my cheeks to my toes. "Did you think about me?"

The *look* he gave me. Hot and dark and dirty, like he was reliving every torrid thing we did in his imagination. I swallowed hard.

"Tell me to go, Chloe." He came closer. "Tell me to get the hell out of here, lock the door behind me, and make use of that vibrator I've heard buzzing all week."

Impulsively, I captured his wrists, just to see if my fingers could reach all the way around. They couldn't. A delicious shiver of anticipation ran down my spine. "Now, why would I do that?" I asked.

His eyes met mine, jaw tight with barely leashed restraint. "Because if you don't, then the only man you're going to fuck tonight is me, princess, and right now I'm past caring if you hate me for it."

All the air whooshed out of me on a single word. "Please." My hands scraped up his arms, my fingernails dragging against the flannel, up over the curve of his shoulders until I looped my arms around his neck. "Please, Steven."

He was so rigid it was like embracing a rock. He stood there, not moving, not even breathing, every muscle tense as he fought himself. I didn't know what to do with that, so I rolled up on my toes and gently kissed his cheek. His hand shot to the back of my head like a vise and he held me there, twisting his neck to give me an incredulous look.

And then he slammed his mouth to mine.

It was a desperate, hungry kiss that made me needy for more—more touching, more skin, more of *him*—but unwilling to release his mouth for even a second to get it. He arched over me and I arched back to stay with his mouth, and he hooked his hands behind my thighs, boosted me up, and pivoted to the bed, kicking the door shut behind him.

We landed with me beneath him. He hovered over me, all his weight braced on his arms and his knee outside my thigh. My hips tipped up to his, desperate for friction, and he shifted to lower himself closer, but jerked away again before I got what I wanted. I slipped my hands to his belt on either side of his hips and tried to tug him closer, growling with frustration when he resisted.

"What if I hurt Radish?" he said against my throat.

"You're not—" I started but then stopped. I wasn't a pregnancy expert, and Steven was a big guy. For all I knew, he'd squish Radish like a pancake. I huffed. "Fine."

I pushed at his shoulders. He rolled to his back, then shifted back against the pillows so he was half reclining, and I scrambled into his lap, straddling him. My skirt floofed out around me.

His gaze skimmed over me. "You look like a treat," he said, the words tinged with hunger and disbelief, like he couldn't believe I was here.

Honestly, I couldn't believe it either, but I didn't want to think about it. I wanted to *do* it, hopefully before my brain turned back on and put a stop to this nonsense.

I kissed him. The first brush of my lips was almost timid, a mere question of a kiss. But then his lips parted, his hand spasmed on my knee, and a low, aching sound emanated from him as our tongues touched, and it was no longer a question. It was an answer.

I got the top two buttons of his flannel undone but then I was too impatient to do the rest and tugged it off over his head, then sat back a little to take him in. He looked even better than I remembered, all those hard ridges of muscle impossibly more defined. I traced the ridges and valleys of his abs with my index finger, my lower lip caught between my teeth.

When I met his gaze, I found him watching me with a big ole smile on his face. Not smug. *Happy.* It stole my breath. "What?" I asked.

"Nothing. I'm just...glad you like it." He gestured to his

abdomen. "I've been doing core work every morning. Just in case."

"In case of what?" I asked.

"In case of you," he said. He swallowed and looked away, suddenly shy. "Not that I expected…I didn't even really hope for it. I just wanted you to like me."

I felt like I was melting inside. I turned his face back to mine and kissed him again. "I *do* like you, Steven. I like you a whole lot and only a little bit of that is because of your abs."

The truth of it knocked the breath out of me. I genuinely *liked* him. It shook me to my core. Now was not the time to catch feelings for my roommate. I was pregnant. My friends hated him. It was the worst possible timing, and Steven was the worst possible man.

And right now, I didn't care about any of that. All I cared about was that he kissed me with my face cupped in his hands like I was something precious. The way his fingers gently skimmed down my throat, traced the vest's deep v neckline, calloused fingertips rough against the soft skin of my breasts, and met in the middle at the top button.

"Still yes?" he murmured against my mouth.

"Yes," I breathed back.

"Thank fuck," he said, and popped open the first button.

He tilted his head to kiss the base of my throat, then laved his tongue down my cleavage while his quick fingers undid the rest of the buttons. I gasped and panted, my nipples tingled, and I arched my chest into his face. He nuzzled closer, not seeming to mind that at all. I felt his lips curve in a smile as he maneuvered me out of my vest.

He pulled back to look at me. "Interesting. I had you pegged as a fancy lingerie kind of girl. But I like this." He tugged at the strap of my plain white cotton bra.

"Cotton is all I can wear now," I confessed. "My breasts are too sensitive for anything else."

His hands stilled. "Good sensitive or bad sensitive?"

I liked that, that he cared about what felt good for me and what didn't. "Good sensitive." *If you like walking around permanently horny.* "I could probably come just from you playing with my nipples."

"Really?" He eyed my breasts speculatively. "Let's find out."

He dipped his head and licked over my nipple through my bra in one broad stroke. The sound that came out of me was unholy.

His head snapped up to look at me, his eyes nearly black. "Jesus, Chloe."

And then his mouth was instantly on me again, hot and hungry. He circled my nipple with slow, sucking kisses while I writhed on his lap, caught between agony and plea-sure. When he finally drew my nipple into his mouth, I nearly sobbed with relief. His hot tongue toyed with me through the fabric until it was damp and clinging to my skin and then shifted to my other breast.

My core turned to molten liquid. I could actually come

from this. Just this. Just his mouth on my breasts and my fingers digging into his scalp.

He pulled back and stared at my nipples, peaked and rosy through the translucent white cotton. "Look at you," he whispered, rubbing his thumbs over the wet spots. "Fuck, princess, *look* at you."

"Don't stop," I panted, pushing on his temple to urge him back down.

With a low laugh, he complied. He snaked one hand behind my back and unclasped my bra and tossed it aside. My hips rocked as he took my breast in his mouth again. I couldn't stop the noises I made, the low moans and wanton gasps.

He tore his mouth from my nipple on a groan as his hands frantically worked at his belt. If I hadn't been every bit as desperate as he was, I might have laughed. I had never seen him clumsy before. The instant he freed himself from his jeans, my hand wrapped around him, my fingers not quite meeting, and squeezed.

He froze.

"Still yes?" I teased, sure of the answer.

"No," he gritted out.

I reeled back. "What?"

"I don't have a condom." He thunked his head against the headboard. "I mean, I do, but about a thousand feet away in my bedroom."

Oh. Thank god. "I can't get more pregnant than I already am, and I had the battery of STI tests. I'm safe."

"But I might not be. It's been several months since I've been with anyone, but I haven't been tested in a year."

I dragged my mouth up his throat, sucking at the pulse point beneath his jaw. "I'm sure it's fine."

He laughed hoarsely and clamped his hands around my hips, stopping their movement. "Chloe, it is *not* fine. Please don't tempt me, princess. I would do anything to keep you safe, but my brain is operating on a very low blood supply right now."

I whimpered with frustration. "So go get a condom. I'll wait. I promise I won't change my mind while you're gone."

A growl rumbled in his chest. "No one's going anywhere until you come." He pushed his hand between us and situated his cock against the gusset of my cotton panties. "Use me."

I couldn't think straight. My nervous system was on overload. "What?"

He bent to my breast again, craning his neck to look up at me with half-shut eyes as he lapped my nipple. "Use me, Chloe. Keep your panties on and ride my dick."

I shifted my hips, then shifted again, searching for exactly the right angle. When I found it, we both shivered. I rocked my clit against his length, hard, again and again while he played with my breasts, biting, licking, kissing. My movements became clumsy as I got closer.

"Don't stop," he muttered around my breast. "Don't you dare fucking stop, Chloe."

I didn't. I couldn't. I edged closer and closer to the brink and then suddenly I was there. I cried out, sinking my nails into his scalp to hold him to me as waves of plea-sure wracked my body. Just before I went limp, he stiffened beneath me. His hands spasmed on my breasts and he buried his face into my cleavage on a deep groan as his orgasm pulsed between my thighs.

We stayed that way for a long moment, neither of us moving except for the air sawing in and out of us as we tried to catch our breath.

His forehead dropped to the crook of my neck. "I feel like I should apologize for making a mess, but you know what? I'm really not sorry," he mumbled.

I laughed and held him closer. "Neither am I."

For any of it.

24

———

STEVEN

Apparently, I did care if Chloe hated me because after the orgasm returned enough blood flow to my brain for me to function, I took one look at her sleeping face and knew that if I had to watch her wake up with regret and self-loathing when she saw me in bed with her, I'd escort myself straight off a cliff.

I gently replaced my chest with a pillow and left her there making adorable sleeping sounds that made me feel soft and achy inside. I paused in the doorway and looked back. She had curled herself into a ball under the covers, and I couldn't see much of her beyond the dark hair that spilled out in all directions. It was so hard to resist the urge to climb back into bed with her despite the uncomfortable wetness in my jeans.

Jesus, fuck, this woman. What the hell was I going to do about her?

Other than make a doctor appointment for every STI check under the sun. That was happening immediately. And then I was going to clear her schedule and keep her in bed with me for a solid twenty-four hours.

As soon as I figured out how to keep her from hating me after.

CHLOE HAD CUT BACK SLIGHTLY on her hours at Jo, working four days a week instead of five or six. I hated that she was still working there at all, spending six hours on her feet before commuting to her office in the city where she put in another four hours, minimum. She intended to help Jo replace her before the baby came in May, but right now she wanted to take advantage of the free rent and stockpile as much money as possible so she could move out of my house and into a place of her own.

If I was honest, I hated that, too.

I had the feeling she'd been avoiding me since the night we had dry humped each other like randy teenagers who hadn't figured out where all the parts go, but she spent more time working than at home, so it was hard to tell for sure. But it wasn't a great sign that she had Saturday off, yet I hadn't seen even a glimpse of her since Friday morning.

Fine. If that was how she wanted to play it, I would avoid her, too. It wasn't like I didn't have shit to do.

I spent the morning in town, running errands and getting the groceries for the week. But no matter how hard I tried to fight it, the thought of Chloe incessantly tugged my attention back home. After two hours, I gave up. Maybe I could lure her out of hiding with food or something.

She was on the front porch when I got home. Her wind-whipped skirt billowed out behind her like a sail, molding itself to the front of her body. Her full breasts, the round curve of her belly, her strong thighs. For the first time, she looked obviously, undeniably pregnant. Fuck, she was beautiful.

She rested one hand on the top of her belly and lifted the other to her forehead to shield her eyes from the sharp sunlight. She was looking for something, or someone.

And suddenly I couldn't breathe for wanting.

Wanting her to see whatever it was she was looking for. Wanting it to be me. There wasn't a cell in my body that wouldn't turn itself inside out to become whatever made her happy. *You want a giraffe, princess? I'll be a giraffe.*

I fucking *yearned* for it. For her.

And then she turned and caught sight of me staring at her. Her face lit up.

"There you are!" She hustled over to me.

Me. She had been looking for *me.* Warmth exploded in my chest.

"You will not believe what happened. You know Bernadette from Sunshine Rescue? She called here. Said they have an emu that needs a temporary place. They already have a permanent home, but they need a week to get it ready." Chloe tugged at my arm and looked up at me expectantly. "An *emu*, Steven. It's not an ostrich but that's probably for the best. I don't think an ostrich will let you play dress up. They are way more mean than emus."

I stared down at her eager, upturned face. It took everything I had not to kiss her. "You already said yes, didn't you?"

"You *said* you wanted an emu. Of course I said yes. Anyway, you have the space," she reminded me. "And it's only for a week."

She was right. In addition to the chicken coop and pig pen, there was a four-stall barn and small pasture. Although I fully planned on getting horses someday, right now it was empty.

"I wonder why Bernadette thought of me," I said. "I don't know the first thing about caring for emus."

Chloe shrugged. "Neither did the so-called petting zoo who had him for the past two years. If he could survive that, he can survive a week with you. Bernadette will be here later this afternoon, and she promised she'd walk you through all the care and feeding." Then she grinned. "Apparently, emus get along great with pigs."

"I'm going to have a whole damn menagerie," I muttered, loading my arms with groceries from the truck. When Chloe reached for one, I handed her the toilet paper instead. She rolled her eyes but allowed it.

"You hungry?" I asked as we headed up the steps.

"Starving." She shot me a mischievous grin over her shoulder. "You got home right on time. I was about to make myself a bowl of cereal."

Well, look at that. I didn't have to turn myself into a giraffe, after all. Somehow, right now, I was already exactly what she wanted. Just me. Just for this moment. I knew that.

But I wanted so much more.

25

———

CHLOE

At this point, I was just stalling.

I was well into the second trimester now and full of energy (and horniness). Every doctor appointment I had so far had determined that Radish and I were in perfect health—and there had been plenty of appointments, as Dr. Davidson tended toward caution, and my extreme level of nausea in the first trimester had worried her. Slowly but surely, the feelings of doom had receded. I still worried about being a good mom and bringing a new life into a fucked up world and what the hell was going on with Radish's dad, but at least I had stopped worrying that Radish would slip out when I peed.

But I still hadn't told my family.

One reason I hadn't told them was because I knew they

would have questions about the baby's father, and I couldn't answer those questions yet. I still hadn't heard from Gabe and now I really was starting to worry. Maybe he had lost his phone, but maybe he had gotten into a terrible motorcycle accident and was in a hospital somewhere, or maybe he had gone straight over a cliff. The nightmare scenarios were endless.

The other reason I hadn't told them was because I was chickenshit. Not because I was scared of how they would react. I knew that would be fine. Mom would be out-of-her-mind thrilled to be a grandma. Terry would be a little bit uncomfortable at first with the incontrovertible evidence that his unmarried, thirty-year-old daughter was no longer a virgin, but he'd rally. Grams would be her ghostly self. My brothers might have strong feelings about Radish's dad not being around, but what could they do about it?

But I was terrified to tell them things had to change. I was already spread too thin. Once Radish was born and I was a full-time licensed clinical social work therapist, there was no way I'd be able to help them every week. I felt like I was letting everyone down.

And now I couldn't stall any longer. Steven and Amy had been invited to join us for Thanksgiving dinner, and even though I was wearing a loose sweater over my black leggings, my bump was no longer invisible. I'd been able to hide it strategically until now, but over the last week it was like my belly had suddenly popped out like a balloon.

"Come on, honey," Steven cooed like I was a horse that needed calming. "Get out of the car."

I narrowed my eyes. "Don't use that tone with me, Steven. I will bite you."

His dark eyes flashed like he was remembering something sinful. "If you're a good girl, maybe I'll bite *you*," he murmured for my ears only.

I flushed, remembering how much I had liked the feeling of his teeth on my nipple. But he hadn't shown any interest in a repeat. He had been so damn polite the past two days, I wanted to wring his damn neck.

When I still didn't move, Steven gave a beleaguered sigh. "There's pie, Chloe. You like pie. Do you want to come inside and have potatoes and pie, or do you want to stay in the truck and starve?"

My stomach rumbled plaintively. My appetite had been making up for lost time. "Fine," I said, unbuckling. "But you've gotten mean, Steven."

"That seems to be the only thing you like," he muttered.

Mom pounced on us the second we walked in the door. "We're having snacks and drinks to tide us over. The turkey should be done in another hour. Hang up your coats and come join us. Can I get you anything to drink? Amy, we have tap water, sparkling water, and iced tea."

Mom didn't stop bustling around while she talked, refilling the nut bowl, slipping a coaster under Terry's beer, checking the timer on her phone. She looked good. Happy and healthy. I let out a relieved breath.

"Sparkling water would be great," Amy said. "Let me help you."

Mom nodded. "Steven? Anything for you? We have beer and wine. Chloe, I'll get you a glass of white—"

"Just water for me," I cut her off. "I'm pregnant."

My announcement sucked all the noise out of the room. The only sound left was the incessant clacking of Grams's wooden knitting needles as she relentlessly soldiered on. My parents, my brothers, even Amy all stared at me with comically stunned expressions. Then they swiveled like weathervanes to look at Steven.

Steven, completely unperturbed, grabbed a plate. We all watched him load it with slices of cheddar cheese, gherkins, and crackers. He handed it to me with a little smirk, like it was all the same to him that everyone assumed he had knocked me up, and then smiled at my mom. "I'll take a beer, thanks, Angie."

"I'll take an explanation," my stepdad said mildly. "Is this a joke?"

"It's not a joke," I said. "I'm really pregnant, and Steven is *not* the dad, so you can all stop planning our shotgun wedding."

I frowned at him like the misunderstanding had been his fault, like I wasn't imagining his big, competent hands cradling a delicate newborn. I should never have let him put those hands on me. I should never have let him put his mouth on me and make me come.

Because now? Now I was standing in my parents'

house, telling them Steven wasn't the father of my baby while a part of me wished he was.

"You're pregnant?" Mom whispered, lifting her hands to her cheeks. "Really and truly? If you're joking, Chloe Anne, I swear to god—"

"I promise it's real, Mom." I swallowed past the lump in my throat. I knew what this meant to her. To both of us. "I'm pregnant. Fifteen weeks. The doctor said it's sticking around for the long haul."

Mom burst into tears.

DINNER WAS a barrage of congratulations and questions. Where would I live? Was I going to take time off from work when the baby came? Did I want a boy or girl? What would I do for childcare when I had to go to work? Did I want my brothers to drag Gabe's ass back from Argentina?

I answered as best I could.

I don't know. (Steven: "She has a home with me for as long as she wants."

Yes, if I can afford it. (Steven: "She can afford it.")

Either, honestly. (Steven: "Oh, do they allow you to choose now? Do you have to put in a request up front?")

I don't know. (Steven: silence.)

Hell, no. (Steven: "We'll see.)

By the time we finished eating, I was feeling jittery from the *I don't knows.* I had been so focused on work and keeping my food down that I hadn't even started to look for a place to live.

Mom and Terry packed up the leftovers while I washed dishes. Grams sat silently at the breakfast table with her pillbox and a glass of water.

"You know, your room is here anytime you want it," Mom said gently. She divided the cranberry sauce into three small plastic containers for my brothers to take home with them, and a larger container for the household. "We can turn Ellis's room into a nursery. I think it's safe to say he's flown the nest for good."

"Thanks, Mom, but I'm fine." I scrubbed at a bit of orange peel stuck to the pot. "You don't have to worry about me."

"I'm not worried. I'm excited. Don't you see? Moving back home is the perfect solution. You can work part-time for your dad until the baby is in school. I would much rather watch my grandbaby than do financial paperwork. Once he's in school, you can go to work managing a farm or doing consulting like you'd always planned."

This again. Frustration bubbled up, mingling with the already present anxiety. It made my stomach hurt. "The plan changed when Gramps died. You know that. Social work is what I need to be doing. Not farm management."

"So, what, then? You're going to let a stranger raise your baby?" Mom protested. "That's not what you want."

My chest felt tight. I didn't see daycare that way, but the truth was, there wasn't an abundance of childcare options in Aspen Springs. As a farming and ranching community, most families had a parent staying home.

Steven's hand landed on the small of my back with reassuring pressure. I looked up at him with wild-eyed panic.

"We'll work something out," he said. "I make my own schedule, and so do you. I have a neighbor—"

"Oh, Steven, that's so sweet of you," Mom interjected. "But don't put yourself out for us. It would be much more convenient to have Chloe at home."

Steven's eyebrows slammed together. "Convenient for who?"

Grams pushed back her chair with a loud scrape. She straightened, and for once her green eyes—the same shade as my dad's, the same shade as mine—did not look past me. They saw right into mine. "Selfish," she spat.

The room fell deathly quiet, so quiet that I could hear Grams's soft footsteps as she retreated to her bedroom down the hall.

I looked at my mother, who was staring after Grams like she had seen a ghost. I forced a smile.

"Well," I said. "That's the first thing she's said to me in eight years."

STEVEN

"Wʜᴀᴛ ᴅᴏ ʏᴏᴜ ᴍᴇᴀɴ, sʜᴇ ʜᴀsɴ'ᴛ sᴘᴏᴋᴇɴ ᴛᴏ ʏᴏᴜ ɪɴ ᴇɪɢʜᴛ years?" I asked incredulously. "You're here every week. You *lived* with her."

"She found a way," Chloe said flatly. "That's Grams for you. She's resourceful."

"Chloe," Maggie said. Her forehead pinched with concern. Concern—but not surprise.

Chloe's hands flexed with agitation before she pivoted to the sink. "It's fine, Mom." She smacked the faucet on and then stared blankly at the empty sink. There weren't any more dishes to wash.

I silently handed her a dishtowel and grabbed a second one for me. She blinked at me and reached for a pot in the drying rack. "It's fine," she repeated, more calmly this time, like she was soothing her own fractured nerves.

"It's not fine," I said. "There's nothing *fine* about your

grandmother not speaking to you for eight years. What happened?"

Chloe paused for so long that I wondered if she was going to answer at all. Then she glanced at her parents still seated at the table, like she was looking for their permission. Her mom nodded and Chloe sighed. "Eight years ago, I was a senior in college. I was about to graduate with a B.S. in agriculture, but I was already working part-time for my grandfather at the Adams' farm. It had been in our family for several generations. Wheat and corn. That's what we grew."

Her hand moved the towel in quick circles around the pot, despite it no longer having even a speck of water on it. There didn't seem to be a reason to point this out to her, so I just nodded.

"At first everything seemed fine. I thought the farm was turning a decent profit. Nothing that would make us rich, but enough money that we could weather a few disappointments, as long as they didn't happen back-to-back. But of course the disappointments hit like a one-two punch. Too little rain followed by too much rain followed by political bullshit." The circles got faster and angrier. "The thing was, though, on paper, it seemed like we were still doing okay. And that didn't make sense at all. I got curious and followed paper trails Gramps never intended me to see."

Her hands stilled. I gently took the pot from her and set it on the counter.

She blinked rapidly. "It turned out the farm was not

okay and hadn't been for some time. By that point, even selling off everything wouldn't pay the debts. It was so far beyond my knowledge and capabilities. I knew we needed help, but I didn't know who to go to. I told him we at least needed to tell Grams and Mom and hire a lawyer. Gramps begged me not to say anything, to give him more time. He said he was on the verge of making a partnership deal that would bring an influx of cash. I agreed. God, I was dumb." She laughed harshly. "That was the stupidest thing I could have done. It kept him isolated and ashamed. I didn't understand that at the time."

An awful, sinking feeling lodged in my gut. I glanced at her parents. Angie clasped her hands on the table, fingers woven so tightly together her knuckles were white, while Terry rubbed her back.

"That May, I discovered Gramps hadn't paid the taxes back in March like he had promised he would. It was a Sunday. I told him I was done hiding. He agreed we would tell Grams together that evening when she came home from church. He seemed...relieved. So I went ahead to my stupid school luncheon for magna cum laude graduates." She gave a derisive snort. "While Grams was at church and I was laughing with my friends, Gramps laid a tarp down in the barn and shot himself in the head. I found him there, with a note that said he was sorry for the mess."

"Chloe," I said hoarsely.

She frowned. "Suicide is always a mess in one way or another. I never could get the blood out of the walls. When the barn was finally torn down, I was relieved I never had to see it again." She twisted the dishtowel in her hands. "Grams never forgave me for any of it."

"What?" My brow furrowed as I studied her. "She blames you? What for?"

Chloe shrugged. "For not telling anyone the farm was in trouble. For not being able to save the farm. For leaving my grandfather alone that afternoon. Any of it. All of it."

I shook my head. "You didn't kill him. You're no more at fault than she is."

"That's the thing, isn't it? When you're left picking up the pieces and have more questions than answers, and you can't blame the person who died because they've clearly already suffered enough. So who does that leave? If she didn't blame me, she might have to blame herself."

"Or no one," I said. "No one is to blame."

Chloe smiled sadly. "That's harder to live with. All that pain and anger...Someone needed to carry the weight of it so it didn't crush her."

I stared at her. I couldn't wrap my mind around it. "Eight years," I said. "She's blamed you for eight years so she doesn't have to question why she knew nothing about her own home and husband and—" Anger licked up my spine and I whirled to face her parents. "And you let her? She hasn't spoken a single word to your daughter in eight years, and you thought that was fine? You let her get away with treating Chloe like that under your own roof?"

Angie looked flustered. "We couldn't—I don't—Grams cannot be reasoned with," she stammered. "But *we* don't blame Chloe."

Like that made it okay.

Terry's mouth flattened. "What exactly would you have had us do? It kept the peace. You don't know how hard things were for this family back then. Angie's sickness, the bankruptcy. We all did the best we could, but it was a heavy time for all of us."

"So you let Chloe carry the extra weight. Like always. Not because you *have to*, but because she can. It's easier that way." I split a look between them, and they stared back in shock. Fuck that. My jaw clenched hard. "Get your things, Chloe. We're leaving."

"You can't leave yet," Angie protested. "We haven't had pie."

I almost laughed. "Angie, I like you a lot and I know Chloe thinks the world of you, but your priorities are seriously out of whack if pie is what you're worried about right now."

Angie flushed.

I took Chloe's elbow. She stared up at me with wide eyes, her lower lip falling open. "Do you want to stay here and have pie with the people who thought it was perfectly okay for you to carry the blame of your grandfather's death for eight freaking years, or do you want to come home with me and I'll make you something sweet?"

Her gaze shifted over my face and then her lips firmed. She nodded. "Take me home."

I steered her out of the kitchen and through the living room. "Let's go, Amy. We're leaving," I said as we made for the door.

"Without pie—" Amy said in consternation, glancing up from UNO. One look at my face and she jumped to her feet. "Right. Coming. Thanks for dinner. It was great."

I brushed aside her brothers' protests and helped Chloe into her coat while Amy hastily grabbed her jacket and bag, and then we were out the door.

Chloe didn't lose that dazed expression until we pulled onto the highway. She shifted in her seat to face me. "What you did back there...the way you stood up for me?" She shook her head slowly, disbelievingly. "No one's ever done that. Not once in eight years. I can't believe you did that."

My hand found hers in the space between us. "I can't believe you put up with anything less."

THE KNOCK on the door was so faint I thought it was wishful thinking. I froze, every cell in my body on high alert, my heart beating out of time in my chest, my breath stuck in my throat. A moment passed, and then another. Hope ebbed like a July snow field.

The second knock was louder and unmistakable.

I kicked free of the covers, launched myself across the room, and wrenched open the door. Chloe stood there, wrapped up in her fluffy robe, her feet bare.

"What are you doing here?" I asked, my voice rough and breathless like I had run a ten-mile race instead of crossed a tiny ass bedroom.

She fidgeted with the belt on her robe, looking uncertain. "Do you want me to go?"

I reached around her for the doorknob and pulled the door closed. "Don't even fucking think about it, princess."

One eyebrow flicked upward. "Good."

She gave one quick tug on the knot at her waist and shimmied her shoulders. The robe tumbled to a heap at her feet.

I stole one fevered look at her luscious naked body and slammed my eyelids shut with a groan.

"Steven," she said, and I could hear the bafflement in her voice. "What are you doing?"

"I can't think straight when I look at you."

"Then it's a good thing I'm not here for thinking," she said.

Her hands landed gently on my bare pecs, making me tense, but I still didn't open my eyes.

"We should talk," I managed, clinging to my resolve by a gossamer thread as her fingers trailed over my stomach, tracing the squares of muscle, following the V-line to my groin. God, her hands felt good on me.

"I don't want to do that, either."

The air fluttered around us as she went to her knees. My stomach tightened with anticipation. When she curled her fingers around the waistband of my boxers and dragged them down my thighs, I inhaled sharply. I stopped breathing altogether when she palmed my dick with one hand.

"Hmm," she purred. She rubbed her lips with the head of my cock.

"Fuck, Chloe," I groaned. I ground the heels of my palms into my eye sockets. "You're going to break me." What I didn't say: *You're going to break my fucking heart.*

Her tongue swiped my slit. "Should I stop?"

I tried to breathe. Tried to think. This wasn't fair. We weren't on an equal playing field. She just wanted sex, and I...

I was fucking in love with her.

I opened my eyes and looked at her. Fuck, she was pretty, all that creamy skin and the dark cloud of her hair, her baby bump curving over her thighs. She sat back on her heels and stared up at me with pale green irises that didn't hold a hint of hate. With her eyes locked on mine, she lifted my cock to her mouth and pressed a slow kiss to the tip.

My control shattered. I grabbed fistfuls of her hair and pushed my cock between her sweet lips. When she gave a satisfied hum, the sound vibrated straight through my dick and up my spine. My body clenched as I dragged my cock from her mouth, then plunged in again with a snap of my hips.

Fucking hell, her mouth was heaven.

Her tongue swirled around the head and flicked the frenulum. My eyes rolled back in my head and my hands tightened in her hair. She made an eager little sound that damn near had me coming right then and there. Her hands slid from hips to my ass and she grabbed hold, pulling me deeper into her mouth.

"Fuck, shit, goddammit, princess." My voice cracked on a stream of curse words. "I'm going to come."

That only encouraged her. Her mouth moved further down my cock. She was swallowing me down like my dick was her last meal. But I didn't want it to end like this. I wasn't done with her, and if after tonight she was done with me, I needed to make it worth it.

It took everything I had, but I gently pulled out. "Not like this," I murmured. I swiped my thumb over her swollen lips and then helped her to her feet. "Please let me fuck you. I have condoms, and I was tested. You're safe with me."

She looped her arms around my neck and rolled onto her toes so her mouth was a breath from mine. "No condoms. Just you."

"Chloe," I said achingly. My forehead dropped to hers. "Are you sure?"

"I can't get more pregnant," she reminded me.

"I'm so fucking turned on right now, *I* might get pregnant," I muttered nonsensically.

She laughed and pressed her mouth to mine. The scent of her strawberry shampoo was all around me. My arms banded around her waist, and I lifted her off her feet. Her bump nudged against my abdomen. And why, of all things, was *that* what made my knees turn to jelly?

I backed her up until her knees buckled against the mattress and eased her onto her back. She wiggled backwards a bit and propped her heels on the edge, her thighs wide enough to give me a view that made my mouth water.

She stretched her arms behind her and touched the wall. She arched her neck to look behind her and gave a little laugh. "Why did you choose this tiny room? You're a big man. Do you even fit in this bed?"

"It's cozy," I said. "I like it."

"Hm." She cocked her head, desire all over her face as she looked at me. "Come here," she ordered.

And because she fucking owned me, I went.

"You want me?" I roughed out. I wondered if she heard the uncertainty in it, the neediness. I fucking hoped not.

Her gaze locked on mine. "I want you, Steven. So damn much."

I groaned and ran my thumb down the seam of her pussy, feeling her clench and tremble beneath me. She was so wet already. I pushed my thumb inside to verify and found her drenched.

"Fuck, princess. You're soaked. What do you think I should do about that?" I licked my lips, staring down at her. She stared back at me, looking messy and delicious, and god*damn*, I wanted to taste her.

But Chloe had other ideas and was already reaching for my cock. "I think you should fuck me. *Now*." Her hand wrapped around my shaft, her fingers not touching. "God, you're thick," she muttered. "How did I get this into my mouth?"

I couldn't stop a snort of laughter. "You're talented that way."

She swiped the head of my cock against her silky core. My eyelids fluttered and I dropped my chin to my chest on a heavy exhale.

"Steven," she said. "Now."

I pushed into her, slow and steady, inch by inch, filling her up until I was balls deep in her sweet body, my arms braced on either side of her ribcage. She lifted a leg and wrapped it around my back, bringing me impossibly deeper.

"Chloe," I groaned.

She ran her hands up my arms, squeezing my biceps. "You're trembling," she whispered.

I couldn't answer. All I could do was kiss her, feel her, breathe her in. I pulled out as far as she would let me, loving the way she resisted, her heel digging into my ass like she couldn't bear the separation, and then pushed back inside.

"Is this okay?" I panted. I glanced down at her bump. "Am I hurting—"

"Harder," she commanded.

I pulled out again, and again she resisted, and slammed back home. My body shook as she clenched around me with a wanton moan. Every point of contact between us feels like a spark. The brush of her belly against my happy trail. Her calf against my back. The side of her breast against my thumb.

I fucked her hard, my eyes locked on her face, watching her for any sign that it was too much. But all I found was hunger for more, so that was what I gave her.

Her moans pitched higher, her pussy tightened around me. Thank fuck, thank fuck, because I was so close I was in danger of needing a distraction like reciting football stats, and I didn't want a damn thing pulling my attention from her.

Now I wasn't the only one shaking. Her thighs vibrated and her hands moved restlessly across the bed, searching for something to hold onto. I leaned forward, still keeping my weight off her belly, so that her soft breasts ghosted against my chest.

"Hold onto me, princess," I murmured thickly.

Chloe Adams never did a damn thing I told her, but she did this. She clung to me, pressing quick, desperate kisses to my throat, and that made me go even harder, even faster.

"Steven," she cried, her whole body going rigid, her pussy pulsing around my cock, sending me straight over the edge with her.

I groaned into her hair as I emptied myself inside her. The relief of it...fuck. I damn near collapsed on her but had just enough sense left to twist to my side and land on the bed instead. I lay there completely limp and sated, trying to catch my breath.

Her hand flopped to my head, and she sifted her fingers through my hair.

"That," she said softly, "was delightful."

27

CHLOE

"Peanut butter or chocolate chip?" James asked as she piled flour, sugar, and salt—the ingredients needed for either cookie—onto the counter.

"Peanut butter," I decided. "My doctor says I need to eat more protein. Peanut butter has more protein, right?"

James consulted the label on the jar of peanut butter. "More than chocolate chips, anyway. But probably not as much as, say, lentils."

I made a face. "The baby doesn't want lentils, James. The baby wants cookies."

"Peanut butter it is," James said.

"Good choice," Adam said approvingly.

"Peanut butter is his favorite," James explained. She made a shooing motion at her fiancé. "These cookies aren't for you, cowboy. They're for Chloe and her fetus."

"And, um, Steven and Amy," I mumbled. I nibbled my lip. "I can't walk in there with freshly baked cookies and not share. That would be rude. Since he won't even let me pay rent."

"Hell, no." Adam glowered. "That asshole isn't getting my cookies."

"They're not your cookies," James reiterated. "Chloe can share her cookies with whoever she wants. Even if," she added sweetly, "that someone is a giant douche canoe."

I opened my mouth to defend Steven, then snapped it shut, feeling guilty for even considering it. Was I really going to stand up for the man who had gotten her bucked off a horse?

Yes, my heart whispered. Or maybe it was my pussy. That was the problem with having mind-blowing sex with your best friend's enemy. It divided your loyalties right along with your legs.

But Steven was more than my best friend's enemy, and more than a casual fuck. He had done so much for me. And he hadn't meant for James to get hurt. That counted for something, didn't it?

Great. Now I felt guilty for *not* defending him, too. I couldn't win.

James pivoted to the refrigerator, glancing at me over her shoulder before opening it. "You don't have to pay rent? That's nice of him." When Adam scowled, she rolled her eyes. "What? It *is*. I don't like him, either, but you know he's not pure evil. He's not even the worst person in Aspen Springs. Remember that guy Essie stole the horse from? Way worse."

I grimaced. James wasn't exactly setting a high bar for

Steven to clear. And the thing was, I didn't think he was a bad guy at all. Not anymore. Steven was a good guy who had done a very bad thing.

"It's just temporary," I reminded all of us. I rubbed my forehead. "Mom wants me to move back home and work for my dad while she babysits." We hadn't spoken since yesterday when Steven had dragged me out of there. I wondered if she was waiting for me to call her to apologize. If she was, she'd be waiting forever because I wasn't sorry.

James frowned. "What about your clients? I thought you were pushing the clinic to expand its telehealth options."

"Obviously, she's hoping I'll come to my senses." I fiddled with the bag of chocolate chips. If we weren't using them for cookies, I might as well eat a handful. "She's never liked running the business. It would be great for her if I took over."

James's frown deepened. "It's your life, Chloe. What do *you* want?"

I sighed. "I just want everyone to be okay, you know?"

James stood behind me and wrapped me up in a tight hug. "I know. I get it."

I knew she would. I squeezed her forearm that rested across my clavicle. "Thanks."

She released me and got back to work on the cookies.

"So, what are you going to do, really? If you move back in with your parents, you know you're gonna be there for at least a few years. You don't want that, do you?" James asked.

When I shook my head, she continued, "But you don't want to stay with Steven after the baby is born, either."

"Right," I said uncertainly.

But...what if I did? Would I live there as his roommate, or something more? And what would that mean for my friendship with James? She wasn't going to step foot in Steven's house to see me or Radish. It was one thing for this to be temporary, but permanent? I was going to live somewhere she didn't feel comfortable visiting? No. Our friendship wouldn't survive that kind of betrayal.

"Right," I said again, with conviction this time.

"So, where are you gonna go?" James asked. "Have you started looking?"

"I started this morning. There really wasn't anything yet. A one-bedroom rental above the hardware store on Second Street." My pulse ticked anxiously. I was fucked.

"You know, one of the ranch hand cabins is empty." Adam rubbed his jaw. "I wouldn't say it's a suitable option for a woman and a newborn baby, but...When are you due, again?"

"May," I told him.

He nodded. "We could get it in shape by then. Build a small addition for a second bedroom. Hell of a commute to your office, though."

"If the clinic agrees to my telehealth proposal, I'll mostly be working from home," I said.

"Huh." Adam tilted his head thoughtfully. "We have strong wi-fi. That could work."

I stared at him. "Are you serious? I could live here at Lodestar?"

James squealed and threw her arms around Adam. "Of course he's serious! Oh, my gosh, that would be perfect! And I bet Ted wouldn't mind pitching in with childcare while you're working."

Adam laughed. "Dad does love babies."

"It's perfect," James said again, her big dark eyes sparkling with excitement. "You won't have to live with Steven anymore."

I should have felt nothing but relief. I had a plan. Problem solved. Everything would go back to the way it should be.

So why did I feel so sad?

I WISHED this glass of water was wine. Or, better yet, whiskey. Because the feelings tornado-ing in my chest when I watched Steven out the kitchen window weren't the kind of things someone should have to suffer through sober.

He disappeared from view and I sighed, knowing what was coming next. The back door opened and closed. I stayed where I was, sipping my useless water, listening. A thump as he removed his boots. Footsteps. Then there he was, looking like a cowboy and smelling like pine trees and cold air. And I was supposed to *not* touch him? Honestly. How was that even reasonable?

His stride faltered when he caught sight of me. "You're home," he said. "Your car was gone when I woke up. I thought you were at work."

I shook my head. "Holiday hours. I don't go back until Tuesday."

He came right to me and my heart fluttered in my chest. Then I realized he wanted the sink. I moved aside to give him space to wash his hands.

"Where's Amy?" I asked.

"Out hiking with friends. Some kind of tradition they have instead of hitting the Black Friday sales." He dried his hands on the towel hanging off the refrigerator door. "You hungry?"

"No, I had cookies." I gave him a wide berth as I moved to the counter and pushed the plate of cookies forward. "James and I made them this morning."

He tensed and then slowly rolled his neck. "She still likes to bake, huh? How is she?" The words sounded reluctant, like he had to drag them from his mouth.

"Good," I said. "You can have one, you know."

He considered the plate. "Why do I feel like I shouldn't?"

I snorted. "Because you know it would piss Adam off."

"Fuck that guy," Steven muttered and snagged a cookie off the top.

"Fuck that guy?" I repeated. My eyebrows went up. "For

what? Firing you after that shit you pulled with James? For breaking your nose?"

A muscle ticked in his jaw. "No. I don't blame him for any of that. I would have done way worse, if it had been…" His gaze dropped along with the words unsaid.

"Then what?" I pressed. "What do you have to be mad at him for?"

His shoulders jerked slightly, like he was trying to shrug something off. "It feels good to hate him, okay? It feels good to be angry at someone else instead of just myself. What does it matter, anyway? He hates me, too."

My lips flattened. "I'm not taking your side on this."

"Yeah, no shit," he bit out. "I never thought you would. I didn't ask you to."

The words cut deep, even though they shouldn't have. Of course I couldn't take his side. James and Adam hadn't done anything wrong.

"Adam is a good man," I said, almost pleading. For what? For Steven to figure out time travel and go back and fix everything? Some things couldn't be fixed. It was a hard pill to swallow for someone who believed every problem had a solution.

Steven's eyes narrowed. "So I've heard."

I give up. My shoulders slumped. Whatever this thing was between us, it didn't work. I had always known it wouldn't. But that didn't make it hurt any less. Because part of me had hoped that somehow, some way, it would all work out.

"Adam offered me a cabin at Lodestar Ranch," I said,

looking everywhere but at him. "I can move there with Radish in May."

Steven froze. "Lodestar Ranch? You're going to move to the one place in Aspen Springs I can't go? What the hell, Chloe? Did I fucking imagine last night, or was that you begging for my dick?"

I flushed. Oh, shit, he was furious. The tendons in his throat bulged as he stared me down, his dark eyes nearly black. Well, that was fine, because I was mad, too. Mad at him for hurting James. Mad at him for not being able to fix it. Mad at myself for thinking even for a second that we would end up anywhere but right here, in this moment, with all these bad feelings and disappointments swirling around us like an inferno.

"Where else am I supposed to go, Steven?" I demanded, slapping a hand on the counter. "Home?"

He growled. "You *are* home, Chloe. *This* is your home. Even if you never let me into your bed again, this is still yours. Hell, you can turn my room into a nursery. I'll sleep in the basement if that's what you want. Just don't—" His voice cracked. "Just don't go where I can't follow. Please, princess."

Oh, god, the hurt I saw in his face was so much worse than anger. "Steven," I choked out. My chest felt like someone had taken a sledgehammer to it, cracking me open. "What am I going to do with you?"

"Anything you want." He rubbed a hand over his hair, disheveling it. "Anything you want. I love you, Chloe, and I think you could love me too, if you let yourself. Hell, I'm a reasonable man. If you need to hate me a little, I can live with that so long as you call me yours. Because that's what I am, princess. I'm yours."

My heart banged itself against my ribcage like it was trying to fling itself at him, but I held myself back. Held tight to my anger. If I caved now, where would that lead us? Right back here again. "Steven. I *can't.*"

"You can. You can forgive me, Chloe. I would do anything. Ask me to crawl over broken glass on my hands and knees. I'll do it."

That was what people said. *I'll crawl over broken glass* or *I'll walk across hot coals.* I dragged my index finger along the rim of my water glass in a slow circle.

People *said* that, but they didn't *do* that. They didn't mean it.

I tipped the glass to my lips and swallowed the last gulp of water, then hurled the empty glass to the floor. It shattered between us, the sunlight glinting off the water droplets and reflecting rainbows on the walls.

"So crawl," I said.

Because he *wouldn't.*

A heartbeat, and he dropped to his knees.

Another, and he flattened his palms on the linoleum tile.

I stared at him. No. He wouldn't.

Oh, god.

He moved forward.

"What the hell, Steven! Don't crawl!" I gasped. "What is wrong with you?"

He looked up at me and had the nerve to fucking *smirk*. "I'm getting mixed messages, princess. But you're there and I'm here, and one way or another, I'm getting to you."

"Stop!" I shrieked. I instinctively leaned toward him like I was going to take a step.

"Don't you fucking move, Chloe," he commanded, and I froze. "You're barefoot."

He crawled toward me like a lion stalking his prey. He didn't look weak or chastened, down on his hands and knees for me. He looked strong. Determined. *Relentless.*

I was the one who was begging. "Steven, please get up."

The way he looked at me made me grip the counter for support. Like he would crawl a mile over broken glass for me, not just across the kitchen floor. "It's just a little blood, baby."

He was at my feet now. I grabbed fistfuls of his henley and tugged, trying to get him to stand. I might as well have tried to move a boulder. He didn't budge.

"Say I'm yours, Chloe." He looked at me with his heart in his eyes.

The answer lodged itself in my throat. *Yes* was terrifying, but *no* was dishonest.

His mouth twisted. "I know. You still can't forgive me. How could you? You don't even know how to forgive yourself. You haven't learned how to live with something terrible without punishing yourself every day. You're too good, that's what it is. It's all right. Stick with me, princess. I'll show you how to be a villain."

My lips parted on an exhale. "I don't know what you're talking about."

"Yes, you do."

Yes, I do.

I shook my head. "Give me your hands," I said.

I ripped off a handful of paper towels and ran them under the faucet. He turned his palms up for me. Shards of glass sparkled in the light. A smear of blood crossed one palm, a small red bead on the other. I tenderly wiped it all away with the damp towels.

"I can't believe you did that," I said, running my thumbs lightly over his palms to make sure I hadn't left anything sharp behind.

He gave me a sardonic look. "When have I ever said no to you, Chloe?"

"You were supposed to say no to this," I said sternly. "This was supposed to be your limit."

"I don't have limits when it comes to you." He took the towels from me and tossed them on the counter.

His hands bracketed my hips, then clenched around the hem of my t-shirt and pushed it up, exposing my stomach. He pressed his forehead there and took a shaky breath that he released on a long exhale. I stared down at his dark head, stunned, unsure how to respond.

"Don't go," he said thickly. "Please don't go."

He kissed my navel, then trailed his mouth lower and kissed the sensitive skin along the waistband of my stretchy maternity pants. A tremor shuddered through him and he held my body a little tighter.

"Chloe...can I..." He pressed the words to my skin with heated kisses, tongue, and teeth. "Can I taste you?"

My hips answered yes before my brain could comprehend what he was saying, tilting toward him eagerly. I shouldn't let him. It was so selfish, taking pleasure when I couldn't give him everything he wanted in return.

Like he was reading my mind, his head tilted so he could meet my eyes. "At least let me have this."

I nodded. "Yes," I whispered.

He dragged my pants and underwear down my legs, helping me step out of them with my hands on his shoulders for balance. Then he hooked one leg over his shoulder, pressed his face to my pussy, and made me see starbursts with one perfectly placed lick.

"Oh, *god*!" I shouted, from shock and pleasure and need. My hands dove into his hair, and I held on for dear life.

I felt his lips curve into a smile just before he sucked my clit into his mouth more firmly. My senses sparked to life. I wanted to memorize all of this. The silky feel of his hair between my fingers. The rough scratch of his hand palming my ass and the bruising pressure of his fingertips digging into my skin, holding me to his mouth like a starving man.

And his mouth. Oh, my god, his *mouth*. It should be registered as a lethal weapon.

His tongue flicked softly at my clit, then worked straight into me as he fucked me with it, plunging in and out of my pussy as he made hungry noises. My release barreled down on me like a freight train, no matter how hard I tried to push it off, to prolong this obscene pleasure as long as I could.

"Steven, I'm going to—"

I couldn't even finish the sentence before pleasure roared through me. I shattered like the glass on the floor. My knees buckled from the force of it, and he caught me as I fell, cradling me into his lap.

I rested my cheek against his chest. Felt his heartbeat, quick and hard.

You're mine, I wanted to say.

But I didn't say anything at all.

28

CHLOE

MOM

Hi, honey. Are you working today?

CHLOE

No, I have the weekend off. Is everything ok?

MOM

Everything is definitely not ok. Do you have a minute.

CHLOE

I'll be there in 30.

MOM

I'm already here, in your driveway.

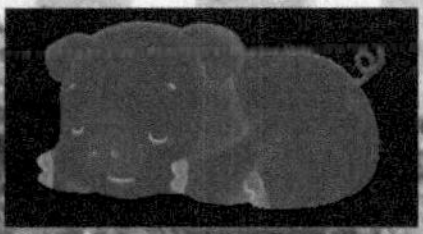

"MOM?" I RAPPED MY KNUCKLES ON THE DRIVER'S SIDE window. "What are you doing?"

She rolled down the window so we could hear each other. "I needed to talk to you, so I figured I should come to you for once but then I got here and realized that you're a busy person, and maybe I was only making things worse by showing up unannounced like this. Maybe you don't have time today. I should have called first."

I blinked. Mom wasn't a rambler. I was starting to worry.

"Mom." I rubbed my arms for warmth. I hadn't grabbed a jacket before running outside when I got her text. "Come inside."

She rubbed her nose. "I don't want to face Steven yet. Not after what happened at Thanksgiving. I'm too embarrassed."

With a sigh, I rounded the car and climbed into the passenger seat. "What's going on, Mom? Are you sick? You didn't have to drive all the way out here. I would have come to you."

"You always come to us, Chloe." She pursed her lips, her forehead pinched in a frown. Then she shook her head like she had come to a decision that she didn't particularly like. "Do you know what I realized? We visited you only once at the bungalow, and that was when you first moved in. We've never been to Steven's place at all."

"It's fine," I said. "It makes more sense for me to go to you. It's easier."

"It's not fine. You have been making things easier for us

for too long. I cannot..." Her hands twisted on her lap. "I'm so sorry, honey."

I searched for the right words, opening and closing my mouth like a fish searching for air. I wanted to tell her it was all okay. That I didn't mind, because this was what families did for each other. We had all done the best we could, hadn't we?

But the truth was, it wasn't all okay. Some of it was, some of it wasn't, and it all got mixed up together somehow. I hadn't set the boundaries that I should have. It had never occurred to me that I *had* boundaries I wanted to set.

"You never asked me to take care of my brothers when you were sick," I said slowly, carefully, still working through it myself. "I did it because it needed to be done. And I'm glad I did. I wouldn't change any of that, except that I hated you were sick. If I had to do it all over again, I would. But asking me now to live my life on your terms..." I shook my head. "That's not fair. If you don't want to do the paperwork, hire someone. I can help with that. But I have my own life, and it's mine to live as I see fit."

"Terry said the same thing," Mom admitted. "He felt terrible about what Steven said. You know he has always loved you like his own, and you were the only one of the five that showed any interest in the horse business. The idea of working with you every day...that was hard for him to let go of. But we are both so proud of you, no matter what you choose to do."

"I know." My eyes stung. "I know. It's okay, Mom. Can we go inside and have hot chocolate now?"

"Yes—no. Darn it, I'm doing it again." Mom cleared her throat and sat up straighter. "None of this is actually what I came here to talk about. I owe you an apology, Chloe. I should never have allowed your grandmother to treat you like that."

"No," I said hastily because, oh, god, I did *not* want to talk about this. Not now, not ever. "No, you don't have to say anything, Mom. You can't force Grams to talk to me. You can't force her to forgive me. We can let it go."

"I can tell her she can treat her granddaughter with basic kindness and respect, or she can find somewhere else to live," Mom said bluntly. "You're bringing her great-grandchild into the world. Is she going to ignore him, too? No. Enough is enough. We've coddled her longer than we should have." She blinked rapidly. "Steven was right. We took the easy way out at your expense."

I felt sick. "You can't do that. You can't send Grams away."

"Honey, your grandmother is eighty-two. She's fully an adult and can make her own decisions. We're not sending her away. We're telling her has a choice to make."

My pulse beat a panicked staccato in my throat. "But she's not wrong. I should have known. I should have said something when I first found out. I never should have left him alone that afternoon."

"Oh, honey." She stroked my hair back from my forehead. "You don't really believe that, do you? You didn't know. You're judging your past self based on what you know now, with a degree in mental health and hundreds of clinical hours under your belt. That's not fair. You have to forgive yourself, Chloe."

You can't forgive me. You don't even know how to forgive yourself. Steven's words echoed in my head. I squeezed my eyes shut.

"I think when we let Grams blame you for his decision, we let you blame yourself, too," Mom said softly. "We should never have let you shoulder the blame just to keep the peace."

"If I could just—" My voice faltered.

"Turn back time?" Mom suggested drily. "If only. But you can't. It doesn't matter how hard you wish otherwise. You made a judgment call, and it turned out to be the wrong one. I'm so sorry you have to live with that. We all wish we had done differently. We all think *if we had only,* then Gramps would still be here. You have to forgive yourself for what you didn't know."

"I don't know how," I confessed.

Have you ever done something you can't take back, no matter how much you want to? You can't fix it. You just have to live with it like a bad tattoo.

Stick with me, princess. I'll show you how to be a villain.

I sat very still as his words collided in my soul like an earthquake. I felt rearranged by it. Suddenly I understood what he meant. Forgiveness didn't mean rationalizing a bad thing away. It wasn't condoning or excusing. It was acceptance and letting go. That was all.

Steven had figured that out when I couldn't. He had learned to live with himself. He was putting good in the world not to punish himself for being bad, but because that was who he was and who he wanted to be. I hadn't done that. I had let Grams treat me like shit because I believed that was what I deserved.

Shit. Shit.

I couldn't breathe.

"We talked it over, me and Terry," Mom said. "We want you to know that the offer is still on the table, but the terms are different. You can still come home anytime you want. I'll babysit no matter what job you choose to do."

"Thanks, but I…" My voice trailed off as Steven jogged out the front door. He did a double take when he saw us sitting in the driveway, and then slowly raised his hand in a wave before grabbing something from the bed of his truck and heading behind the house. I sighed.

"But you'd rather stay put with the big, handsome farrier?" Mom snickered. "Yes, I can relate."

My cheeks heated. "But I'm an adult and need to be on my own. Steven has nothing to do with this."

Mom patted my knee. "Oh, honey. Your dad is his boss, and that still didn't stop him from telling us exactly what he thought about our treatment of you. From the way you two look at each other, he has everything to do with this." She glanced at the clock. "I should be getting back, but here." She reached into the back seat and handed me a loaf of bread in plastic wrap. "I baked it this morning. You know how punching dough helps me work out my feelings."

I laughed. "Thanks. And thanks for the loaf you sent

me through Steven a couple months ago. I meant to call and thank you, but I completely forgot."

Mom tilted her head quizzically. "What are you talking about?"

"You asked Steven to bring me a loaf because he would be in my neighborhood anyway, remember? It was back in early October."

"No," Mom said slowly. "I never did that. I gave him a couple loaves of bread for winterizing the house. It was the only payment he would accept."

All the air whooshed out of my lungs. "No. That was Jaxson."

"Jaxson helped. Steven wrangled him into it, but it wasn't that hard. Jaxson idolizes the man, so he was happy to help."

"But that was..." *When he hated me.* Didn't he? I stared blindly past the house, like I could see him there. "Mom, I have to—"

"Go," she said, looking amused.

I was unbuckled and halfway out the door before she got the full syllable out.

"Not about the farrier, my big white butt," she muttered.

GODDAMMIT, where was that man?

Steven's house sat on a seven-acre lot, most of it

pasture. I had expected he'd be hanging out with the pigs, but he was nowhere to be seen. Frustrated and cold, I turned to go back into the house when a noise caught my attention along the side of the house.

And there he was. Four stakes and string created a square-shaped boundary, with Steven in the middle, his back to me and a shovel in his hands, turning up sod.

"Steven McAllister, I have a question for you," I announced.

He froze, his shoulders bunched up to his ears. "All right," he grunted.

"Turn around, please. I don't want to have this conversation with your backside."

He slowly turned to face me. Whatever emotion had been on his face was immediately replaced with agitation. "Where's your coat?"

"Inside." I crossed my arms over my chest in a way I hoped looked defiant but was really for warmth.

"Then you should be, too," he snapped. "We can talk in there."

"We're talking now," I insisted.

A muscle bulged in his jaw. "For fuck's sake, Chloe."

He drove the shovel into the earth with both hands so it stood upright on its own, then shrugged out of his puffer jacket. Three long strides and he was standing toe to toe with me. He settled his jacket on my shoulders. "Put this on."

"But then you'll be cold," I protested.

"So talk fast."

My gaze flicked over his annoyed face. "This right here. What you're doing now, giving me your coat. What is this? Am I your penance?"

"You're a pain in my ass, if that's what you mean," he muttered. His hands followed the zipper down the front of the coat until he got to the bottom, where he lined up the parts and latched them together.

"You winterized my parents' house," I accused.

He fumbled the zipper momentarily but then kept going, dragging it up to my chin. "Yeah, I did. They needed the help, and I was happy to do it. They're not just your parents to me. Terry is my mentor. He took me under his wing, and I'll be a damn good farrier because of him. And Angie…I just like her, okay? Of course I helped them."

It all sounded so reasonable. So believable. Except for one thing. "It was *my* list. You knew they weren't going to do it themselves. You knew it would be me." I tried to shake my head, but my hair was stuck in the coat with me, holding me still.

With a soft chuckle, Steven slipped his hand underneath my hair and gently pulled it free. "There you go, princess." He squeezed the back of my neck.

"And *that*," I said. "You keep taking care of me. The bread that you said was from my mom but it really wasn't. Grocery shopping and making me take the pregnancy test. Driving me to that first appointment and holding my hand. I'm your penance, aren't I?"

"Are you serious right now?" he demanded.

"Yes, I'm fucking serious!" I shouted in his face.

"Because none of this"—I gestured to myself—"can possibly be fun for you. I was *mean.* Steven...*you caught my vomit in your bare hands.* On purpose! If that's not penance, what is?"

"You're not my penance, Chloe." He cupped my face in his hands, thumbs stroking over my cheeks. "Don't you understand? Taking care of you is not a punishment. It's my reward."

My lower lip trembled. "What?" I whispered.

"I have worked really hard to be a better man than I was two years ago. I didn't do that for you. I did that for me, to be someone I could respect. If I have to live with myself another sixty years, then I'd rather not hate myself every goddamn minute of the day. But you... Even before I fell in love with you, I wanted to be near you. For two years, you wouldn't give me the time of day. Kicked me out of your presence like a princess exiling riffraff. But things changed after that night we rescued Stevie. You let me stay. You let me help you, when you don't accept help from anyone. I never expected it, but I craved it. You're my reward, and I'll never stop trying to earn your love."

I drew in a shaky breath. "You've earned it a thousand times over. I love you so goddamn much." My eyes held his as I looped my arms around his neck and dug my hands into his hair. "You're mine, Steven McAllister, and I want the whole fucking world to know it."

And then I crushed my mouth to his.

29

STEVEN

Chloe Adams was kissing me.

Chloe Adams loved me.

Chloe Adams called me hers.

There was an asshole voice in the back of my mind telling me it wasn't true, that this wasn't real, that I wasn't good enough. I told that voice to fuck all the way off.

Chloe Adams was no liar.

She had me by the collar of my flannel, hauling my face down to her demanding mouth. Her lips were cold and clumsy, but her tongue was warm and soft. The entire world disappeared. It was just her and me and—

I yelped as her icy fingers grazed my neck. I ripped my mouth from hers. The moment she lost the warmth of my mouth, her teeth started chattering. I swore softly. "Let's get you inside."

I didn't give her the opportunity to respond, just scooped her up behind her knees and carried her to the door. She didn't protest. It seemed like a miracle that she didn't protest so I didn't stop there. I braced her against my raised thigh so I could open the door without dropping her, and she did her best to distract me, nuzzling her cold nose against my neck.

"Chloe," I growled, and she laughed.

Down the hall. Into her bedroom, kicking the door closed behind us, bypassing the bed for the bathroom.

"What are we doing?" she asked.

I reached into the shower and spun the knob. "Getting you warm. Getting me clean."

We stripped off our clothes. I took her hand and helped her step into the tub, then turned us around so she was under the hot spray. She faced me and tilted her head back, letting the water sluice down her hair, her strong shoulders, her full breasts, her round belly.

I couldn't breathe for all that beauty.

She opened her eyes and caught me staring. She smiled—the smile I had been waiting for, the smile that meant I was worthwhile.

"It's cold out of the water," she said. "Come here."

I came.

I knelt.

Her green eyes glowed as she looked down at me. Fuck, she was beautiful. "I really love seeing you on your knees," she murmured.

"Good," I said. "Because I don't want to be anywhere else."

I wrapped my hands around the backs of her thighs. "Open your legs, princess. Let me eat you."

She widened her stance, bracing her feet against the sides of the tub. I pressed my face between her legs and nuzzled against her sweetness. A low groan rumbled out of me as I slid my tongue between her lips. Warm. Swollen. Fucking delicious.

"Oh, god, Steven." Her head tipped back on a moan. Water splattered her face. "Oh, *god*."

I buried my tongue deep inside her cunt and inhaled the scent of her. Her pussy muscles clenched around my tongue like a heartbeat. My dick pulsed and leaked in response. I needed to get her there before I fucking exploded.

Her hands tangled in my hair. "Yes, yes," she chanted. Thank god she was close.

I laved the bud of her clit with the tip of my tongue and her hips surged forward, her cries muffled by the running water. Her legs trembled against my cheeks. And then I sucked hard, remembering how it sent her over the goddamn edge last time, and am rewarded with a gush of wetness on my tongue.

Chloe slapped one hand to the wall, her other to the glass door, and rolled her hips to my mouth, her pussy convulsing around my tongue as she came.

I kept at her until the last tremor subsided and then pressed a kiss to each shaking thigh.

"Steven." She said my name like a prayer. "Fuck me." She said *that* like a goddamn queen.

I pushed to my feet and joined her under the hot spray. Water pelted our bodies as she melted into my arms. Soft and sweet and all mine. The swell of her belly bumped against my abdomen and my heart nearly exploded from my chest. I kissed her, knowing she could taste herself on my lips, and cupped a heavy breast in my palm. She moaned when my thumb grazed over her nipple.

"Still a good sensitive?" I asked against her mouth.

"*Very* good sensitive," she breathed back.

I did it again. Her mouth moved to nip my Adam's apple.

"Fuck me," she said again, this time more plea than command.

I said a silent prayer of thanks for the anti-slip patches on the bottom of the bathtub and turned her carefully to face the wall. The curve of her ass bumped against my already aching dick, and I sent another prayer heavenward, this time for help holding my shit together.

Leaning over her body, my mouth on her earlobe, I growled, "Hands on the wall, princess."

"Yes," she hissed. She slapped her hands to the wall, fingertips finding the coarse grout between the tiles for extra leverage.

"I won't let you slip," I promised. "I've got you."

She looked at me over her shoulder, her pretty eyes full of fire and trust. "I know."

Her words were a balm to my self-inflicted wound. I couldn't stop touching her, running my hands down the muscles on either side of her spine, molding the shape of her hips, sliding forward to gently hold the curve of her belly. A fucking miracle, every inch of her.

Water beat down on us as I took my cock in hand and guided it down the crack of her ass and then lower to her entrance. She mewled softly as I played with her there, dragging my cock through her wetness and teasing her clit.

And then I couldn't stand it a second longer. I gripped her hips and thrust into her. She was soaked, and I slid right inside like we were made for each other.

"Tell me if anything hurts," I panted. "If I go too hard or too fast or—"

Her response was to push against the tile to slam her hips back on me. We both groaned loudly.

We liked it so much that we did it again, me thrusting into her, her rocking back to me, again and again and fucking *again*. Steam rolled around us in a damp cloud. Water pelted our bodies. Flesh smacked against flesh.

And somehow, my hands found their way once more to her round belly. I held her there, supporting the weight of it in my palms, my heart pounding with every slide of my cock, and dropped my forehead to the juncture of her shoulder.

"I love you," I choked out, because I couldn't stop myself.

She looked back at me, curled an arm around my head, and dragged my mouth to hers. "I love you, too."

My hands dropped from her belly to her clit and she gasped, sending her hips slamming back to mine with a ferocious eagerness that had me seeing stars.

"More," she sobbed. "Harder."

Her pussy clenched around me like a vise. I groaned and scraped my teeth against the nape of her neck. With my right hand still playing with her clit, I brought my left hand to her breast and tweaked her nipple.

"Come for me, princess. Come with me." My voice was tinged with desperation.

She met me there, matching my savage thrusts with her own. And finally I felt it, the rhythmic, clenching pulse of her orgasm. I surged into her one more time and let go. She bucked against me, gasping, crying out curses and my name. My orgasm hit me like a lightning strike, blinding and brilliant.

We managed to make it out of the shower without killing ourselves despite our shaking muscles. I wrapped a towel around her and rubbed it over her arms. She looked up at me with a sweet, sated smile.

"So," she said, "when are you moving back into your bedroom?"

I blinked. "What?"

"Come on, Steven." She gave me a sardonic scowl. "I know this is really your room. I appreciate you letting me use it, but when I moved in, you thought it would be temporary."

"When did you figure it out?" I asked, toweling my hair.

She laughed. "Around the time I realized your feet hung off the end of your bed in the other room. If I'm going to stay, you need to take your real room back. I don't feel right keeping it."

"Tell you what," I said, pulling her in close. "You stay. I'll move back in when you call it ours."

CHLOE

PREGNANCY WEEK 20: RADISH IS THE SIZE OF A BANANA

"I see you brought your emotional support Steven with you," Dr. Davidson greeted us.

Steven, standing at my shoulder, smirked down at me, clearly pleased with the designation. I rolled my eyes, but I couldn't argue. I loved having him here with me.

Dr. Davidson smiled warmly. "How are you feeling, Chloe?"

"Good," I said. "Like I have more energy than I know what to do with, but then I crash and need a two-hour nap."

Dr. Davidson nodded. "That's perfectly normal. Remember to focus on protein and fiber. Fruit is great. I would never tell a pregnant woman to avoid all treats, but try to keep the sugar intake low, because it will make those energy crashes much more intense. And, of course, too much can lead to gestational diabetes. We'll test for that in another six weeks or so. It's easy. You drink a disgustingly sweet orange drink and then we check your blood sugar."

Steven squeezed my shoulder. I nodded.

"So, today we're going to do the anatomy scan," Dr. Davidson continued. "The ultrasound technician will look at every organ of your baby's body to make sure there are no defects and everything is growing properly. We'll also look at the umbilical cord and where it attaches to the placenta and measure your amniotic fluid. What's really exciting for the parents is that this time, your baby looks like a baby. We can also tell you the sex if you want to know." She glanced at both of us and pushed to her feet. "Okay, I'll go get the technician."

I stared down at my baby bump. A boy or a girl? Mostly I had been referring to it as *it*.

"Do you want to know?" Steven asked. "Or do you want it to be a surprise?"

"It's a surprise either way, isn't it?" I said. "I'll be surprised now, or surprised after I push it out."

"Are you...hoping?" he asked hesitantly.

There was something odd in his tone that made me look up at him quizzically.

He shrugged. "When Amy was born, I remember my dad ranting about how useless girls were. He was so sure he would only have boys because of his virility or whatever. My mom cried. It would have been better if they had found out earlier and to give him a few months to adjust, instead of when she was cut open on the operating table in an emergency c-section."

I rubbed my belly. "Someday," I muttered, "I am going to meet your dad and we will have *words*."

He snorted. "Chloe, you will *never* meet him. I love you too much for that."

I kept rubbing my belly, thinking about what was inside. *Who* was inside. It was hard to imagine. "Is it weird that I can't picture either a boy or a girl? In some ways, I'm still stuck on thinking this can't be real." I looked up at him. "I want to know. I don't care what I'm having, but I think knowing will help me feel connected in some way."

The technician came in and squirted goo on my belly. He dragged the transducer across my belly, pushing harder than I expected but not so hard that it was painful, and an image appeared on the screen.

"There you go," he said. "There's your baby."

I couldn't speak as I stared at the screen. Big head, little body with its knees drawn up, tiny hands and feet, adorable baby features. Everything swirled together like images in a kaleidoscope as wetness flooded my eyes.

That's my baby.

He didn't say much as he kept moving the transducer. Sometimes he drew a line across a various body part like a tape measure. Time floated by in a haze. I couldn't look away from the screen.

"All right," he said finally, standing. He handed me

some wipes to clean the gel from my belly. "Dr. Davidson will be in to go over everything. I took a couple pictures that you can take home with you."

I blinked, dazed. "Thank you."

Steven looked every bit as dazed as I felt.

"All right," Dr. Davidson said, bustling in. "Everything looks great. Congratulations, Chloe. You have a perfectly healthy baby in there. Do you want to know the sex?"

I nodded.

Her smile widened. "It's a boy."

"You hungry?" Steven asked for the third time, his fingertips beating out a nervous rhythm on the steering wheel.

"No," I said, also for the third time. In the silence that had stretched between us, I had lost my appetite.

Other than asking me if I was hungry, Steven hadn't said a word since we left the doctor's office. At first I'd been too excited at seeing a real baby-shaped image on the screen to notice Steven getting quieter and quieter. He had stopped talking altogether sometime around when Dr. Davidson announced I was having a boy.

And there he was on the screen, a real boy looking very much like a human baby instead of a splotch. It was suddenly all so very real.

Maybe that was the problem.

Maybe it had suddenly become real for Steven, too.

And maybe...maybe he wasn't ready for that. And maybe I should have expected as much. We had gone from enemies to being roommates to being in love in only five months, and in another four months I was going to be a mother to another man's son. That was...a lot to process.

"Hey." My voice cracked. I cleared my throat and tried again. "Hey. We should talk."

His gaze whipped to mine and then back to the road. His lips pressed in a grim line. "All right."

My mouth went completely dry. I couldn't even get a squeak out.

"*Chloe*." His jaw ticked. "Say it."

I licked my lips nervously. "You know that day outside Jo's, when I spilled my coffee and you bought me a new one? I was pregnant and I didn't even know it."

"Okay," he said slowly.

"What I'm saying is, this whole time we've been getting to know each other, I've been pregnant. Most couples have a time that's just them. We don't have that. We are *never* going to have that. And that's okay, isn't it? I mean, we don't have to follow the same trajectory. We can slow things down now and take our time figuring it all out."

His knuckles turned white as he gripped the wheel. "Slow things down?"

"Yeah. I know it's weird because technically we live together, but that doesn't mean we have to *live together*, live together, right? We can keep separate bedrooms. We can be roommates who date." I rubbed my damp palms on my pants and stared straight out the window. "You don't have to be a de facto dad just because we're together." *Please, please say you want to be together. Say this isn't too much for you.*

The truck swerved slightly, then quickly corrected. I grabbed my seatbelt and looked at Steven with wide eyes. "What happened?"

"Shit. Shit," he muttered. He rubbed his temple, checked his mirrors, steered us onto the shoulder, and threw the gearshift in park. "I knew you were going to say that, but I still didn't...I need a minute, okay?" He pressed the heels of his palms to his eyes.

"Steven?" I stared at him in genuine confusion. Water leaked down his wrists. "Are you...are you *crying*?"

"No," he said huskily. "Listen. Listen." He inhaled sharply, then exhaled, his hands still covering his eyes. "I understand Radish is your top priority. That's the way it is. That's the way it *has* to be. You want separate bedrooms, fine. I can live with that for now. But we're not roommates, Chloe, and we're not fucking dating. I don't even know what that means. I understand why you're scared. I know I'm not his dad. But I can be *something*. You don't have to take my word for it right now. Just give me a chance to prove it. Don't shut me out."

"I'm not...I don't... What the hell are you talking about? I'm not scared. *You're* scared." I grabbed his wrists, dragged his hands from his eyes, and literally gasped. "You *are* crying! Why are you crying?"

"Because you're trying to cut me out of Radish's life.

That really hurts, Chloe. I understand, okay? I do. I wouldn't take a chance on me, either, if it were my kid on the line. But it still hurts like hell."

I unbuckled and clambered over the console to him. He reached under his seat for the lever and sent his seat careening back, then hauled me onto his lap. "Steven," I whispered, cupping his face in my hands. "Aren't you scared?"

He laughed hoarsely. "I'm terrified," he confessed.

I nodded. "It's so much. You don't want to get trapped parenting a kid who's not even yours. I get it. So let's go slow. Until you know what you want."

"For fuck's sake, Chloe. *No*," he said, exasperated. "I know what I want, and it doesn't scare me at all. I want you. I want this baby. I want the life we'll build together. That's not why I'm scared."

I scanned his face and what I saw there shook me to my core. He meant it. "Then what is it?"

"Chloe." He sighed, thunked his head back against the rest, and contemplated the roof of the truck. "My grandfather was an asshole who raised an asshole. My dad was an asshole who raised an asshole. I would really, really like to break that cycle, and I am *terrified*—" His voice wobbled, and he swallowed hard. "I am terrified that I can't."

"You already have." I kissed his face, first one cheek, then the other. "You're not an asshole. You have been a good son, a good brother, a good friend, a good farrier, and a good partner. Do you know what that all adds up to?" I dropped my forehead to his. "A good man. You're a good man, Steven. I am so damn lucky to have you in my life and so is this baby."

He cupped the sides of my throat in his large hands, his thumbs pushing under my jaw to angle my mouth to his. He kissed me like he couldn't get enough.

When we broke away, his eyes were shiny and wet, but he was smiling. "Shit." He laughed and rubbed his eyes with the backs of his hands. "No one told me I could cry from being fucking *happy*."

I swallowed thickly. "I still want you to take some time to think about all this."

He shook his head. "Chloe. I'm in."

"I might not be able to have more kids. Getting pregnant once doesn't mean I can do it again." I ran my hands over his chest, fidgeting with the buttons.

"I'm in."

I fisted his shirt in my hands. "Please think about it. Don't just say things because you think that's what I want to hear, or because you wish it were true. I don't want to be five years into this with you and you suddenly feel your biological clock ticking for something I can't give you."

"I am fucking *in*, Chloe." His hands wrapped around mine, his eyes glowing at me like I hung the moon. "I was ambivalent on fatherhood before I met you. I am so glad this baby is coming, but you would have been more than enough for me. Just you. Radish is an amazing bonus. Whatever other babies come along or don't come along, I don't care. They're not real. You're real, and Radish is real. I'm all in, princess. All I need to know is if you're in it with me."

"I'm in," I choked out.

"That's my good girl," he muttered against my mouth.

It took us a long time to get back on the road.

31

STEVEN

PREGNANCY WEEK 21: RADISH IS THE SIZE OF AN ENDIVE

WHAT THE HELL WAS AN ENDIVE? I soaped my hands at the kitchen sink, my attention diverted by the chart stuck to the refrigerator by a magnet and the sonogram photo next to it. It had been a week since the sonogram, but I still felt a shiver of awe when I looked at the baby Chloe was growing inside her.

"Hey." Chloe strolled into the kitchen, dropped a kiss on the back of my neck, and unlocked the fridge.

"What are you still doing home?" I glanced at the microwave clock to verify the time. I had spent more time than I intended to out back on a special project. "Shouldn't you be at the library for your sewing circle now?"

"Not going," Chloe mumbled, her head in the fridge, her hips pushed back.

I dried my hands on the towel and swatted her ass, because it was there and I couldn't help myself. She smirked at me over her shoulder.

"If you're hungry, I can make you something," I offered. "Are you feeling okay?" Chloe never missed a sewing circle, not even during the first trimester when she was throwing up breakfast, lunch, and dinner.

"I'm okay, I just want a little snack." She closed the fridge and waved the container of hummus and bag of baby carrots—because according to Chloe, the vibes were off on full-sized carrots. I was morally opposed to baby carrots on the grounds that they were a marketing scam, but Chloe could squish my morals into whatever shape she wanted.

"Why aren't you with your friends?" I asked again.

She pried the lid off the hummus. "Because I'm not sure if I have any friends left and I'm scared to find out."

"Wait, what?" I scanned her face. I knew how much Chloe's friends meant to her. "What happened?"

The look she gave me suggested she harbored doubts about my intelligence. "*You* happened, Steven. I don't know if you realize this, but my friends are not your biggest fans."

She took her snack to the table and sat down cross-legged. I followed her like a dog on a leash. "But you've been living here with me for four months. What's different now?"

"We're different. It's one thing for me to live here temporarily because my only other choices are living with my parents or homelessness. It's another thing entirely to live here permanently because I'm head-over-heels in love with you."

"You're head-over-heels in love with me?" I couldn't stop a goofy-ass grin from spreading across my face.

"Yes. Which is wonderful but also does not bode well for my friendships." She dragged a carrot through the hummus and popped it into her mouth with a loud crunch.

Her embroidered shoes laying by the back door taunted me. I felt sick. "I never asked you to choose."

She stopped chewing and took a large gulp of water. "I know you didn't. Neither did James. What difference does that make? I still have two people I dearly love who cannot be in the same room together, and that means I have to make a choice." Her face was soft when she looked at me. "I'm choosing you, Steven. I hope that doesn't cost me my friends. But if it does..." She swallowed hard, heartbreak all over her pretty face. "I still choose you."

"That's not fair." I wrapped my hands around the edge of the table hard enough to leave a mark across my palms. "I'm the one who screwed up. Not you."

"Who told you life was supposed to be fair? Because I never got that memo," she mocked. But then she reached across the table and wiggled my fingers loose one by one. "I'm not giving up on my friends. I'll talk to James and try to work it out."

I didn't know what to say. *Sorry I purposefully spooked*

your best friend's horse and got her bucked off with bruised ribs wouldn't cut it.

Chloe unfolded her legs and pushed to her feet. "I told Amy I'd help her study after I ate something." She rounded the table and dropped a kiss on my upturned face. "Don't worry, okay? I'll take care of it."

Because that was what Chloe did. She took care of the hard parts. The messy parts. The parts no one else wanted to deal with.

Jesus fucking Christ. I was no better than her parents, letting her take care of things because it was easier, because she could. Why hadn't it occurred to me that Chloe would be the one to pay the price for my mistake?

I had never once tried to apologize to James. I had decided it would be better for both of us to pretend we didn't live in the same town and know the same people, so that's what I did. Because I knew she couldn't forgive me, so why bother trying? It was impossible.

The truth was, I simply didn't want to. Not because I wasn't sorry; I was *so* fucking sorry. But the broken little boy in me couldn't tolerate the idea of saying it out loud and hearing that it wasn't enough. That nothing I did would ever be enough.

Maybe that was true. Maybe nothing I did would ever be good enough to earn James's forgiveness. But I could live with that, as long as Chloe wasn't punished for it. And her son...hell. I knew what it was like to not be loved. Chloe's son could have the opposite of that. There were so many people in her life ready to love this kid. I sure as fuck was not going to ruin that for him before he even took his first breath.

He mattered so much more than protecting my own hurt feelings. Chloe mattered more. I refused to protect myself at their expense.

I mean, Christ. I hadn't even fucking *tried*.

I shot off a text before I could think better of it.

Then I grabbed my keys.

THE SIGN HANGING above the gravel road said *Welcome to Lodestar Ranch*.

The three large men standing side-by-side directly underneath, blocking my path to the ranch, said *The fuck you are*.

I probably should have gotten my affairs in order before driving out here like I had a death wish. Finished the project out back, drawn up care and feeding instructions for Stevie and her friends, taught Amy how to actually use that dang car battery charger I got her. Definitely should have fucked Chloe one last time. Give her something to remember me by.

Oh, well. It was too late for all that now. I was here. The Hale brothers were here. Time to get it over with.

No one said a word as I killed the engine and got out. It felt like even the mountains were holding their breath.

I made it a whole two steps before Adam drove his fist straight into my gut. I keeled over and dry heaved.

"I owed you that," he informed me.

"Fair," I gasped out, remembering the sucker punch I had landed after he broke my nose.

"Dammit, Adam." Brax pinched the bridge of his nose. "I told you to let him throw the first punch."

"You only said that because you knew he wouldn't," Adam said. "I'm not waiting around for something that is never going to happen."

"Me, either," Zack said and the next thing I knew, his fist connected with my jaw.

The force of it sent me rocking back a couple steps, windmilling my arms for balance like a jackass before I righted myself.

"Jesus, Zack. What did I ever do to you?" I touched my tongue to the corner of my mouth and tasted blood. I spat on the ground and glared at him. "Feel better now?"

"Not particularly." Zack flexed his hand, frowning. "That's going to leave a mark. Not sure bruised knuckles are worth hitting a man who won't fight back. Less fun than I thought it would be, truthfully."

"Damn shame you couldn't have had that epiphany before you punched my face," I muttered. "I thought we were friends. We were on the circuit together."

"You're mistaken." Zack Hale had the reputation of being a happy-go-lucky, always-down-for-a-good-time kind of guy, but the way he looked at me now with no trace of humor in his expression made me take note. "I'm not a friend to any man who hurts women."

Damn. His words hit harder than his fist. I flinched and rubbed at the sudden tight feeling in my chest. "That's why I'm here. I didn't hurt her on purpose, but I do owe her an apology." I looked to Adam. "If you could tell her I'm here, I'd be obliged."

Adam snorted. "Not going to happen. So how about you get on back in your truck and get the hell off our property?"

It wasn't like I had thought this would be easy.

But shit, I really hoped I at least survived it.

"No," I said.

Three sets of identical blue eyes regarded me with stunned disbelief.

"I could hit him again," Zack volunteered. "It might be more fun this time."

Brax scrubbed a hand over his face. "Fuck."

Adam stepped forward, the look on his face downright menacing. "You have a lot of fucking nerve, McAllister."

I put my hands up. "I'm not going to fight you. Chloe would kill me. All I'm asking is that you tell James I'm here to talk. If she wants me gone, I'll get gone and never bother any of you again. You have my word on that—"

Adam snorted. "Your word isn't worth shit."

My temper went off like a rocket. "Fuck you, Adam," I spat. "I did something terrible, but that doesn't mean *everything* I do is terrible. I never broke a promise to you or anyone else."

"What you did to James was worse," Brax pointed out mildly.

"Yeah, it was," I agreed. Frustration rolled through me. "But that still isn't everything. Are you honestly going to stand here and say you have never done anything terrible? Do you let that one terrible thing define who you are as a person?"

Brax looked like he was actually considering the question, but Adam's eyes narrowed. "Give me one good reason why I shouldn't fold you into a pocket square and mail you to China."

"Because Chloe won't be moving to Lodestar Ranch. Not this spring. Not ever." I looked him dead in the eyes. "She's staying with me. For good."

Adam let loose a stream of curse words. Zack looked ready to throw another punch. Brax shook his head.

"You don't deserve her," he said.

I laughed. I couldn't help it. "Shit, Brax, I know that. She's way too good for me. I've known that since the first moment I saw her. I spent a long fucking time feeling like I wasn't good enough. But what I deserve, that doesn't matter anymore. Because *she* deserves *me*. She deserves a man who will show up for her every day. A man who will show up for her son. She deserves a man who will fucking *try*, and when he inevitably falls short—and I know I will —he tries again and keeps right on fucking trying until he gets it right. She deserves a man who loves her. She deserves to have everything in this whole world she wants, even if that includes a jackass like me."

They stared at me like I had sprouted an extra head, and that extra head happened to be particularly upsetting.

"Oh, goddammit," Adam muttered with deep disgust. "I'm going to be pissed if we have to invite him to the picnic."

And then he took out his phone.

32

CHLOE

"I can't believe how big she's getting!" I cooed, stroking Belle's velvety pink nose.

James gave the mare an affectionate pat on the neck and grinned at me. Belle was special to her, and her pregnancy meant big things for the breeding operation at Pedestal Ranch.

"My two favorite mamas-to-be," James said. She placed one hand on Belle's belly, and her other on mine. "I can't wait to spoil both babies rotten. Within reason, of course. Foals can be real brats, and you don't want to reward that behavior no matter how cute they are, because when they get big—hey, what's wrong?" James's big brown eyes got even bigger as she took in the tears leaking down my face. "Why are you crying?"

"Because you're an amazing friend, and I am the *worst*," I wailed. "The literal worst."

"Don't be ridiculous." James wrapped her arms around me. "What's going on?"

"I can't move to the ranch." I gulped back a sob and hiccupped.

James rubbed my back soothingly. "Okay. That's okay."

"It's *not* okay," I said. "It's really not. I did the worst possible thing. It's Steven's fault, really. He made me go and fall in love with him."

James did a slow blink. "Say that again?"

"I'm in love with Steven."

"McAllister?" she asked dubiously.

"We don't know another Steven."

She wrinkled her nose. "Ew."

My eyes narrowed. "Careful," I warned.

"He is hot," she admitted. She cocked her head, studying me. "But he's still the guy who spooked my horse and called me a slut."

"I know." I rubbed my forehead. *Fuck, fuck, fuck.* "I could give you a hundred other things he's done. Good things. Sweet things. I mean, the man caught my vomit barehanded to save the shoes you embroidered for me because he knew how much they meant to me. But I'm not going to sit here and try to balance out his soul for you. You don't have to like him. But if you could learn to *tolerate* him..." My voice wobbled and I slid to the ground in a pathetic heap. "Goddammit, James, I love him so much."

"Oh, honey." James sighed. She sat down next to me, and we leaned back against the stall wall. "I really hope you landed on clean hay."

"I tried really hard not to love him, James. You have no idea. I fought it for weeks."

"Weeks," James echoed drily. "You don't say."

"You haven't seen that man's abs. It was a Herculean effort on my part, and I want credit for it."

"I'll take your word for it." She snickered.

I sighed. "I really did try, you know. You mean the world to me, and it felt like such a betrayal of our friendship. I feel terrible about keeping it a secret from you. But I'm also..." I struggled to find the words. "I'm also *glad* I love him. I wouldn't want to be in love with anyone else. He's so...*Steven*."

She studied me. Stroked my hair off my damp cheek. "You really do love him, huh?"

I nodded. "So much I can't remember what it felt like to hate him. It's not really his abs, you know. He's so good to me that it's almost embarrassing. I could list all of it, but you still wouldn't understand. Because all those nice things, that's not why I love him. I..."

The enormity of the emotion rolled over me like a tsunami. "It's the strangest thing, falling in love with someone. The strangest damn thing, James. I know *why* I should love him, but that's not really why I do."

James linked her elbow through mine. "All right. I'm listening."

"It's all these little moments, you know? I love him because he's infatuated with a pig and because he refused to come inside after a bad day because he didn't want to take it out on his sister. I love him because the more he cares, the grumpier he gets and you know what? That's adorable. I go so soft every time." I felt soft right now, just thinking about it. "And I love him because he tries. He tries so fucking hard."

James squeezed me closer. I knew she understood, but I also knew that might not be enough.

I hesitated before asking the question I knew I had to ask. I wasn't sure I was ready for the answer. "Do you think someday you could be okay with that? You don't have to be his friend," I added hastily. "But maybe you could come over sometime? Visit the baby?"

She rolled her lips together, thinking. "Honestly, I don't know. I want to say yes because I love you so much, but the truth is, I'm not sure how I feel about him. What I do know is that I love you enough to try."

"Really?" I asked hopefully.

She nodded. "Really."

Her phone buzzed and she pulled it out of her pocket. Her eyebrows shot up. "It's from Adam. Steven is here."

"Steven is *here*?" I squawked. "At Lodestar Ranch? And Adam knows?" I scrambled to my feet. "Oh, god, they're going to kill him."

James pushed herself up the wall. "Chloe, wait—"

But I did not wait. I couldn't.

I left the stables at a sprint that quickly devolved into an awkward jog. I wrapped my hands underneath my belly for support and hustled toward the house, looking this way and that for any sign of Steven or the Hale brothers or blood.

When I saw Steven's truck parked in the circular driveway, I picked up speed...and then immediately slowed down again because Radish was somehow taking up all the space in my lungs and I couldn't pull in a full breath.

"Chloe!" James hollered behind me as I made for the front door. "Back deck!"

I changed direction, huffing and puffing. James finally caught up with me and we skidded to a stop as we found them. Steven, Adam, Brax, and Zack had each claimed a rocking chair with a beer in hand.

I grabbed the deck rail and wheezed.

"Chloe?" Steven was on his feet in a flash. "What happened?"

"I thought...you...I ran...fuck," I wheezed.

That goddamn grin of his could power the whole earth. It lit up his face, the sky, the mountains. *Me.* "Aww." His arms went around me, loosely because I was still panting. "Were you worried about me, princess?"

"YOU JUST HAD to go and fall in love with that asshole, didn't you," Adam said, pushing a glass of water into my hand.

I took a long, grateful swallow. "His *abs*, Adam. Have you seen his abs?"

Adam made a face. "It's a good thing James likes you so much."

"Yeah. It really is," I agreed.

We both looked to where Steven and James were talking quietly, far enough away that we couldn't hear their conversation, but still close by. I shifted anxiously. I wanted everything to be okay so badly, but I had to let them work it out for themselves.

Adam sighed. "I know he didn't mean for her to get hurt the way she did, but every time I look at him, all I see is James unconscious and crumpled on the fence."

I winced. "I'm sorry. I know this isn't easy to accept."

"No. It's fucking hard." He paused, tipped his beer to his mouth, and then looked at James again. "But good things are worth the hard."

Feeling our eyes on them, they looked up. Steven's lips moved, and James nodded. They headed back to us.

I stood. Steven's arm wrapped around my waist like I was a missing limb. I glanced from his face to hers, trying to get a read on how things were between them. "Should we get going?" I asked hesitantly.

Steven looked to James, who looked to Adam and then back to me. She smiled.

"Stay awhile," she said.

33

CHLOE

Pregnancy Week 22: Radish is the size of a carrot

GABE

Chloe? Is everything ok?

CHLOE

You're alive! JFC, Gabe. You scared me.

GABE

I'm fine. Better than fine. It's a long story.
What's with the crazy texts?

CHLOE

Right. We need to talk.

GABE

Like on the phone?

CHLOE

Unless you're going to be in Aspen
Springs anytime soon, yes.

Give me an hour. I'll call you.

THE HAZY, lazy week between Christmas and New Years was my favorite. No social events, no work, no rules. I spent the afternoons sprawled on the couch with a plate of cookies and apple slices balanced on my increasingly pronounced baby bump, a book open but mostly unread next to me, a crackling fire in the fireplace because Steven knew I loved a good fire, wearing nothing but a soft sports bra and itty bitty sleeping shorts because baby plus fire meant I was too hot. *Bliss.*

Gabe's texts popping up on one such afternoon felt entirely surreal. I considered putting on proper clothes for the very adult conversation we were about to have, but then decided against it. It wasn't like he could see me over the phone. Anyway, my skin felt too itchy for clothes.

He called an hour later exactly like he said he would, which only surprised me because Gabe had never been known for being punctual.

"Chloe? Are you okay?" he asked straight off when I picked up, concern evident in his voice.

It was a reminder that Gabe wasn't a bad guy. He might not be the love of my life—scratch that, he definitely was not—but we'd had some good times together. There were worse people to co-parent with.

"I'm good," I said, and meant it. "Better than good, actually. I'm pregnant."

There was a brief pause, and then "Oh, shit. Listen, I'm happy for you. Really. You don't have to worry about me. Whoever the guy is, I'm happy for him, too. You and me, we were never officially together, so you don't have to officially break up with me. I get it. In fact—"

It took me a stupidly long moment to realize he didn't understand what I was telling him. "No, Gabe. You're the dad," I broke in.

This time the silence was longer. I let him have it. After all, I had been throwing up for a solid week before I came to terms with the fact that I was pregnant.

"Chloe. Shit," he muttered. I could hear the sound of muffled voices around him, a door being shut, and then more silence. "Are you sure?"

"Very sure," I said. "You were the only one I had sex with. Assuming it's not immaculate conception, the baby is yours."

"Chloe, I—" He exhaled heavily. "Are you keeping it?"

I blinked down at my round stomach. "Well...yeah. I mean, you know I'm twenty-two weeks pregnant, right? The decision-making part is past."

"Sorry, I'm just so surprised. I don't know what to say."

"It's okay," I assured him. "You don't have to say anything right now. I'm okay. I mean, I don't *need* anything from you. You're the father, and I want you to be involved for the baby's sake, but I know this wasn't the plan for either of us. I made my choice, and now you can make yours."

Another pause. "I need to think about this."

My stomach sank a little, but only a little. Did I want Radish to know his dad? Of course. But families came in all different sizes and shapes. We would be fine either way. "Sure. I understand."

Gabe blew out a breath. "The thing is, Chloe, I met someone."

"Oh." I cleared my throat. "I don't want to marry you, Gabe. In case I wasn't clear on that. I'm actually...I met someone, too."

"I mean, I met someone here. In Argentina. Cordoba, actually. I crashed my bike and ended up in a hospital here. She's a nurse. You'd like her, actually. She's really sarcastic, but—" He babbled on a bit before I could get a word in.

"Gabe. Are you saying you're staying in Argentina?" I asked.

"Well...yeah. I'm staying."

"Huh," I said. That wasn't something I'd considered at all in the hundreds of times I'd imagined this conversation.

"When are you...when are you due?" he asked hesitantly.

"In early May," I told him.

"Oh. That's really soon," he said, sounding surprised.

"Well, it takes nine months to grow a baby, and it's been

five months since we had sex. That's how math works," I said.

He laughed. "I'm sorry. I'm still in shock."

"I know. It's okay."

There was another silence while we both considered our next words.

He cleared his throat. "Is it all or nothing? I mean... could I send cards, come and visit when I can, do video calls?"

I thought it over. What would Radish want from his dad? What would he *need* from his dad? I knew the stereotypes of kids who grew up with an absentee father, or worse, a father who bounced in and out and broke promises. But stereotypes were not guarantees. Wasn't it better to try?

"It doesn't have to be all or nothing," I said finally. "Text me your address and email. I'll send you the sonogram photos."

"Thanks. I'd like that," he said.

My phone dinged with his text. "Got it," I said.

After a few more minutes of updates, we hung up. I stared into space for a long time, my hands wrapped protectively over my belly.

That wasn't how I had wanted the conversation to go, but it was what it was. More than anything, I wanted Radish to be healthy, happy, and loved. And that was exactly what he was.

What a lucky kid.

We were going to be just fine.

"Whatcha doing, princess? Sleeping?" Steven asked, coming in from outside. He kicked off his boots, tugged off his gloves, and added another log to the fireplace. The fire roared back to life.

I blinked my eyes open and stretched, smiling at him. "Not sleeping. Daydreaming."

"Yeah?" He came closer. "Can I dream with you?"

"Always."

He chuckled softly. "Careful, princess. I might take you at your word."

Maybe I want *you to take me at my word. Maybe I want always.*

Maybe the baby hormones had eaten my brain.

Steven scootched in behind me so we were sitting my back to his chest. He reclined against the armrest with me snuggled between his thighs. "This good?" he murmured against my temple.

"Mm," I agreed. "Can you hand me the body butter? It's on the end table behind you."

"Feeling itchy again?" he asked.

I felt him move behind me, then settle back in. When I heard the lid being unscrewed, I craned my neck to look at him. "What—"

"I've got it. Just relax."

I wiggled deeper into his body. "Okay."

He scooped out a palmful and gave it an appreciative sniff. "I don't know which I like more. Your strawberry hair or your cookie batter stomach."

"It's the cocoa and shea butters. That's what makes it smell so good." I made a sound of pure pleasure as he worked the cream into my parched belly. Colorado air was always dry, but it was especially brutal in winter. Add in all the stretching to accommodate a growing baby, and my skin was constantly dehydrated and uncomfortable.

Behind me, Steven's shoulders shook with laughter.

"What's so funny?" I asked.

"Remember that first dinner at your parents' house, and you accused me of buttering you up so you wouldn't tell your dad I was the world's biggest asshole?" His shoulders shook some more. "And I said I didn't know you *could* be buttered. Now here we are, snuggled up on the couch, and I'm literally buttering you."

I smiled down at his big, strong hands on my round belly. My eyes went misty. God, I loved this man so much. "Who would have thought?"

He snorted. "Not you. That's for damn sure." His hands moved in slow, thorough circles.

"So, guess what?" I didn't wait for him to reply before immediately answering my own question. "Gabe finally surfaced. I talked to him about an hour ago."

His hands stilled and his body stiffened behind me. "You did? That's...that's good."

I tilted my head to look back at him. "Why do you say that like it's opposite day?"

"Because I'm jealous, Chloe." He nudged at my cheek with his shoulder, trying to get me to turn back around. "Don't look at me right now. Pretend I'm a good person."

I rolled my eyes but settled against him again. "You *are* a good person, Steven. Tell me you're not actually worried about a guy I was never really with to begin with."

"Family is a powerful motivator," he said. "I wouldn't blame you if you decided you owed it to Radish to see if you could make it work with his dad."

"I couldn't even if I wanted to. Gabe is staying in Argentina. He met a nurse there." I shook my head. I still couldn't entirely believe it.

"You told him about Radish? That he has a baby here in Colorado?" Steven asked.

"Of course I did," I said. Steven's hips tilted, briefly dislodging me, as he fished his phone out of his front jeans pocket. "What are you doing?"

"Looking up flights to Argentina so I can kick some deadbeat ass."

"Be serious."

"I *am* serious. Radish deserves better than this. *You* deserve better than this."

"Steven." Exasperated, I took his phone away. When he reached for it, I slid it across the floor. "We *have* better than this. We have you."

He gripped my chin and forced my face back to look at him. "Say that again," he said quietly.

I swallowed hard at the emotion I saw in his eyes. "We have you."

"Damn right you do."

He lowered his head and kissed me slow and deep. I whimpered into his mouth as his tongue rubbed mine. When he pulled back, I stared up at him, dazed. The corner of his mouth crooked up as he studied me. Then he reached for the body butter again.

"I'm not done buttering you up, princess."

He drew a circle around my belly button, then rubbed the butter in with his palms. I leaned back against him with a happy sigh, my hands folded between in the valley between my breasts and bump.

"What were you dreaming about?" he asked.

"Hmm?"

"When I came first came in. You said you were daydreaming. What were you dreaming about?"

I laughed lightly. "Oh, you know. Baby things. Planting peonies so we can enjoy them on the porch. Introducing Radish to his uncles and grandparents." My voice got softer when I said, "You teaching him how to ride."

"I dream of that, too." His hands moved to mine, separating them from each other, massaging the leftover butter into my skin with tender care. "You want to know what else I dream of?"

"Yes," I said.

He hooked his pinky around my left ring finger like a wedding band. "This," he said huskily.

I stared down at our linked hands. My heart pounded like a winged bird against my ribs. "You want to marry me?" I asked, stupefied.

"More than anything in this whole wide world, princess."

"Steven," I whispered.

"This isn't a real proposal, but that's coming soon. I don't even have a ring because I had no idea if I should get one that fits you now or two months from now or a year from now. But yes, I want to marry you. I can't imagine a better way to spend the rest of my life than loving, honoring, and cherishing you."

Tears blurred my vision. "Are you sure? Even if I can't have another child with you?"

He touched his forehead to my temple. "You're having this one with me. The three of us, we all belong to each other. How could that not be enough? You and Radish are my whole world."

"Steven." My voice trembled. "Ye—"

He smashed his mouth to mine. "Don't answer now. Save it for the real thing."

I broke away, laughing. "Steven McAllister, you *are* the real thing."

And I got to call him mine. Forever.

EPILOGUE
STEVEN

7 months later

Maybe if I held my breath, I could sneak Grayson into his bassinet without waking him up. Third time was the charm, right? With one hand cradling his downy head and the other cupping his diapered butt, I bent over the bassinet, said a silent prayer to the god of exhausted but horny newborn parents, and gently detached his warm body from my bare torso.

Please, Gray, I need to fuck your mom.

I didn't breathe as I laid him on his back. His rosebud mouth sucked at the air like he wanted the bottle again, but then he settled. I waited, still not breathing, and looked down at him. His dark eyelashes fanned across his round cheeks, dusting over a pink splotch where he had pressed his face against my chest. My heart squeezed. God,

I loved him. Only three months of him being in the world, and already I could no more imagine life without him than without my right hand.

Chloe was watching us through half-drooped eyelids when I turned around. I set the empty bottle on the night-stand. Grayson got most of his meals straight from Chloe's boobs, but every night I rocked him to sleep with a bottle. It was our special moment together, and I wouldn't trade it for the world.

"You think he's really asleep?" Chloe asked, not bothering to whisper.

Grayson struggled with falling asleep, but once he was really and truly out, a brass band could march through here and he'd keep right on sleeping. For the next four or five hours, anyway. He wasn't quite sleeping through the night yet, which meant we were both sleep deprived and euphorically happy. Newborn delirium, Angie called it.

I crawled across the bed to her. "He's out."

"Hmm."

Her hair slid over her chest as she leaned sideways, reaching for the nightlight. Her hair was longer now and thicker, gleaming like oiled leather in the dim light. It gave me ideas about how it would look wrapped around my fist. Not tonight—we were still feeling our way through the changes to her body and the realities of having a baby sleeping six feet away—but someday soon.

"Leave the light on," I said, shucking my jeans. "I want to see you."

I hated that she hesitated.

"Please," I said. "You're so fucking beautiful, Chloe. Let me look at you."

She gave me an eyeroll and a sarcastic little smirk like she didn't quite believe me, but her hand fell away from the light, leaving it on.

"Are you tired?" I asked, helping her pull her tank top off over her head and then slid her gray cotton shorts down and off.

"I'm always tired." She smirked again, and this time there was a sexy playfulness to it. "I can be tired and want to fuck you at the same time, Steven. It's called multi-tasking."

I chuckled as I moved backwards down her body and settled between her thighs. "You always were a great multitasker."

"That's because—"

I pressed my palm between her legs and she gasped.

"Too much?" I asked, looking up. The first time we had sex post-birth, her pain had surprised us both. We had taken it slow since then. Lube helped, and going down on her first helped even more.

"No, it's perfect." She widened her legs invitingly, giving me more space to play.

I slipped a finger down the seam of her lips. She wasn't wet yet, and it might take a bit to get her there, but I wasn't in a rush. There was nowhere else I'd rather be than right here between her thighs. I took my time touching her, letting her grow the slightest bit impatient. When her hands finally stopped sifting sweetly through my hair and nudged my head down, I grinned. *There it was.*

I lowered my mouth and feasted.

"God, you taste good," I muttered, circling my tongue around her clit. I pumped my fingers inside her, in and out, in and out, and sucked gently.

Her orgasm was quick and light, pulsing around my fingers in rhythmic spurts. With a last savoring lick, I slid my fingers from her pussy and rose up on my knees to look at her. God, she was a sight. Flushed pink from her orgasm, her breasts swollen and full, her dark hair mussed across the pillow. My hand wrapped around my dick and squeezed.

Her eyes dropped there and she bit her lip, her mossy green irises darkening. Wordlessly, she handed me the lube.

I worked a small amount inside her and she hummed, her back arching. I kissed her navel, licked the line of her sternum, then dragged my tongue on the undercurve of her breast. I loved her body before, and I love it even more now. Her wider hips, softer belly, the lines and squiggles that are starting to fade to pale pink. Her hips moved restlessly beneath me and then she reached between us, found my cock, and lined it up with her opening.

I slid in slowly, carefully, pressing kisses to her jaw like that might distract her from any pain I caused. But she grabbed my ass with both hands and brought me home.

"I won't break," she whispered in my ear, right before she bit my earlobe.

I groaned into her neck. My hips snapped against her again and again. Cupping her breast in one hand, I squeezed, and felt a warm, wet slide of milk against my palm.

I froze.

"Oh! Shit," Chloe mumbled.

She tugged at the sheet, trying to cover herself, but I grabbed both her wrists with one hand and held them over her head as I stared down at her, at her full breasts and leaking nipples. My cock pulsed inside her. I licked my lips, unable to tear my gaze away.

"Can I?" I husked.

"Yes," she whispered.

I lowered my head and licked at the tight pink bud, lapped up the spilled milk from her breast, but that only made me want more. I drew her nipple into my mouth and sucked until warm sweetness coated my tongue.

"Oh, fuck," she gasped.

My hips moved and I sucked and she moaned and I sucked and this time her orgasm was slow and so fucking deep, dragging my own from me before I knew what was happening. We came together in a messy explosion and then lay there panting.

I had never felt so sated. So loved. So fucking cared for.

I looked at her. "Am I yours, Chloe?" I asked, just to hear her say it.

A smile bloomed across her face. "You're mine. Always."

Want more Steven and Chloe? Sign up for Elizabeth Bright's newsletter to receive a bonus epilogue! https://BookHip.com/WJZPAZW

ABOUT THE AUTHOR

Elizabeth Bright is a USA Today best-selling author of small town romance with heart, humor, and heat. When she's not dreaming up new stories, she can be found hiking or rock climbing. She lives in Washington, D.C. with her two daughters and very needy dog.

Sign up for Elizabeth's newsletter at elizabethbrightauthor.com

ACKNOWLEDGMENTS

Every time I sit down to write the acknowledgments, I am overwhelmed with gratitude and the sheer number of people it takes to get a book out of my head and into a reader's hands.

Lori and Nicole, who have cheered me on since the very first book in 2017.

Jonathan, who always understands that when I'm staring off into space, that counts as writing.

My daughters, who remind me to put on real pants before I leave the house.

Liana and Lisa, who keep me sane in this increasingly crazy publishing world.

Debra and Colby, who create amazing graphics and videos so readers can actually find me.

The bookstagrammers and booktokkers and reviewers who have shouted about my books—no one would know who I am without you!

Maybe—a BIG maybe—I could have done this without you, but good lord, that would have sucked. Thank you all.

www.ingramcontent.com/pod-product-compliance
Lightning Source LLC
Chambersburg PA
CBHW020228010826
48973CB00006B/1414